The New Neighbours

The New Neighbours

CLAIRE DOUGLAS

MICHAEL JOSEPH

PENGUIN MICHAEL JOSEPH

UK | USA | Canada | Ireland | Australia
India | New Zealand | South Africa

Penguin Michael Joseph is part of the Penguin Random House group of companies
whose addresses can be found at global.penguinrandomhouse.com

Penguin Random House UK,
One Embassy Gardens, 8 Viaduct Gardens, London SW11 7BW

penguin.co.uk

First published 2025

001

Copyright © Little Bear Artists Ltd., 2025

The moral right of the author has been asserted

Set in Garamond MT
Typeset by Couper Street Type Co.
Printed and bound in Great Britain by Clays Ltd, Elcograf S.p.A.

The authorized representative in the EEA is Penguin Random House Ireland,
Morrison Chambers, 32 Nassau Street, Dublin D02 YH68

A CIP catalogue record for this book is available from the British Library

HARDBACK ISBN: 978–1–405–95763–2
TRADE PAPERBACK ISBN: 978–1–405–95764–9

Penguin Random House is committed to a sustainable future
for our business, our readers and our planet. This book is made from
Forest Stewardship Council® certified paper

www.greenpenguin.co.uk

For Laura

PROLOGUE

He's always known that he loves her too much. Nobody else has ever compared to her. They haven't even come close. If there are such things as soul-mates, then she is his. The way he feels about her is both a blessing and a curse. He's sometimes wondered if this need for her, this *obsession*, is all to do with growing up without a mother, without any kind of strong female role model. But no, his feelings for her go way beyond that. It's primal, almost spiritual. When they first laid eyes on each other there was this spark, this mutual recognition that they'd finally found their person, their kindred spirit, and a sense of calm had washed over him because he was no longer alone in the world. He'd finally met someone who would understand him completely. All of him, even the bad bits. *Especially* the bad bits.

But lately another emotion has begun to creep in. Something unwanted, insidious, playing over and over in his mind until it's impossible to ignore.

Fear.

He's realized he's scared of the power she has over him. And of what she can make him do.

PART ONE

I

LENA

July 2024
Bristol

The new neighbours are in their front garden. I stay in my car a little longer just to observe them, the aircon blowing in my face. They moved in just a few days ago so I haven't met them properly yet, but I've heard on the grapevine (well, Phyllis at number fifty-two) that they are a 'retired, well-to-do couple in their late sixties'.

Their front door is open, allowing me a tantalizing view of the newly refurbished hallway and the huge chandelier that catches the late-afternoon sunlight. Our houses are set on a pretty Victorian terrace on a tree-lined street in the Redland area of Bristol, although theirs is at the end of the row and is larger, with a loft conversion and modern glass extension at the back. It once belonged to Joan but when she went into a nursing home her daughter sold it to a developer, who renovated it to a high specification and must have sold it on to this couple. Ours feels like the less attractive smaller sibling. The runt of the litter.

For the last ten days the weather has been getting progressively hotter and every move I make causes sweat to break out in places I never knew you could sweat. Yet the neighbours look cool and fresh: she is slim in a pale-yellow linen sundress that contrasts with her dark auburn hair and he is in chino shorts and a linen shirt, not a drop of perspiration in sight. He's tall and handsome in that old-Hollywood matinee-idol way, his white hair slicked back from his perma-tanned face that screams of hours spent on golf-courses and beaches in the Caribbean. Parked outside their house, just behind my car, is a classic blue Jaguar that my teenage son, Rufus, is already coveting.

The woman notices me and smiles warmly. I wave, embarrassed to be caught gawping but this could be a great opportunity to introduce myself. I step out of the car, my dress already sticking to the backs of my thighs, and go to the boot to retrieve two paper bags of groceries for my movie night with Rufus. Every Thursday we do the same and I cherish it more than ever, especially as next year he'll be leaving for university. Our house, which had once felt so poky and overcrowded, will seem as empty as a beach out of season.

I close the boot with my elbow, and as I turn towards their house ready to welcome them to the neighbourhood, I'm startled to see the woman just inches away from me, a bright smile on her face.

'Hi. I'm Marielle Morgan. We've just moved in next door.' She holds out a hand but laughs when she realizes both of mine are taken up with shopping bags and drops it down by her side.

'So lovely to meet you. I'm Lena,' I say, sounding higher-pitched and more excitable than I was aiming for. I've never been very good at giving the impression of aloof or cool. I immediately warm to Marielle. She has beautiful greeny-grey eyes, symmetrical crow's feet that fan towards her temples, high cheekbones and a honeyed voice, like Joanna Lumley's.

'Henry!' she calls to her husband. 'Come and meet Lena!'

The bags are heavy but I adjust them in my arms as her husband joins us. He seems more reserved than Marielle and softly spoken, but he has a calm self-assurance. He says hello, then stands silently by his wife.

'Do you have any children?' she asks. 'I've seen a teenage boy coming and going.'

'Yes. Rufus. He's seventeen. He'll be off to uni next year.' I grimace and Marielle nods knowingly.

'It's so hard when they fly the nest. Is it just the two of you?' I think of my husband, Charlie, who moved out late last year and say yes. She must notice the tension in my face, as she moves swiftly on. 'It seems like a lovely neighbourhood. We're new to the area and wanted to be close to family. We've recently become grandparents.' She flushes with pride as she says it.

'Oh, wow, congratulations. That's lovely.' I feel a small tug of envy. I love babies. I'd wanted a house full of children but sadly it wasn't to be, which makes Rufus extra special and why I've always been a little overprotective of him.

She beams and Henry gives a half-smile tinged with embarrassment, then glances at his feet. He looks a tad uncomfortable and I'm reminded of my dad. He always hated small-talk too.

'You must come over for a drink one evening,' continues Marielle. 'Rufus too.'

'Thank you, we'd love to.'

'Great. Well, we'll let you get on.' She turns to Henry and they are about to go back into their front garden when one of my bags decides to split open and my shopping spills on to the pavement. I stare down at it in dismay.

'Oh dear,' says Marielle, as I thrust my leg out to prevent a bottle of Coke from rolling into the road. 'Hold on, I'll go and fetch another bag.' She dashes into her house, leaving Henry and me alone, my shopping strewn on the pavement. I'm mortified by all the junk food.

'Here, let me help,' Henry says, picking up a box of Jaffa Cakes and a packet of custard creams and handing them to me.

'It's a Thursday-night treat,' I say, flustered. I set the other bag on the pavement. 'For me and Rufus. There *is* fruit in this bag.'

'Hey, I'm not judging.' He chuckles, which illuminates his whole face. 'You should see the junk Marielle and I get through. My wife has a very sweet tooth.'

'My mum's coming this weekend, and she's also got a sweet tooth, so this is for her too . . .' He looks slightly bemused as I blabber on about my mum and how she can only stay for one night because of her dogs, even though her partner, Mick, will be at home to look after them. I'm totally over-sharing but there is something about him that makes me feel like a child, not the forty-three-year-old mother of one that I am.

Marielle emerges from the house holding a hessian bag from the posh deli around the corner. Between us we scoop up my multipack of biscuits, the family-sized bag of crisps, a huge slab of Dairy Milk, and deposit them in the bag.

'Thank you so much. I'll go and dump this lot now but it's so lovely to meet you both,' I say again, aware I'm gabbling.

'You too,' says Marielle.

I let myself into the house and close the door behind me, my armpits damp. God, that was embarrassing. What a great first impression they'll have of me, flapping, sweating and over-sharing.

I notice Rufus's trainers chucked by the doormat and I'm pleased he's home from college already. I carry the shopping to the kitchen and Phoenix, my latte-coloured Cavachon, trots over to greet me, acting like I've been gone all day and not just an hour at the supermarket. I put the shopping on the worktop and throw open the patio doors. Our rear garden is a sun-trap and the lawn is already patchy and dry after the last ten days of intense heat. According to the forecast we can expect the heatwave to go on for another week or two.

Rufus is in the sitting room with the blinds closed. When I come in, he pauses the TV on a close-up of James Stewart's face and turns to me, looking guilty. He's watching *Rear Window* again. Tonight it's *The Third Man* because Rufus is doing a *film-noir* module for his media-studies course. I love how we've made watching a movie a regular Thursday-night event since last November, which coincided with Charlie moving out. I know it's Rufus's way of

9

offering his support: our love of movies has always been our thing. With his father it's music.

'Have you started without me?'

Rufus shakes his head. 'Ah, sorry, Mum. I can't tonight. I totally forgot, Dad's got that gig later and he asked if I'd help out. He's gonna pay me and Freddie to be his roadies.' Freddie is a new friend from college whom Rufus has been talking a lot about these last few months. He seems a nice enough lad. Rufus had got in with the wrong group in year eleven and one of his supposed 'friends' bullied him so I'm pleased he's making new ones. It was unfortunate he didn't go to the same school as my best friend Jo's son Archie as the two of them always got on, despite being quite different. Rufus couldn't wait to move to sixth-form college instead of staying on.

'But it's a Thursday night and you have college tomorrow . . .'

He runs a hand through his thick mop of hair. 'I know, and I'd never usually miss it but Dad said this gig's important. It's, like, a really big crowd.' I brush away my disappointment. Rufus is young: he should be out with his friends, not stuck in with me.

'Okay. What time will you be back?'

'I'll stay at Dad's tonight and he'll drop me to college in the morning.'

My heart sinks. I hate being in the house at night on my own, even though I'll have to get used to it when Rufus leaves.

To hide my feelings, I move to the window to open the blinds. Marielle and Henry are still in their front garden.

'Also, Mum, been meaning to ask. Could I have some guitar lessons?'

I turn to face him. 'Isn't your dad teaching you?'

He pulls a face. 'Dad only knows the basics and I need someone . . . more experienced.' Charlie is a brilliant drummer but not so great on guitar.

'How much are the lessons?' Since Charlie and I split up money has been tight. I don't earn much as an adviser at Citizens Advice and the modest inheritance my dad left me eighteen months ago has dwindled.

He gets up from the sofa and turns off the TV. 'Not much. This guy is offering discounts if we sign up to a term. I shouldn't need that many lessons. Dad knows the guy. He's said it's okay by him but I have to ask you too.'

'I'll talk to Dad about it,' I promise. In my peripheral vision I can see Marielle pulling out a weed. 'Hold on a sec. I need to give a bag back to the new neighbours before I forget. Long story,' I add, when he frowns. 'They seem nice. Older. Posh.'

I leave the room and go to the kitchen, grab the bag off the worktop and rush out of the front door. I'm about to cross to our boundary wall when Henry's expression makes me hesitate. Marielle has her back to me, her shoulders slumped.

'I've already said, we can't discuss this now,' he hisses. 'It's too dangerous.' He notices me and lowers his gaze. Without saying another word he stalks off into the house. Marielle turns to face me and . . . Is it my imagination or is her smile a little wobbly?

I walk towards her, holding out the bag. 'Sorry for interrupting. I just wanted to give you this back.'

'Oh, you weren't.' She leans over the wall, takes it from me and clutches it to her chest.

'Oh, okay, good. Thanks.' I give a pathetic little wave and retreat into my house, wishing I'd waited before returning the bag.

I wonder what they were talking about and why Henry was so cross.

2

Rufus is in the back garden with his recording equipment. He's had it on loan from college for the past few days, and we've had fun using it to gather sound for his project. I'm not very technical but Rufus patiently showed me how to use it and last night we managed to pick up the cries of foxes and the hoot of an owl, which he was really pleased with.

'What time are you going to Dad's?' I ask, joining him on the lawn, where he's faffing with the fluffy boom microphone. 'I thought you were going soon.'

He adjusts the height of the mic's pole, frowning in concentration. 'I was hoping to do some more recording before I head off. When's the next bus?'

'Six forty.' The bus stop is only a street along, but Rufus still hasn't packed his bag. He has no concept of time, just like his dad.

'Ah, okay. It's just this is quite urgent.'

He's been home from college for more than an hour and of course he's trying to do it now, ten minutes before his bus. 'Here, give me that.' I sigh. 'Go and get your stuff and I'll do it for you. You'll miss the bus otherwise.'

He hands me the pole. 'Thanks, Mum.' He smiles ruefully. 'I've only got night sounds.' He winces at the high-pitched shriek of a far-off child and laughs. 'But I could do with more stuff like this.' He throws up his arms as though to encompass the cacophony that makes up this summer evening on a Thursday: the buzz of a lawnmower, an aeroplane overhead, the tinkling of cutlery, the sizzle of a barbecue, the splash of a paddling pool, the low murmur of conversation and the excitable squeals of children playing.

'No problem, I'll do my best. Remember Bess is coming this weekend. She won't want to miss seeing you so make sure you're around a bit on Saturday, won't you?' He's called my mum by her Christian name since he could speak as she always refused to be called Nan or Gran. Says it would make her feel ancient, and I don't like to break it to her that, at seventy-one, she's not exactly a spring chicken even if her partner Mick is nine years her junior.

'Sure.' He unravels the tape deck's strap from around his neck. When he'd first brought it home we'd laughed at how archaic it was, how it reminded me of the one I had in the early 1990s when I used to record the Top 40 every Sunday night.

I take it from him, surprised again by its bulk. 'God, can't they at least get some more up-to-date equipment at that college?'

He helps thread the strap over my shoulder. He's shot up in the last year and towers above me now. 'I know, right. And they've only got, like, five, so we have to share them. Harrison's group are having it next. I promised him I'll be done with it by Saturday so he can use it.'

'Lucky them.' I reach up to kiss his head, resisting the urge to hug him so tightly he's forced to stay with me. I smile to hide the sorrow that has lately been sitting just below the surface. 'Now go, or you'll miss the bus.'

He waves as he does a backward jog across the lawn then darts into the house. I can hear him thundering up the stairs, Phoenix chasing him, thinking it's a game. A few minutes later he calls goodbye and I hear the front door slam behind him. For a few beats all is silent, then Phoenix trots out to greet me and I bend down to cuddle him. 'He's gone, I know,' I say quietly, into his fur. Then I stand up, leaning on the boom mic. Right, I can't wallow. I might as well get on with this. I clamp the headphones over my ears and fiddle with the dials, like Rufus has shown me, and press record. I move across the sun-bleached lawn, nearly tripping over Phoenix, who is running in circles around my legs, as I point the mic towards the cloudless sky. The microphone instantly picks up the amplified sounds of a clunky piano, the slam of a car door, the low thrum of drum and bass, and . . . something else. Voices speaking in hushed, urgent tones.

'. . . I don't know, Mari . . .'

'You promised me you'd take her. I've got everything ready. The room . . .'

'I know . . . but . . . after what happened before . . . should we really try again?'

They're coming from the direction of next door. Marielle and Henry. I lower the microphone, mortified that I'm picking up my new neighbours' private conversation, and move towards my back gate, determined to put distance between the microphone and where they might be.

I can see their upstairs window is slightly ajar, and a shadow moves behind the glass. They must have gone into the house. I move further back so that I'm almost in the bushes. When I think I'm far enough away not to pick up any more of their conversation I tentatively raise the mic again.

'. . . *we have no choice* . . .'

Damn it, I can still hear them. I press stop on the tape deck so I'm no longer recording.

'. . . *You said you'd see this through to the end. You promised. And you know what I think about broken promises, Henry?*'

'*Marielle, please* . . .'

'*It's not going to go away. And I'm not going to forget about it. This has to happen as we planned. It's the only way.*' Her voice takes on a high-pitched, almost wheedling tone, at odds with the strong, independent woman I had taken her to be. '*I don't know what I'll do if you break your promise, Henry. I don't know how I'll live* . . .'

She sounds genuinely upset and I'm flooded with shame. God, is my life so boring that I have to get my excitement from listening in on someone else's private conversation? I'm just about to lower the microphone when Henry says something that makes me freeze.

'*It's too risky. We could get caught, Mari.*'

'*We didn't last time.*'

My pulse quickens. Getting caught doing what?

Their voices are replaced by a rustling sound. Slowly, I turn and look up at their house, and see Henry moving at the window. Shit, has he seen me? I lower the boom mic with a prickle of unease and, head down, I hurry back into my kitchen.

What on earth are they planning?

3

NATALIE

It's been happening for weeks now. The sensation that she's being followed. Whenever Natalie turns around, nobody is there, yet sometimes, like when she's mooching around the shops or waiting to catch the bus to work, the hairs on the back of her neck stand up, as though some-one has blown very softly on the skin of the nape. She's being paranoid, isn't she? It's been years. She thought she was finally safe. She's forty-nine now and she knows she looks a mess half the time, with her dirty-blonde hair always pulled back in a scruffy bun and no make-up. She doesn't have to dress up for work so usually spends most days in jeans and a T-shirt or jumper. She calls it her invisibility uniform. And for a while that's exactly what she's been. Invisible. Or at least that's what she's hoped. But as she hurries through the park, the sun pressing into her back like a child's hot, sticky hand, she can't shake the sensation. Yet when she glances over her shoulder it's just the shadows of the branches that dance on the pavement behind her.

They can't have found her after all this time, can they?

No, that's impossible. She's kept a low profile. Retrained. Moved cities numerous times, even changing her name. What more could she do? And it might all have been for nothing anyway.

Then she remembers the photograph. That stupid photograph in the local paper. The electrical company she works for had won some industry award. She's their only female electrician so she knew they'd want her in the photo, despite her best attempts to get out of it. When she realized she couldn't, she'd made sure to stand right at the back, behind Big Dave so she wouldn't be visible. But then the ageing male photographer with the earring and dyed black hair had insisted she move to the front. 'A pretty, petite girl like you,' he'd said, smiling in a way that he obviously thought was charming but she considered downright creepy. And she'd been propelled to the front, in full view of the camera.

But she had hoped nobody would see the photo. Who even reads articles about industry awards in a local newspaper with a dwindling circulation?

As she exits the park her T-shirt is already clinging to her, despite it not yet being 9 a.m. She's always been an early riser, although lately she's wondered more and more what she's got to get up for.

Although after last night there might be someone. *Finally.* Someone who made her heart quicken, whom she found interesting and handsome. Whom she could imagine going to dinner with, sitting up all night talking with, maybe even having sex with.

She smiles to herself at the memory. The way his fingers

had brushed hers as he passed her a pint. His crooked smile, his kind blue eyes.

For the first time in ages she feels hopeful and less alone in the world. Even if she knows that nothing will ever come of it because she can't allow herself to get too close to anyone. But the possibility is there and for now that's enough.

The shops aren't open except her favourite deli on the corner, so she grabs a latte, then wanders the city's sun-soaked pavements, yet the sensation of being followed persists. She'd had quite a few drinks last night at the bar. She's always been lucky to escape a hangover, never mind how much she'd necked. Alcohol makes her twitchy, paranoid, as though all her limbs are too sensitive, as though all the electricity she works with has seeped into her every nerve ending, and she has to keep moving to rid herself of the feeling until she eventually conks out and sleeps it off.

Natalie passes a woman pushing a pram. She looks sleep-deprived, and the sight causes her insides to shrivel a little. She's instantly transported back to a time when that was her life. Crying babies and frazzled new mums. A humid ward that smelt of urine, bleach and blood. So much blood. The memory is so strong that Natalie is forced to stop for a second to grab the nearby wall and catch her breath, warding off the sudden bout of nausea. Maybe she's getting too old for late-night drinking binges after all.

She straightens, inhaling a lungful of the fresh summer morning, and makes her way back into the park. It's a little busier now. People are dotted on the grass, faces turned up to the sunshine. One woman sits alone on a bench reading a book, her legs crossed, a foot bobbing up and down to some inaudible tune. Natalie continues walking, her nerve endings still fraught and fizzy, not helped by the injection of caffeine into her system. It's cooler as she heads further into the park, the trees providing a canopy shielding her from the sun, which glints through the leaves. She'll make three more circuits of the park, she decides, and then she'll head back to her sparse little flat above the kebab shop, which has been her home for the last year.

She's carrying her favourite cross-body bag that she's had for the past twenty years. It's a chestnut-coloured leather Mulberry that she'd treated herself to after everything that happened. It's the only luxury item Natalie has ever owned, and she wears it everywhere. The leather now smells faintly of last night's lager and the dry ice of too many gigs, but sometimes she's sure she still gets the whiff of her mother's perfume. She feels it buzzing against her thigh and realizes with surprise that her phone is ringing. She receives hardly any calls as she rarely gives out her number. She slows down to rootle inside the bag, and when she pulls the phone free she notices an unfamiliar number flashing on the screen. She debates whether to answer it but curiosity gets the better of her.

'Hello,' she says tentatively.

For a few moments there is silence and then a voice says her name – *her real name* – and her airways tighten in terror.

4

LENA

The house feels silent and empty now Rufus has gone. I used to yearn for my own company when he was little and the house was a revolving door of Charlie's band mates, NCT mums and their toddlers, but now I'd give anything to have those days back. I'm not someone who needs constant companionship – I like my own company up to a point – but the trouble is that lately I've been on my own more often than not and, when Rufus leaves, it'll get worse.

I glance at the recording equipment I've placed neatly by the patio doors. I gave up trying to get sound for Rufus after overhearing the neighbours' conversation. I'll have to try again in the morning before work.

It's too risky. We could get caught, Mari . . .

I can't stop wondering what they were talking about. Maybe something sexual – they could be swingers – or it could be something illegal. Although it's probably much more innocuous than I'm imagining. Anyway, it's none of my business. Not everyone is up to no good. I have to remind myself of that. I hear some dark things in my role at Citizens Advice – domestic violence, coercive control, fraud, cheating spouses – and I have to be mindful that it doesn't warp my view of the world.

On a whim I decide to call Jo. She answers on the second ring. 'Lena! This is a nice surprise on a Thursday evening.'

'I haven't interrupted anything, have I?'

'Just a sex-sesh with Paul . . .'

'Jo!'

'Kidding. Of course not. He'd be so lucky! He's on the Xbox with Archie.' Archie is Jo's eldest, the same age as Rufus. I'd met her at an overpriced baby singing and dancing class in Clifton when our boys were only six months old. It was midway through us skipping around the room to a hideous rendition of 'Three Blind Mice' and wafting scarves around our heads when she murmured over her shoulder, 'I can't believe I'm doing this. I'm a grown-ass woman, for crying out loud.' I warmed to her instantly, and over the years a deep friendship has evolved between us. It had taken me a long time to trust someone again after what had happened with Simone, a friend I'd had while training to be a midwife a long time ago. I'd ended up quitting my training in my second year and I never thought I'd get close to a girlfriend again, until I met Jo. She's a sharp-tongued barrister, solid and dependable. I really don't know what I'd have done without her, especially after Charlie left.

I hear her closing a door and the laughter leaves her voice. 'Is everything okay?'

'Yeah . . . all good. Listen, I know this is last-minute, but Ruf is now with Charlie tonight and I wondered if you fancied a drink.'

'Hell, yeah! The boys are busy with their gaming and Charmaine is on a school camping trip,' she says, referring to her fourteen-year-old daughter.

My heart lifts. 'Great. Where shall we go?'

'I fancy that new place in Clifton. I've been meaning to go for a while. Paul can drop us in town.'

'That would be great. Thanks, Jo. Give me half an hour to get changed.'

I race upstairs and have a quick shower, then throw on a fresh pale pink maxi dress. The air is so still and humid that I can't face drying my hair so I gather it up in a top-knot instead. While I'm waiting for Jo and Paul I head into Rufus's room, something I've ended up doing a lot recently when he's with his dad. It has that typical teenage-boy smell of balled-up old socks, fabric softener, Lynx de-odorant and sweat.

I pull my cotton dress over my knees, the fabric brushing my ankles and the tops of my feet, which are now cold. I sit watching the shadows dancing on Rufus's ink-coloured walls, remembering when I painted them four years ago. He'd just turned thirteen and wanted something more fitting to his new teenage self. Charlie and I had spent the day decorating it together, Radiohead playing in the background, while reminiscing about the first time we'd painted our son's bedroom, not long after we'd bought the house. He'd been a toddler then, with his cot bed, his array of dinosaurs and trains with smiley faces. Charlie always laughed at me when we decorated because by the end of it I had paint everywhere, including in my hair and between my eyebrows, while he didn't have a spot on him. If only I'd known then how our lives would turn out. That I'd be facing up to living here without either of them.

If I squint I can almost see those sky-blue walls and the rubbery triceratops and diplodocus that used to line his shelves, and his bed with the *Thomas the Tank Engine* duvet. I can almost see Charlie as he was then, his unlined face tipped back in laughter, a roller in his hand. I can almost feel the love we had for each other. Now the walls are full of posters from Rufus's favourite movies: Tippi Hedren cowering from a flock of birds takes up half of one wall and there's another of Cary Grant and Joan Fontaine in *Suspicion* by the window. Above the bed he's stuck modern posters of films like *Nightcrawler* and *Shutter Island*.

My mobile buzzes to say Jo is outside. She lives a few streets away from me, at the Gloucester Road end of Redland. I say goodbye to Phoenix, grab my bag and leave the house. As I reach the gate I see Marielle getting something out of the boot of their Jaguar. She's alone and I hope she's okay. Whatever she and Henry were talking about had sounded heated and she had seemed upset.

When she notices me she stops and smiles. 'You look lovely,' she says. 'Off somewhere nice?'

'Thank you.' I blush at the compliment. 'Going to a new bar with my friend.'

'Oh, what happened to your movie night with your son?' She lifts a leather tote bag from the boot. I catch a glimpse of a syringe and a medical kit.

Their conversation flitters through my mind again and I briefly wonder if they were talking about drugs.

'It's too risky. We could get caught, Mari.'

'We didn't last time.'

But I discount this straight away. They don't look like the drug-pushing type. Maybe one of them is ill. I try to concentrate on answering Marielle's question. 'Rufus had to go and help out his dad. He's in a band.'

She closes the boot with a smile. There is no hint of distress in her expression. No sign that an hour ago she was having a heated discussion with her husband. 'Oh, well, at least you get the night off.' The night off. This niggles me. Rufus isn't a chore. He's not work. I love spending time with him. Then I remember she's a new grandmother and looking after a baby is different. I'm being overly sensitive because my time with Rufus is running out.

'Anyway, I'd better go. My friend's waiting . . .'

'Of course. Have a lovely time.' She smiles again and walks back into the house, clutching the tote bag tightly.

The bar is surprisingly quiet for a Thursday evening. Most people are sitting on the large terrace outside, but Jo and I choose a spot inside in the corner. We haven't caught up properly all week. Jo has a big case on that is taking up quite a lot of her time. I only work three days a week and my job doesn't have the same kind of pressures as Jo's, even though they both involve people and their problems. The strain from the last week is evident in the creases and dark circles under her eyes. She won't talk about work, though. She never does. I get the sense that some of her cases are particularly harrowing as she works in family law, plus she's bound by confidentiality.

She's wearing a bright orange sundress that clashes with her dyed burgundy hair, and she lights up the dull room. She once told me that she can't help a small act of rebellion in most aspects of her life. Dyeing her hair and wearing bright clothes is her way of going against people's expectations of how a barrister should dress. It's one of the many things I love about her.

We spend a good hour or so catching up on what's been going on in our lives: our kids, our parents. She knows all about my complicated relationship with my mum and how much I miss my dad and, likewise, I listen when she pours her heart out to me about her parents' declining health.

And then I tell her about the Morgans and the conversation I overheard.

Her eyes light up with interest. 'Juicy!' she exclaims, when I've finished.

'Maybe . . . or they could have been talking about something boring, like taking driving penalty points for each other.'

'Which is illegal . . .'

I laugh and hold up my hands. Sometimes Jo can become a bit head-girlish. 'I know. But not exactly juicy.'

She downs the rest of her wine. 'Did you manage to record any of their conversation?'

'Only the first bit.'

'Ooh, can I listen? Why don't I come back to yours?'

I'm relieved. The wine here is expensive and I've got a bottle in the fridge that we could be drinking.

'Good idea.'

Jo gets out her phone to book an Uber while I finish my drink. Just as we're about to leave I notice a group of men walk in and recognize some as Charlie's bandmates. The gig must have just finished. I'd forgotten they were playing around the corner. I haven't seen them since we split up. Charlie must have gone straight back to his flat with Rufus and Freddie. They don't notice me as they head for the bar, and I nudge Jo, who has spotted them too. I'd instigated our break-up, and if I hadn't we would probably still be together, but only because Charlie prefers the easy route in life. I'd pushed it in the hope that he'd decide what we had was worth fighting for. Well, that backfired! They are Charlie's friends, and they would have heard only his side of the story. I don't want to be seeing them now for the first time.

'Let's go out of the side door,' I say to Jo. She nods in understanding and we weave our way through the tables. As I follow her, I almost collide with her when she suddenly stops. My stomach drops when I see what she's staring at.

It's Charlie. And he's kissing a very attractive brunette.

5

Charlie must sense our stares because he pulls apart from the woman and turns to us. His shocked expression mirrors my own. The woman appears oblivious and obviously has no idea who I am. I assess her. She's younger than me and is petite and attractive with big dark eyes and long conker-coloured hair. Charlie certainly has a type. She's trendy too, more so than I am, in her short black skirt and black lace top, like a pretty Goth doll.

A whoosh of heat rises.

Charlie moves away from the woman, his face flushed. 'Uh . . . Lena . . . Jo . . . hi. This is . . . um, Rosie, and, Rosie, this is Lena, my . . . er . . . ex-wife.'

'We're still married,' I say coldly. 'Separated,' I add to Rosie, who smiles awkwardly. I turn back to Charlie. 'Where's Rufus?'

'He's gone back to the flat with Freddie. I'm about to go home.'

I feel like I've been punched in the stomach. Seeing Charlie with someone else hurts more than I'd thought it would. Foolishly I believed he was far from ready to date anyone else. I should have known they'd be around here after their gig.

'Anyway,' says Jo, 'we'd better go. Our Uber is here.' She steers me away from Charlie to our cab. I can't speak as I climb into the back seat, but as we drive away I notice Charlie and Rosie staring after us.

'God.' I lean back against the seat. 'He's moved on quickly.'

'Hon, it's been over seven months,' Jo says gently. 'But he should have told you.'

I close my eyes to hide the film of tears, and nod, unable to say anything else.

She grips my hand, and we don't speak until we arrive at my house. Once inside she goes to the fridge and pours us both some wine. 'Do you want to talk about him?' she says, handing me my glass.

'No.' I take it and gulp a mouthful. 'I wonder if Rufus knows.'

A mix of emotions passes over Jo's face. 'Well, he should have told you first.' She's always liked Charlie and has never spoken ill of him, but I can see she's struggling to keep her opinion in check.

We stand in silence for a few moments and her eyes go to Rufus's recording equipment by the patio doors. Her face lights up. 'Ooh, let's hear this convo, then.' She puts her glass on the counter, goes to the sound monitor and lifts it onto the kitchen table.

'I don't know . . .' I feel bad about it now. They seem such nice people, and I've violated their privacy.

'Oh, come on. You didn't mean to record them. Don't you want to know what they were talking about?'

I laugh. She knows me too well. And I could do with the distraction to stop myself thinking about Charlie with another, much younger, woman.

'Okay, go on, then.'

She turns back to the monitor and rewinds the tape.

'Not too far,' I warn her, 'or all you'll get is owl and fox sounds.'

She laughs and presses play. Immediately Henry's voice fills my kitchen.

'. . . *should we really try again?*'

'Rewind a bit,' I say. 'Budge over, let me do it.'

Jo steps aside and I rewind the tape a bit more, then press play. At first we don't hear anything, just the far-off sound of an aeroplane, and then their voices ring out. Something about hearing it again in my kitchen brings me out in goosebumps.

'. . . *I don't know, Mari . . .*'

'*You promised me you'd take her. I've got everything ready. The room . . .*'

'*I know . . . but . . . after what happened before . . . should we really try again?*'

'. . . *we have no choice . . .*'

Silence follows and I turn to Jo. 'That's when I stopped recording.'

'They sound quite intense. What did she mean by "You promised me you'd take her"? Take who, where? And the room being ready?'

'I don't know . . . the baby, maybe? They have a grand-child.'

'So what did they say next? Can you remember?'

I think back to their conversation. 'Something about seeing it through to the very end. And broken promises. Marielle seemed obsessed about that. She got quite upset and started talking about how she couldn't live if he didn't do what she wanted.'

'Shit.'

'I know. And that's when Henry said about it being too risky and they could get caught. Marielle then said something about how they had got away with it before.'

Jo leans across me to play back their conversation. She presses the stop button and looks at me, an eyebrow raised. Last year, when she turned forty-five, she'd had it pierced. 'My midlife crisis,' she'd called it. 'We need to try to record them again.'

'Wait, what? No. We can't, Jo.'

She stands up straighter, pushing her shoulders back. I tease her that this is her 'barrister pose'. She always does it when she wants to make a point, although it loses its power as she's swaying slightly. 'It could be illegal . . .'

Trust Jo to think that, her being a barrister. But an uneasy feeling washes over me. She's right. This could be something. And, if it is, I can't ignore it.

Not like you did before.

I push away the thought. That's not fair, I tell my subconscious. Yet that started in exactly the same way, with a suspicion I talked myself out of. If I'd acted on it, I could have saved lives.

'Lena?' Jo is staring at me. 'Come on! It's doubtful we'll hear anything, but it's worth a shot.' She suppresses a hiccup. She's a bit drunk and I know she's enjoying the drama, the laugh of it all. I might as well go along with it, even though I'd sobered up the moment I saw Charlie kissing another woman.

I sigh. 'Okay. Come on, then, how shall we do it?'

'This is what I think you should do . . .' She grabs the sound monitor and hands me the microphone before walking out of the kitchen. She has a habit of leaving rooms mid-sentence so that I have no choice but to follow. She heads upstairs and I trail behind her with the microphone, which keeps getting caught on the ceiling. When she reaches the top of the stairs she turns to me. 'Rufus's room? It's the one that looks out onto the back garden, right?'

I nod. She takes the mic from me and enters my son's bedroom. It's bathed in a silvery light and she moves stealthily across his floor with exaggerated movements and pulls up the sash window. 'If we rest the mic here and set the tape to record we might pick something up,' she says, wedging the microphone between the window and the sill so that it resembles a rodent caught in a trap. 'Just leave it running.'

'Fine. Just don't tape over Rufus's background sounds. Use the other side of the tape.'

Jo hides the end of the microphone behind the curtain, plonks the monitor on the floor and turns to face me, looking pleased with herself.

'Careful with that. Rufus's college mate is picking it up on Saturday. I don't want a bill for broken equipment, even if it is nearly thirty years old.'

She places a finger on her lips and giggles, then presses record on the monitor. She grabs my arm and wordlessly leads me from the room. It's not until we're back downstairs that she speaks again. 'How long is the running time on the tape?'

'I have no idea. Two hours? It's eleven seventeen now.'

'Listen to it in the morning. You just never know.'

I resist rolling my eyes at her.

We head downstairs and I put on some Taylor Swift (Charlie hates her music: too jolly for him!), light some candles and pour ourselves some Coke to sober us up as we have to get up for work the next morning. We spend the next forty-five minutes theorizing over what the Morgans might have been talking about, each idea becoming more and more outlandish and absurd. We've got them involved in everything from spying on the government to being the biggest swingers in town, to Bristol's answer to Fred and Rose West. Then, just before midnight, Jo calls Paul to come and pick her up. She must notice my worried expression at spending the night alone as she adds, 'You'll be okay, won't you? Do you want me to stay the night?'

I bite my lip to stop myself saying yes and shake my head. 'I'm fine. I've got Phoenix. But thanks for scaring me half to death with your theories on what the Morgans could be up to,' I say.

Just five minutes later a pair of headlights beam through the glass of the front door. Jo gathers up her bag and reaches over to hug me. 'Let me know if anything else happens,' she says, brushing her lips against my cheek. When she pulls away she says, softly, 'I know seeing Charlie tonight must have been really tough, but remember, you were the one who wanted the split. And it's for the best. You weren't happy, hon.'

And then she's gone.

*

The house feels even more silent now that she's left, and I go around blowing out candles, turning off the music, making sure every downstairs window is shut and the patio doors are locked. I think about the microphone upstairs, recording into the dark, humid night, and can't help but smile to myself. If nothing else, Rufus should get more background noise, although I'll have to get up extra early tomorrow to record day sounds before work. From outside I hear the cries of foxes and trudge up to bed with Phoenix at my heels. Since Charlie moved out I've allowed the dog to sleep on the bed with me, and as I slip beneath the sheet I feel reassured by the heavy weight of him against my legs. I turn off the light and try to sleep, but every time I close my eyes I see Charlie kissing the other woman. In a burst of indignation, I sit up in bed, switching the lamp back on. I stare down at my hands and the platinum wedding band embedded with tiny diamonds. Inscribed inside is a short lyric from a song Charlie wrote about me when we first fell in love. I twist it around my finger and then, in anger, I wrench it off and throw it into the drawer of my bedside table among my socks. Fuck him, I fume. Fuck him and his stupid young girlfriend!

I turn the light off and lie in the dark, waves of fury rolling over my body. I toss and turn and must eventually fall asleep because when I wake up it's crushingly dark, and I can hear Phoenix's low, rumbling growl that seems to vibrate through the bed. My heart starts hammering and pressure builds in my bladder. I sit up, listening for sounds, my skin turning clammy. Phoenix's growls grow more insistent as I blink in the darkness, trying to adjust my eyes. I can just about see the outline of his pricked ears, his bared teeth and the whites of his eyes. I pick out the shadows in the darkness. Phoenix's head is now turned towards my closed bedroom door. He isn't one of those barky dogs. We rescued him eighteen months ago from our local cats-and-dogs home – he'd been well trained and adored for the first eight years of his life by an elderly lady who'd had to give him up to go into residential care.

'What is it? What is it, baby?' I whisper, reaching for his head, but he continues his low-level snarling. When Rufus is here I keep my bedroom door open, a habit from when he was little. I swing my legs around and sit on the edge of the bed. Phoenix jumps down and lets out a sharp bark that makes me jump. And then he stands at my bedroom door, growling. My heart picks up speed. This is unlike him. Oh God, oh God. I try to quell my panic that some-one is in the house, but my legs start trembling.

'Sssh, Phoenix, shush.' I listen intently for any sound or movement, but I can't hear anything apart from the dog. I go to the window and pull aside the curtains. The street is dark and silent. I can see the corner of the Morgans' house, but there are no lights on. The clock on my bedside table flashes up 1.06 a.m. Is it burglars?

Phoenix barks again. I scan the room for an object I can use as a weapon. All I can see is my lamp. I pull the plug from the wall, the lead trailing after me as I brandish the lamp in one hand. With trepidation I open the door and grab Phoenix's collar so he can't dart off without me. I stand there for a moment, my heart beating wildly, and then I grapple around for the light switch. I slowly descend the stairs, Phoenix straining against my hand. I can hear my shallow breathing, but everything else is quiet. Phoenix is still growling softly. I've reached the bottom step now. The lamp feels sweaty in my hand, but I grip it tighter. Moonlight or streetlight filters through the fan of glass at the top of the front door, reflecting onto the wooden floor, but everything else is in shadow.

Phoenix suddenly pulls away from me and gallops towards the kitchen, barking madly. Oh God, is someone in there?

'Phoenix,' I hiss, fear making me snap.

I pad down the hallway towards the kitchen and jump when I hear a crash outside, something falling and breaking. My heart thumps painfully. *What the fuck was that?*

From my position in the hallway I can see through to the kitchen and the patio doors ahead. They are closed. No smashed glass or kicked-in lock.

Nausea engulfs me and for a few moments I'm too scared to move. I'm suspended there, in the hallway, clutching the stupid, useless lamp. And then fear is replaced by anger. How dare someone come into my house? My sanctuary. And, with a burst of adrenaline, I rush into the kitchen, growling like a woman possessed, the lamp raised, ready to hit whoever might be lurking in the kitchen.

But it's only Phoenix standing there, looking up at me with his dark eyes.

'What was that crash?' I ask Phoenix. I catch sight of myself in the reflection of the patio doors, in my shapeless PJs, my dark hair a messy halo around my head, my brown eyes huge in my pale face. And then I notice something else. I move closer to the doors and peer through the glass. One of my terracotta tubs is overturned, rolling on its side on the patio. Someone was out there. Someone was in my garden. I click on the outside light, which instantly illuminates the patio, throwing shadows onto the lawn.

A chill runs down my back.

The garden gate that leads to the lane, which is always closed, is wide open.

I'm relieved when it's morning. I hardly slept the rest of the night and took a knife to bed. I'm not sure what I would have done with it had anyone tried to break in. The cry of a baby woke me briefly at five but I dropped off again, feeling safer because the sun was up. Now, in the cold light of day, I grasp at explanations for the knocked-over tub and the open garden gate. Maybe I'd forgotten to lock it. Maybe an animal had knocked over the tub. I'm not convinced.

At seven thirty my room is like an oven, and I reach over to widen the window. The morning air smells of hot car fumes and festering bins. My head is pounding. I shouldn't have drunk so much last night and now I've got a full day at Citizens Advice ahead of me.

I reach for my phone to text Jo but she's already sent a message.

SO? Did you listen?

For a few seconds I wonder what she's talking about and then I remember our plan. I get out of bed and head to Rufus's room, kneeling on the carpet to press play on the tape deck. There is nothing but white noise. I pick it up and take it downstairs, plonking it on the kitchen table.

I let the tape run while I'm making a cup of tea and sorting out Phoenix's breakfast. My limbs feel heavy. Just when I'm about to give up and turn it off I hear something: Phoenix's barking and growling. And then I freeze. What was that? A crash. The same as the crash I heard last night. My eyes instantly go to the tub, still lying on its side.

I rewind and listen, turning up the dial as far as it will go. It's faint and hard to hear behind the fuzz of white noise and Phoenix's barking, but I'm sure I'm not mistaken. It's there, just after the crash of the tub.

A man's voice.

6

HENRY

December 1986
London

Henry didn't want to go to the party. He hated all the false
joviality surrounding Christmas, but it was a new job and
his boss, Stanley, had insisted he went.

'You'll have fun,' he'd said, clapping him on the back,
like they were old chums. 'All the higher echelons of
society will be there. Plus trustees at the hospital. You can
do a bit of hobnobbing.'

Henry hadn't become one of the top surgeons at the
private hospital where he worked to 'hobnob'. If he'd
wanted a job like that he would have been a lawyer. But
he'd looked up into Stanley's shiny, plump, expectant face
and acquiesced, even if he would rather have gone back to
his little rented flat in Marble Arch to immerse himself in
the first and special editions of his favourite books and
drown his sorrows with a bottle of Chablis.

So now here he was, wearing a borrowed dinner jacket,
in the back of the taxi as it darted through the ice-coated

London streets towards Kensington, squashed between Stanley and his garlic breath, and another colleague, Rupert something or other, who wouldn't shut up about advances in cosmetic surgery. The radio was playing that annoying Christmas song by Shakin' Stevens, although he could hardly hear it over Rupert sucking up to the boss.

The party was being held at the V&A Museum, and when Henry got out of the taxi he stood and gazed up at the building with its beautiful intricate mouldings and arches. The entrance was lit up against the dark night, casting a blue hue onto the frost-covered steps, and despite his reluctance to socialize, he marvelled at how far he had come in the last decade. He had escaped his dull little Hampshire town in the middle of nowhere and the father he'd always been so afraid of. Through sheer hard work and intelligence, he'd managed to gain a place at medical school at Cambridge and change his life. Now he was here he just wanted to keep his head down, earn money and his freedom, and exist under the radar.

'Come on, slowcoach,' called Stanley, and Henry steeled himself, as he'd taught himself to do in childhood, to follow them inside.

It was a posh do and the jacket was too tight, the fabric pulling across his back and around his armpits. A string quartet was playing Christmas songs, and uniformed waiting staff were weaving in and out of the crowds carrying silver trays covered with fancy foods he'd never heard of. Someone thrust a glass of champagne into his hand as soon as he entered the room, and Stanley, a hand firmly on his shoulder, directed him to different 'influential' people, but it wasn't long before he found himself adrift, as he always did. He stood in the corner and watched all these people effortlessly work the room. It crossed his mind that he'd never felt more alone. He couldn't do this, he thought. He was a strange, messed-up jumble of nerves and demons and trauma. He wasn't a proper functioning person. It was something that ate away at him when he was alone, burrowing into his mind, like a flesh-eating parasite. At school the other boys had thought he was weird. At home his father hated him. At medical school he kept himself to himself. He studied hard, worked his way up the ranks, but he never socialized. One of his deep-seated fears was that he'd never had the chance to form a personality. That, despite being handsome, he was too buttoned-up. Too strange.

He'd been ten years old when he understood that his mother wasn't coming back. He'd adored her and, so he thought, she him. Yet she'd walked out of their lives without a backward glance, leaving him alone with a man who should never have been a father.

It was no wonder that he found it hard to form relationships with women. He'd had a few girlfriends over the years. Nothing serious, just a string of flings with beautiful women who wanted to change him. To save him. Yet he had nothing in common with any of them and this had made him feel even more alone.

That all went through his mind now, like a galloping horse, as he stood there with his half-empty champagne glass. He should leave. He was never going to be the kind of protégé that Stanley was after. He was a good surgeon, but he was no networker. He lacked the charm.

And then he saw her.

She was standing by the door, alone, in an emerald gown, low-cut at the front, which showed off her long white throat and the diamond necklace that shimmered in her full cleavage. Her auburn hair was swept up in a Grace Kelly do and she looked as lost as he felt. In that moment it was as though all the air had been sucked from the room, everyone else fading into the background. Even the music seemed to stop. He'd never experienced that feeling before. It was more than her beauty that attracted him. Yes, she was stunning, but he recognized something in her. Something that was mirrored in him.

She must have been aware of his gaze because she turned her head towards him, her eyes meeting his, and he inhaled sharply, his stomach dipping with a sudden hungry desire that was almost painful.

Their eyes locked, only for a few moments, but it was enough time for him to feel it. The certainty that she was his other half. The woman he had been missing for all of his thirty-one years.

He'd never believed in love at first sight.

Until now.

7

LENA

'A man's voice.'

'What did he say?' asks Jo. I'd called her straight after listening to the tape. My whole body is still trembling at the thought someone was in my garden last night.

'He said, "*I forgot about the fucking dog.*"'

Jo gasps. 'Oh, my God! Did you recognize the voice?'

I glance towards the patio, where the tub is still on its side. There is a crack in the rim. 'I don't know. It was hard to tell. Obviously it was someone who knows I have a dog.' I feel sick and push away the toast I was nibbling. I stand up and begin pacing. 'I'm scared, Jo. All night I've been thinking about it, going over and over it. I overhear the Morgans talking about something potentially dodgy and then this happens. It can't be a coincidence, can it? My back gate was wide open. I swear it was locked. I'm worried Henry might have seen me with the boom mic.'

'I don't know,' Jo's voice sounds small. 'But even if they had, why would they come into your garden?'

'To break into the house and steal the tape?'

'But breaking in? It's not like you recorded them saying anything particularly incriminating.'

'Yes. True. The part where they said they were worried about getting caught was at the end of their conversation and I wasn't even recording at that stage. But they wouldn't know that, would they? If Henry spotted me he might have assumed I'd recorded more of their conversation. Who knows how incriminating it was? I didn't catch all of it. God, Jo . . . this is a nightmare. For all we know they could be secret psychopaths. A Fred and Rose West hidden underneath a veneer of respectability.'

'Don't panic. I've got to get to work, but I'll speak to Paul about installing a camera in your back garden.' Paul has his own security firm and kindly gave me a Ring doorbell when Charlie moved out. 'Will you tell Rufus?'

I shake my head, even though she can't see me. 'I don't want to worry him. He's been through enough. I just . . .' I swallow and blink back the tears that have come out of nowhere. 'I just want him to feel safe.' If I told him, I know he'd worry. Despite his gangly limbs, which he hasn't quite grown into yet, I still think of him as the little boy who always wanted me to check his wardrobe for monsters before he went to sleep.

'Understandable. You don't think it was one of his mates messing about or that kid who bullied him last year?'

It did enter my mind that it might have been Jackson. But Rufus has had no problems with him since he left school a year ago. Why would he suddenly strike now? 'No. I don't think so.'

'Look, let's put this into perspective. I know we were saying all sorts last night and letting our imaginations run away with us. But it's doubtful you're in any danger from

Henry Morgan. I mean, in the cold light of day the idea is ludicrous. How old did you say he was? Like, seventy?'

'Not quite. Late sixties.'

'Well, there you are, then. Perfectly harmless.'

I know Jo is trying to make me feel better. It's what she's always done. She's like the big sister I never had, a confidence booster and a brilliant sounding board. She always makes me feel better and talks me down when I start to spin out (which seems to be more often since Charlie left).

'I don't know, Jo. I keep thinking about what happened all those years ago when I was doing my midwife training. Remember I told you about Simone? If only I'd spoken up then about what was going on, what Simone and that doctor were up to, instead of burying my head in the sand. If only . . .'

'Look, that wasn't your fault, and neither is this.'

I know it, deep down, but it doesn't stop me feeling guilty.

Jo's voice softens. 'Hon, this isn't your problem. The likelihood of it being anything truly bad is very small. They could have been talking about anything.'

Relief washes over me at the thought of being let off the hook. Jo, the voice of reason, has given me permission not to feel guilty about this. Whatever the Morgans were talking about is between them and nothing to do with me. I have to stop feeling as if I'm expected to do the right thing all the time. The right thing in this case is to do nothing.

But you did nothing once before and look what happened.

47

I push away the intrusive thought. 'You're right,' I say. 'Now, go. You'll be late for work. I've kept you talking long enough.'

'At least you've got your mum coming to stay tomorrow. You can tell her all about it.'

I laugh because we both know my mum isn't understanding. She wasn't born with a sensitivity gene. 'And Rufus will be back tonight,' I say, relieved I won't be in the house on my own. I'm even more creeped out after what happened last night. What if the man comes back?

I decide to take Phoenix for a walk before I leave for work, having recorded more sounds for Rufus. I haven't even allowed myself to think about Charlie kissing another woman. I won't be able to tell Mum when I see her tomorrow. Sometimes it feels as if she loves him more than me and she doesn't understand why we split up. I would have thought – considering she kicked my father out when I was nine – that she'd be more sympathetic.

My father was an artist, which Mum had loved about him, until his lack of conventionality and stability started to frustrate her. He moved to Provence, but I still saw him regularly, and when he died eighteen months ago he left me some money. My mum had been shocked, believing him to be impoverished – 'He didn't even own his home!' – and hinting that he'd never paid a penny for me after they split up. But I'd loved my dad with all my heart. I knew he was flawed: he smoked too much, loved his red wine, was irresponsible in so many ways (he gave me a joint at fifteen, which I'd hated, but my mum had never forgiven him), and by the end had myriad health problems. I loved his spontaneity, his passion for life. It's not a coincidence that I married a man with similar qualities. Mum likes to think she defies conformism by making her grandson call her Bess and dating a younger man, but that's as far as her 'free spirit' stretches.

The street looks pretty in the sunshine, the trees full and vibrant, flowers bright and open despite no rain for weeks. I'm pleased Mum will be seeing it at its best. She can't understand why I fled London all those years ago only to settle in Bristol. She thinks I should have married a lawyer and moved back to Rye, to the idyllic cottage where I grew up and where she still lives.

As I walk out of my front gate, Phoenix jostling ahead, pulling at his lead, my heart sinks. Marielle Morgan is walking towards me, pushing an old-fashioned pram. She has a bottle of water in the cup holder. She's immaculately dressed as usual, this time in a linen A-line shirt dress in mint green and ivory sandals, her auburn hair perfectly set. As she approaches me she smiles. 'Hi, Lena.'

I return the smile, letting the gate close behind me with a creak, and go to peer into the pram. I've always loved babies and Rufus accuses me of treating the dog like one, but before I can do so she reaches for the hood and pulls it down. 'He's sleeping,' she says apologetically. 'My daughter-in-law won't be happy if he doesn't get his allocated nap time. She's doing Gina Ford.'

'Oh, okay.' I step back. 'What's his name?'

She hesitates and I get the strange sense she doesn't want to tell me. But then she says, 'Arthur.' Her face lights up. 'He's only seven weeks old. They sleep a lot at this age, don't they?'

That wasn't my experience of Rufus as a baby but, then, he did have reflux.

'Did you . . . um . . . look after Arthur last night?' I ask, thinking of the baby I'd heard crying in the early hours.

'Yes. Babysitting duties. I love it, though.' She laughs. 'I'd have him all the time if it was up to me. Don't think my son would like that, though, unfortunately.'

'Ah, well, it's nice for them to have a break.'

She glances towards the pram with a proud smile. 'We don't usually have him overnight. Heidi, my daughter-in-law, has gone back to work one day a week so I get to have him every Thursday at least.'

I'm surprised. 'That's a short maternity leave.'

'Ah . . . no . . . well, yes.' Her smile wavers. 'I think she does it to get out of the house, have a break. She loves her job. She's a librarian at the central library. She finds it peaceful.'

'It's good to keep her hand in,' I say, thinking of how I'd have liked to do the same when Rufus was born, but it would have been hard around Charlie's rehearsals and tours. 'I love that library. We went there a lot when Rufus was little.'

'Anyway,' – she clutches the pram's handle – 'best be off before this one wakes up. Have a good day.'

'You too.'

I watch as she continues down the street, the pram bouncing up and down jauntily.

As I walk around the park with Phoenix I can't get the Morgans' conversation out of my head. The more I ruminate on it, the more it morphs and warps in my mind, just as fear can cause a shadow on a wall to turn into a sinister face at dead of night.

You promised me you'd take her. I've got everything ready. The room . . .

I did wonder if they could have been talking about their grandchild. Now I know he's a boy, who had they really meant?

8

On Saturday morning I hear my mum arrive before I see her. She has the kind of voice that carries. She's nosy and will talk to anyone so I'm not surprised when I hear her chatting to someone outside.

I'm in the living room brushing Phoenix's fur from the sofa – my mum has a million dogs yet there is never a hair to be found in her immaculate cottage. I peer through the living-room window. Oh, God, she's talking to Henry. She's become all flustered and high-pitched. Marielle is nowhere to be seen. I'm going to have to rescue him – he'll be there all day otherwise.

Leaving the front door on the latch, I step outside. Mum is practically leaning over the Morgans' wall to talk to Henry. Her sunglasses are pushed back onto her still-dark curls and she is wearing a pretty floral blouse and white capri pants. Henry has a watering can in his hand, which hangs uselessly by his side, and he's nodding politely as Mum natters away.

'Oh, there she is,' Mum cries, when she sees me. 'You never said you had new neighbours, Lena.'

My toes retract in my sandals and Henry gives me a half-smile. It's the first time we've met since I think he might have seen me with Rufus's boom mic in the garden.

'Aren't you going to help me with my case?' She directs this at me, but Henry jumps to attention, swiftly moves out of the gate and is taking it from her while she's laughing and saying, 'Oh, I didn't mean you, but thank you.' I go to take the case from Henry but he insists and follows me inside the house, Mum keeping up a running commentary on the trains and the walk from the station in the heat. I'd offered to pick her up from Temple Meads but she'd refused.

Henry stands awkwardly in my hallway, still clutching the handle of my mum's yellow suitcase. It feels strange having him here.

'You must stay for a cup of tea,' insists Mum. 'Just leave the case there. Lena will take it upstairs for me in a bit, won't you, sweetheart?' She doesn't wait for me to answer as she frogmarches Henry down the hallway and into the kitchen. I wonder what he makes of it compared to his. The cream cabinets are chipped, and the walls need repainting. I had a nose on Rightmove when the developers put next door up for sale and the kitchen had looked spectacular with its glass extension, expensive mink-coloured units, marble work surfaces and pale oak floors. Poor Henry looks completely bamboozled by my mother as he sits at my old oak table while she rushes around after him making tea – as if this is her house, not mine. He laughs at some of the things she says as she chatters on to him, takes the tea and sips it. He's wearing chino shorts, a short-sleeved shirt, blue-and-white boat shoes, and looks the picture of respectability and class. Everything my mum admires in a person.

I notice the boom microphone and tape deck propped up in the corner and my heart drops. Henry doesn't appear to have spotted them, thank goodness. His attention is taken up with Mum.

'So, Henry,' she says, pulling out a chair so she's sitting next to him, 'what brings you to Bristol? You don't sound like you're from the West Country.'

'His grandson is here, Mum,' I say, moving past them to open the patio doors. It's stifling in the kitchen and there is no air, even with the doors open, but I'm also hoping to obscure Rufus's recording equipment. I can smell Henry's aftershave, something expensive and musky.

'Oh, how lovely. How old?' Mum asks Henry, ignoring me.

'I . . . um, a few weeks, I think,' he says, with a frown, while I pour myself a glass of water.

Mum shuffles in her seat. 'Where are you from?'

'All over. I grew up in Hampshire. Moved to London. We lived in Scotland for a bit.' He sips his tea. Mum has put too much milk in it, but Henry doesn't complain.

She looks as if she's about to ask another question when her eyes go to the tape deck and microphone. 'What on earth is all that?'

Henry follows her line of sight, and frowns.

Damn it.

'Oh, that's Rufus's college equipment.'

'Why the huge microphone?' Mum asks. 'What is he planning to do with that?'

'He's just gathering background sound for his project . . .' I surreptitiously glance at Henry. His face is expressionless.

Mum laughs and turns to Henry. 'My grandson thinks he's Steven Scorsese,' she says.

'Steven Spielberg, Mum,' I say. 'Or Martin Scorsese.'

Henry looks up at me, mug in hand. 'I've seen you and your son in the garden with it,' he says mildly, with no apparent edge to his tone, but my stomach flips anyway.

'It's very old equipment. It doesn't pick up much. We managed to get an owl hooting but that's about all.' I laugh, but it sounds forced.

Henry puts down his mug with a small smile. 'Thanks so much for the tea. I'd better get back or Marielle will wonder where I am.' He stands up. 'It was lovely to meet you, er . . .' He glances at my mum.

'Bess. Are you sure? You've not finished your tea.'

'I'd love to stay longer but I promised I'd take Marielle to the garden centre.' He smiles charmingly at Mum.

She leaps up to trot after him and doesn't come back in for another ten minutes. I dread to think what other information she's prying from him. Mum has been known to extract all sorts from strangers, anything from their sex lives to whom they've fallen out with.

When she comes back she looks a little ruffled. 'Such lovely people!'

'You met Marielle too?'

'She was in their front garden. What an immaculately turned-out woman. She was a lecturer at some fancy London university, and he was a neurosurgeon. He went to Cambridge. So clever! They have lovely accents, don't they? Very well spoken. They still have a flat in London. And a country pad in the Cotswolds. Old money. You can tell.' She dusts down her trousers. 'Anyway, where's Rufus?'

'Oh, so you've noticed your grandson isn't here?'

She shakes her head at me in mock exasperation. 'Of course.'

'I thought you were too dazzled by Henry Morgan to notice anything else,' I tease.

'Oh, stop it.' She hides a giggle behind her hand. 'But he's handsome, isn't he? Very debonair. Like Sean Connery.'

'Mum! He looks nothing like Sean Connery!'

'Okay, maybe a taller Paul Newman then.' She bends down to stroke Phoenix, who is nuzzling her leg. 'So where's my grandson?'

'At Charlie's.' I glance at the clock. It's nearly lunchtime. 'He'll be back in a minute.' I'd checked Find My Phone and he was only around the corner. Jo thinks that now Rufus is seventeen I shouldn't be tracking him any more. But I can't help it. I like to know where he is when he's not at home. It's always so reassuring to see that he's arrived at his destination safely.

Rufus had called me while I was at work yesterday, asking if he could spend another night at Charlie's because one of his friends was having a party not far away. I'd been almost winded with disappointment, not to mention terror at having to spend another night alone. I'd hardly slept, waking up at every creak coming from the house, although thankfully there were no repeats of Thursday night. I'm exhausted today and so relieved that the house will be full tonight.

As if on cue I hear the key in the lock and Rufus saunters in. His mass of sandy hair, just like Charlie's, is dishevelled and he looks as though he's slept in his clothes. My heart soars at the sight of him and sinks when he's followed by

Charlie. Why is he here? He hasn't set foot in the house since he left. The living room still looks bare since he took out his huge speakers and sound system, and the study at the foot of the stairs was where he kept his drum kit but now houses only Rufus's guitar.

Mum, who has barely sat down, jumps up again to give Rufus a hug, and then Charlie. I try not to feel offended that she hasn't hugged me since she arrived.

For a few seconds everything feels like it used to: this time last year we might have gone for a pub lunch. We might have sat outside, at that nice place in Clifton Village, filling up on artisan bread. Charlie would have had a lager, Rufus the fish and chips, his favourite, Mum the Welsh rarebit and a glass of wine. Things can change so much in a year.

'How did you get on last night? Was the party fun? And how was the gig on Thursday?' I ask, hugging Rufus and avoiding Charlie's gaze. 'Was it good?'

'Yep,' he replies, opening the fridge and sticking his head inside.

'Meet anyone new at the party? Any nice girls?'

'Nope.' And that's all I'll get out of him as he removes a packet of pre-cooked mini sausages and starts stuffing them into his mouth. Maybe, now he's older, he feels more comfortable talking to Charlie about this kind of stuff. I've always been over-involved. Charlie once called me a 'mama bear' and he didn't mean it as a compliment. I do find it hard to listen to reason when it comes to Rufus because my instinct is always to fight hard for him in a way my mum never did for me. I still remember how she reacted when I left my midwifery course. And then, later, when I moved to Bristol. She was never on my side.

'Goodness, Charlie, don't you feed the child?' Mum asks.

Charlie shrugs. 'You know what he's like. I don't know where he puts it.' Then he catches my eye. 'I . . . er . . . was wondering if I could have a quick word, Lena?' His gaze goes to my mum and then back to me. 'In private?'

Mum looks mildly offended but starts fussing around Rufus so I lead Charlie into the living room.

'I like what you've done in here,' he says, taking in the newly painted pale pink walls and new velvet cushions. 'Very . . . minimalist.'

'That's because most of your stuff used to be in here.' There's a throb of awkward silence.

He clears his throat. 'You look well,' he says, appraising me.

'Wish I could say the same for you.' I laugh to take the sting out of the words.

'And straight to the point, as usual,' he quips. Avoidance tactics, but we play out our usual roles. He thrusts his hands into the pockets of his jeans. His sandy-brown hair is still showing no signs of grey, but I can see flecks of white in his stubble.

'Band going well?'

'Not bad.'

Charlie's band, Moderation, had some early success at the height of the Britpop era back in the mid- to late 1990s with a hit single that Radio 1 used to play endlessly, and a record deal for one album. The band – particularly the lead singer, Sirus – had been young and good-looking, but when they failed to write anything as catchy again they were subsequently dropped and have spent the last twenty-odd years trying to replicate it. Now in their mid-forties, they are still performing at gigs in small venues around the West Country. Charlie also works as a painter and decorator for his dad's company, which he likes for its flexibility, but in the belief he'd be a huge rock star one day, he never bothered with any further education after he left school.

I'd met him after his flurry of success, in November 2004. I hadn't been living in Bristol long and didn't recognize him when I got chatting to him at a pub in Clifton as we stood at the bar waiting to be served. He'd laughed at that, his sparkly eyes crinkling as he acknowledged, 'Nobody remembers the drummer,' which wasn't quite true, but I didn't want to burst his bubble by admitting I just didn't remember *him*. I'd been smitten from that very first meeting. He was tall and broad and, as Jo described him later, 'very manly'. I'd always gone for finer-boned, wiry men with floppy hair and big eyes but there had been something about him, the relaxed way he stood at the bar, as though he had all the time in the world, confidence that was just on the right side of cocky, his gaze, which he fixed on me while I talked, making me feel like the most important person in the room and that I could do anything, be anyone.

It wasn't long before I moved into his swanky flat near the Downs, which he'd bought at the height of his fame, and I became the band's – or rather Charlie's – number-one fan. I preferred their newer music, which was more mature, nuanced, and I believed they would hit the heights of that first single. I really did. Charlie's optimism was infectious. Me, who'd always been a glass-half-empty person, falling in love with a man who truly believed his cup ran over. And things were great, at first, when he wasn't weighed down by responsibility, when he was young enough to think fame could still happen. When he could take off whenever he fancied to play a gig in some random town up or down the country – even abroad – and I could go with him.

I put my own career on hold to accompany him – not that I had much of one by then. Five years earlier I'd left my midwifery training, having become disillusioned after everything that happened with Simone. I'd looked up to her before I started to suspect what she was involved in. It turned out I'd been right about that, but the whole experience had left me depressed. I spent the next few years doing temp work for a recruitment agency. I fell hard for Charlie. But when I found out I was pregnant with Rufus eighteen months after we'd met, when I was twenty-six, things moved quickly. I wanted to put down roots, give our baby a stable upbringing. Charlie had been twenty-seven and I knew he felt he wasn't ready to be a father. He was still a big kid himself. So I was shocked when, just as I'd begun to show, he took me out to dinner in a fancy restaurant in town and slid a blue velvet box across the table.

'You don't have to marry me.' I'd laughed when I opened it and saw the most beautiful emerald ring. 'This isn't 1956.'

'No, it's 2006, and I want you to be my wife.' He'd grinned, although his smile had slipped slightly at the thought

I might say no. I'd loved him for that. His uncertainty. A glimpse at his more vulnerable side, which I rarely saw. And we really did try to make it work. We were happy for a long time. Until we weren't.

There have been so many moments over the last seven months when I've been tempted to pick up the phone and ask him to come home. To beg him to give our marriage another try. But I know it's not what he wants. Not really. And I'm not sure it's what I want either. I can't separate the longing for him from my longing not to be alone.

And now he's met someone new.

'So . . . last night . . .' He looks sheepish. 'I'm sorry you had to find out that way.'

'Is it serious?'

He fidgets from foot to foot. He still wears the same style of trainers as he did when I first met him: black Adidas Sambas. 'It's early days.'

My chest feels tight as it hits home that it's really over between us. 'Right.'

'There's another reason why I wanted to talk to you.' He hesitates, his eyes not leaving mine.

'Spit it out, Charlie.'

'The house.'

My stomach drops. 'What about it?' Our arrangement was that I'd keep the house. Charlie still owns the flat he had when I first met him and which he's now moved back into.

'We need to sell it.'

9

NATALIE

Natalie rushes back to her flat. She can't stay here. Not now. She's blocked the number, but what if they know where she lives? She has no choice but to flee, and her heart sinks at the thought of giving up her job, her life. Again. She'd liked working at Herman, Hardy and Sullivans. The guys were friendly but respectful of the fact she wanted her privacy. They didn't hassle her to go to the pub or try too deeply to get to know her. She did a good job and they knew it. She could live under the radar there, do her own thing, within reason.

And then there was the guy she'd met at the pub. She hadn't wanted to risk giving him her mobile number, but she'd hoped she'd see him there again this Friday night. He'd left enough heavy hints that that was where he'd be if she wanted to meet for a drink.

But now everything has changed.

How have they found her after all this time?

They must have seen that stupid newspaper article. Her photo had been in the paper, even if her name was different. She knew she hadn't imagined being followed. How had they done it? A private investigator?

It had been a man who had called her. But as soon as he used her real name she knew. Everyone she'd met since then knew her as Natalie. She'd abruptly ended the call. But it was them. It had to be.

'Oh, you've really messed with the wrong person this time.' She still remembers those chilling words after they accused her of ripping them off. She goes to the window, pulling aside the curtains, and looks out onto the busy street with its array of independent shops, cafés and the park around the corner. It's still early and there aren't many people around. A half-eaten kebab lies splattered on the pavement below. Is that someone watching the flat? But, no, it's just a woman pushing a pram. A person with a normal life, who isn't on the run like her. This is karma, she knows. She's made some stupid, stupid mistakes in her life. And for what?

She'll have to wait until it gets dark. Less chance of being seen. She closes the curtains with a sigh. She's loved living here. It's not much, just a one-bedroom rented flat above the kebab shop, with the smell of cooked meat seeping through the floorboards, scratchy carpets and the ugly furniture left by the landlord. But she's always felt safe here. Where should she go next? Maybe north. Perhaps Scotland. She could find a small village, somewhere they won't think of looking. She can't risk working for electricians again. Not now they know that's what she's been doing for a living. Thankfully, she's got enough money saved up to tide her over for a bit.

She needs to tell her brother. She hasn't seen him in the last few years, but she keeps in touch sporadically. Just so that he knows she's safe. But she can't contact him yet.

No, the most pressing thing she needs to do right now is flee and then, once she's settled, she can let him know where she is.

She hides in the flat for the rest of the day, and once it starts getting dark, she grabs her suitcase from the wardrobe and starts pulling clothes from their hangers and shoving them inside. She takes only what she needs – she's never been one for fashion and has just a few pairs of jeans, some jumpers and T-shirts, plus some faded bras and old pants. She scoops up her make-up, dumping it in a dusty sponge bag with a foundation mark on the side.

She's suddenly filled with a fire so intense she can feel the heat all the way to the tips of her fingers and flooding her face. She pauses at the door to look back at the flat, the scratched pine table she never used, the old leather sofa where she'd spend her evenings eating a ready-meal in front of the TV, living her life through her favourite shows. And then she grabs her trusty Mulberry bag and closes the front door softly behind her, pushing the key through the letterbox. She's paid up until the end of the month. She'll let the landlord know – when she's far away from here – that she won't be coming back.

She heads down the stairs. The kebab shop is closed so nobody sees her leave. She steps onto the street, looking back over her shoulder every now and again, but there's only a few people around and nobody is paying attention to her. She finally allows herself to breathe when she gets to the end of the street. It's fine, she tells herself. It's going to be fine. They haven't found out where she lives. Not yet. But it's only a matter of time so she's done the right thing. She takes a few deep breaths, her heart still racing.

Yes, she's definitely doing the right thing. It will all be okay. She won't be so stupid in the future. She'll be extra careful. She repeats this to herself as she takes a shortcut through the park to the station, walking as quickly as she can, dragging her suitcase on wheels behind her. It's even darker in the park without street lamps and she quickens her pace, the leaves on the trees whispering overhead. Maybe she should have gone the long way around, but there is no time, she tells herself. It's better she's on the next available train.

And then she hears footsteps.

She daren't turn around. It could be nothing. A stranger. Not someone who means her harm.

But then it could be *one of them.*

She breaks into a run, pulling her suitcase roughly over the uneven pavement, not caring any longer about trying to keep calm. Up ahead she can see the iron gate that leads out of the park. She's nearly there. Just a few more steps . . .

In the distance, just beyond the gate, there is a layby where a black car is parked, lights on and the indicator flashing in the dark. Is it a taxi? She could call to them. Tell them she's being followed. If she *is* being followed. Her hand is on the gate. Finally. Finally. She reaches forward to push it open. The footsteps are closer. They are right behind her now. But the car . . . Someone is getting out of the driver's side.

'Excuse me,' she cries. 'I think I'm being –'

A hand from behind her clamps her mouth shut.

'Going somewhere?' says a voice in her ear.

10

LENA

I stare at Charlie in shock. 'Sell the house! Why?'

'Mortgage rates have gone up.' He throws up his arms. 'Everything has gone up. I'm not making that much money from gigging any more. Royalties from *What Will We Do?* are drying up.' It was their first and most successful album, named after the hit single. 'My dad pays me a pittance, as you know. And,' he says softly, 'we did say when we split up that you could keep this house until Rufus turns eighteen. That's next year.'

'We did, I know, but . . .' A dark feeling of despair grows in the pit of my stomach. I love this house. The memories of Rufus as a child still echo around its rooms. And maybe, on some level, I'd hoped Charlie and I might have reconciled by then. That Charlie would tell me all the things I wanted to hear.

'It's a big house for just one person.' *For just one person.* His words are like a sucker punch to the stomach. No doubt he'll be shacked up with Rosie before long. 'You don't need a three-bedroom house.'

'The third bedroom is tiny. It's not a particularly big house.' My voice wobbles and I bite back my tears. He stares at me patiently without speaking. It's such a familiar gesture that I feel a lurch of anger mixed with regret. 'Okay,' I concede. 'I know I don't need three bedrooms.'

'If you earned more . . .'

'I work three days a week.' I used to supplement my income by working shifts at Collette's café on Gloucester Road. I'd loved the job. Getting to chat to customers and hearing all the local gossip was perfect for me, but I left last year after all the trouble with Rufus. Collette's son, Jackson, was the ringleader in the bullying. It was only when I noticed the bruises on Rufus's back that he confessed to a 'falling-out' with Jackson and some of his other mates, though he tried to brush it off. When I brought it up with Collette she defended him, saying it was between the boys and we should keep out of it. I was furious with her and ended up telling her just what I thought of her son, then I resigned. Rufus begged me not to complain to the school, said I'd make it worse, so I didn't. I still don't know if I did the right thing. I told myself it was only a few more weeks before he went on study leave and then he'd never have to see those horrible kids again. I've boycotted Collette's coffee shop ever since. And Rufus is happy now. The bruises are long gone and he's finally coming out of his shell. During this whole time Charlie left me to deal with it while he mucked about with his band like an unencumbered teenager. It had been one unravelling thread too many in the fabric of our marriage, impossible to mend, and leading to the conversation that ended it.

Charlie raises an eyebrow. 'Yes, but it's not well paid. If you worked full-time we could maybe keep the house longer.'

'I've tried to increase my hours,' I say, 'but there weren't any available the last time I asked.' I love being an adviser at Citizens Advice. I started off volunteering and when a part-time job came up two years ago I applied and got it. I'd put my own career on the back-burner so that Charlie could follow his music. One of us had to be the parent who made sure we were there for our son. Charlie could hardly do that when he was flitting up and down the country gigging.

'I'm not trying to be an arsehole, Lena.' I've always loved the way he says my name in his soft Essex accent. Laynah. He's not an arsehole. I know that. 'Look. I've got enough money for things to stay as they are for the next few months. Gives you time to sort something out. But if we sold it you'd have more money. We've got equity in the house and you can have it. I've got the flat.'

It all feels so final. I bet he's saying all this now because of *Rosie*.

He clears his throat. His hands are still thrust in his pockets, and he can't quite look at me as he says, 'We probably should talk about sorting out a divorce.'

I reel. 'Divorce?'

'That's what you wanted. Isn't it?' His gaze is challenging. Is it what I wanted? What I *want*?

'It was mutual,' I mutter, looking at my feet. It was more of a stance than anything else. I wanted him to take stock. To understand what he was losing by never being here, by being emotionally detached, by living his life through his music instead of facing the challenges we were going through as a family. I wanted it to kickstart him into changing. Instead, he just went ahead and left.

A muscle throbs in his jaw. 'We can't be in limbo for ever, can we?'

'I . . . No, I suppose not.'

He looks annoyed, like I've said the wrong thing.

I clear my throat, the weight on my chest intensifying. 'I'll ask again at Citizens Advice for more hours,' I say, my voice sounding thick.

He gives a curt nod, and my heart feels like it's being squeezed.

I don't want a divorce.

But pride won't let me admit it to him. Instead I leave him standing there and head back into the kitchen without another word. Mum and Rufus are sitting at the table. I can see she's made him a cheese sandwich with the crusts cut off, just like she used to do for him when he was little. He's telling her about a media ethics module he's doing on his course, and they turn when I walk in. 'Everything okay?' Mum asks.

'Yep. All good.' I've never bad-mouthed Charlie in front of Rufus and I'm not about to start now. Charlie pops his head around the door to say goodbye. He avoids looking at me. 'Before I forget,' he says to Rufus, 'I've shared Kit's number with you. He'll do mates rates. A tenner for half an hour. He's happy to come to the house, if it's okay with Mum.' He's acting like I'm not in the room.

'Cool. Thanks, Dad.'

'What's this?' I ask.

'Guitar teacher,' says Rufus, through a mouthful of sandwich.

'The band know the guy,' adds Charlie, finally meeting my eye. 'He comes to a lot of our gigs.'

70

I remember Rufus mentioning it on Thursday. 'Oh. Right, okay.'

'I said I'll pay for Rufus's lessons,' he says.

'You don't need to do that . . .' I begin.

He holds up a hand. 'It's no bother. It's my fault he needs lessons in the first place. If I could play better . . .' He smiles ruefully.

'Okay, well, thanks.'

His eyes soften as he looks at me. 'We can speak again . . . about the house.'

I nod, aware my mother's gaze is boring into me. He waves goodbye and leaves.

Mum turns to me. 'What did he mean about the house?'

'Oh, nothing,' I say, my voice breaking a little. I cough to disguise it. I don't want to discuss it in front of Rufus. Selling the house, divorce, it's all too final.

That evening we watch *The Third Man*, with Mum asking questions every ten minutes because she can't distinguish between the male characters or keep up with all the differing accounts surrounding Harry Lime's death. At one point I look across at Rufus, who has paused the TV yet again while Mum makes another cup of tea, and roll my eyes, making him laugh. As a result it takes way longer than usual to get through a film. I can't really concentrate anyway: my mind is too full of Charlie. We always planned to go to Vienna, where the film is set, but that's another thing we never got around to doing.

When Rufus goes up to bed I drag the sound monitor and microphone into the spare room, where Mum will be sleeping, and prop it against the window. Harrison was supposed to come and pick it up this afternoon but he

71

cancelled and said he'll swing by tomorrow lunchtime instead.

'What are you doing?' she asks, sitting on the edge of the bed in her cotton nightdress, her hair pulled away from her face by a stretchy headband as she applies Nivea Creme to her skin. The smell instantly transports me back to my childhood.

'Do you mind if I leave this running? Background sound for Rufus's project.' I haven't told her about the Morgans' conversation, so I don't mention that I'm actually doing this in the hope I'll catch them talking again. She might go over there and ask them outright. Either that or she'll say I'm over-thinking it all and it means nothing.

'Hasn't Rufus got enough sound now?'

'Might as well use up the rest of the tape,' I say. 'Please don't press anything. I've got it all set up.' Earlier I'd re-played the Morgans' conversation and recorded it onto my phone. It's not as clear as the tape, but I wanted a copy of it. I'm not sure why . . . it's not as if there's much, but I also didn't like the idea of not having proof somewhere in case their conversation turned out to mean they're involved in something murky.

'Wouldn't dream of it,' she mutters, lightly tapping Nivea onto her cheeks.

I glance out of the window at the ink-stained sky, never fully dark due to the pollution. I made sure to bolt the garden gate earlier. Jo promised Paul would find me a camera, and I'll sleep a lot easier once it's installed, although I feel safer knowing my mum and Rufus are in the house with me tonight. The night air is warm and sweet-scented: heat-soaked grass and jasmine.

I close the curtains and turn to Mum. 'Are you sure you can't stay tomorrow night as well? It's a long way to come just for one night.'

She glances up at me, her face shiny. Without make-up she looks paradoxically older and younger. 'You know I can't stay long – the dogs . . .'

'Yes, the dogs, I know.' Mick looks after them when she's away, so it's just an excuse.

She reaches for my hand as I pass. 'Is everything okay, sweetheart?'

The gesture is so unexpected, so unusually tender, that I falter. Mum is not one for outward displays of affection – at least, not to me. As a result, I can't hug Rufus enough. Thank goodness he's loving and lets me. She's different with Rufus, I'm pleased to observe.

'It's all good.'

'You seem sad. Is it Charlie?'

How do I tell her that it's everything? It's my marriage ending. It's Rufus on the brink of adulthood. It's the thought of an empty nest. It's the loss of my identity. How can I explain to her that I feel as though I'm grieving even though nobody has died? She wouldn't understand. She'd start talking about how I'm over-sensitive and how I must have inherited that trait from my artistic father, because, in her eyes, all the negative aspects of my personality must come from him.

I pat her hand. 'I'm fine, Mum. Honestly.'

Why do we say 'honestly' when we're being anything but? I've always done it, especially with Mum. There is so much about me that she doesn't know.

*

I wake up late the next morning. Mum is already up and the kitchen smells of bacon and toast. She tells me Rufus has gone to see Freddie to do more filming, and that she's already taken Phoenix for a walk.

'What time did you get up?' I ask, as I pick up the bacon sandwich she's prepared for me. It's nice to be waited on for a change. I noticed she's already unloaded and re-stacked the dishwasher.

She has a wet cloth in her hand and begins wiping down my laminate worktops. 'I was awake at six. It's so hot in your spare room. Couldn't get back to sleep so came downstairs, took the dog out at about eight and bumped into your neighbour, Marielle.' She stops wiping and looks at me, her brow furrowed. 'They got back late last night from their Cotswold house.'

'They have a Cotswold house?'

'Yes, I told you that before. Weren't you listening?' she chides, and I grin apologetically. I was probably thinking about Charlie. Since I saw him with Rosie I've not been able to get him out of my mind. 'Bourton-on-the-Water. I've heard it's beautiful.'

Charlie and I took Rufus there when he was about seven and let him paddle in the river. It had been an unexpected sunny day in late September. It was just after our last failed IVF attempt. We'd run out of money and couldn't try again. It is beautiful, but I'll always remember how I felt that day: grateful to have Rufus, but sad we couldn't add to the family. We never got to the bottom of why it was so easy to have one baby but never go on to get pregnant again. The doctors called it secondary infertility.

I can tell Mum is still chewing over something. 'What is it?'

She dumps the cloth in the sink, gathers up her empty mug and goes to the kettle to make more tea. I can see beads of sweat above her eyebrows and her hair has gone fluffy with the humidity.

'Oh, it's nothing . . .'

'Mum!'

She shakes her head as though trying to rid herself of a negative thought. Mum likes to give the impression she doesn't bad-mouth anyone, but she loves a bit of gossip. I sit up straighter. 'Is it the Morgans?'

'Well, like I said, it's probably nothing, but . . .' She glances around her guiltily, as though Marielle and Henry are lurking behind the patio doors. She lowers her voice. 'Marielle was pushing a pram. One of those old-fashioned ones. Expensive, no doubt. I asked her if it was her grandchild.'

'Ah, yes, his name's Arthur.'

'Right.' Mum grimaces. 'But when I went to look inside the pram she got really defensive and wouldn't let me. Said he was sleeping, which is all well and good, but what did she think I was going to do? Snatch the baby? I felt quite offended.'

'Oh, don't be. She did that to me too. She's just over-protective, I think.'

Mum turns away to make her tea and a prickle of unease settles over me. 'What?'

Mum turns back. 'I don't know. It's silly, really.'

'Go on.'

'Well, she was so weird about me looking in the pram because I might wake the baby. But the way she pushed past me and hurried on down the street, the pram was really bumping along. It would have woken the baby a lot easier than me peering inside.'

I frown. 'True.'

'Anyway, like you say, she's just over-protective. Such a lovely lady,' she says, clearly relieved that she can now rid herself of any negative thought about the Morgans.

'Interesting she had the baby today. She told me she only looks after Arthur on a Thursday when her daughter-in-law is working. And you said they got back late last night?' I need to listen to the tape to see if the boom microphone picked up their voices. I don't hold out much hope. If they were going to talk about whatever they're planning, they could have done that on the drive home.

Mum waves her hand dismissively. 'That's what she said. Maybe her son and daughter-in-law went with them.' She goes back to making the tea but I'm left with a niggly feeling I can't quite place.

11

The branch of Citizens Advice I work at is on the edge of the city, near the M32. Although there's another office in the centre, this one is always busy, and we've been short-staffed since my colleague Janet retired. I'm in every Monday, Wednesday and Friday. There are only two others in the main office when I arrive. There's a waiting room at the front and side rooms so we can talk privately to those who come in for advice. Kath and Susi are in today: Kath is a volunteer and Susi is the full-time supervisor. She's in her mid-fifties, super-knowledgeable, efficient, and doesn't suffer fools. She has a commanding presence, with a chin-length bob, sharp nose and watchful eyes. Kath, on the other hand, is scatty, always losing things, particularly her glasses (I once got into a car with her and was scared for my life!) and lives alone with her two cats, which she calls her fur-babies. She's just turned sixty and has never been married or had any children. I sometimes think of Kath in her tall blue house in Totterdown with her cats, and long days spent without talking to anyone, and wonder if she ever feels lonely. But you can be lonely surrounded by people. You can be lonely in a marriage with your husband, as I'd found.

When Susi leaves the room I follow her before I lose my nerve. I find her putting out pamphlets in the waiting room.

'Um, Susi, could I have a quick word?' I begin.

She glares at me from behind her glasses, clutching the pamphlets to her chest. It takes a lot to get a smile out of Susi. 'Be quick.'

'I . . . er . . . Well, I was wondering if—'

'Spit it out, Lena,' she says curtly. 'I haven't got all day.' She fans herself with one of the pamphlets.

'I was wondering if it's possible to increase my hours so I'm working more days . . .'

She blinks at me.

'. . . so I'm more full-time.'

She sighs. 'I'm not sure, Lena.'

She always uses our names when she's addressing us, something I suspect she was told to do during training to put us all at ease. And maybe it would if it wasn't coming from her. There is nothing about Susi that would put anyone at ease. She's all sharp angles and clipped words.

'Well –' I shuffle my feet – 'please would you consider me if more hours come up?'

She stares at me, and I can see all the doubts she has about me on her face. She once said, 'You're talented at this job, Lena, but too involved sometimes,' and it wasn't a compliment. She seems to be weighing me up, then her shoulders relax. 'I'll see what I can do, but we have strict budgets.'

'I understand. Thank you.'

I return to the office I share with Kath, feeling dejected and wondering if I could supplement my income by applying for shifts somewhere else, maybe another café. Kath looks up from her desk when I enter. 'Your boyfriend's here again.' She grins. She has a pile of cupcakes with pink icing in a plastic tub in front of her. She makes them every week and brings them in. Usually I'd be the first to scoff one, but I've no appetite today. I notice Kath's bought one of those chains for her glasses, which are hanging around her neck. There is a damp patch on the back of her floral blouse, and a fan whirs on the filing cabinet but isn't doing much to move air around this stifling room.

'Who?' I ask absently, as I shift through the paperwork for the woman I spoke to on Wednesday. I take out my notes, ready to input them into the computer.

'Drew Mayhew.'

Heat inches up my neck. Drew is around my age, attractive in a crumpled, dusty way, like a well-thumbed book. 'Rugged' is the best word I can think of to describe him. 'He's here again?' I didn't see him in the waiting room when I was talking to Susi. Drew comes in at least once a month, seeking advice on a variety of issues. Last month it was to ask about benefits due to his mum, who is a carer for his dad.

She chuckles. 'He popped to the loo, but he was asking for you.'

He always asks for me, which I'm quite flattered by while at the same time trying not to be. I get up – my dress is already damp around my legs even though I've hardly sat down – and almost bump into Drew as he comes out of the Gents. His face lights up when he sees me. The sun has brought out the freckles across his nose, and the T-shirt he's wearing shows off his toned arms from the manual work he does on his parents' farm. I'm surprised to see a tattoo poking out of his sleeve. I can just make out the bottom of it, but it looks like some kind of bird.

'Lena! How are you?'

'I'm good, Drew. And you?'

He grins. 'All the better for seeing you.'

I flash him what I hope is a professional smile and he follows me down the corridor to one of the private rooms. Despite the heat he's in jeans and heavy boots.

The room is airless. It smells of drains and too-warm computers. I throw open the window and turn back to Drew. I'm in for a long session. I know all about his life: his divorce from his childhood sweetheart, moving back in with his parents, helping them out on the farm. He doesn't have children, his parents are elderly, and his father is ill. I sense Drew's lonely, set adrift after his divorce. Sometimes, usually in the middle of the night, I wake up seized by a panic that I'll end up the same way when Rufus leaves home. Will I find myself 'popping in' to places just to see a friendly face? Just so I can talk to another human being?

I make my smile even wider and more welcoming. 'So, what can I do for you today?' I sit down opposite him, a table between us, and start the computer. It whirrs loudly as though angry to have been woken up. I'm supposed to read my advice from the screen, so I click on the benefits link. But no. He doesn't want to talk about which benefits he or his parents are eligible for. Not today. Today he has something to ask which is completely new.

'I need help trying to find someone,' he says.

12

Drew is staring at me eagerly, and disappointment takes root that I'm unable to help him. I shift in my seat. 'I'm so sorry, but I'm afraid Citizens Advice can't help with finding missing people, only financial issues, like what to do about pensions, personal property or life insurance.'

His expectant face falls. 'Oh. Right. Okay. What about resources or who to contact for help?'

'Sure. I can give you a list of organizations. Who are you looking for?'

A slant of sunshine beams in through the window, making him squint. I get up to pull down the blind. 'Thanks,' he says, when I've returned to my seat. He lets out a weighty sigh. 'It's my sister, Sarah-Jane. Sarah-Jane Mayhew. Although she might have changed her name.'

'Why would she do that?'

He rolls his eyes. 'Every time she makes a mess of her life she changes her name and runs away.'

I'm amazed that he's never told me about his sister before when he's been so open about all the other aspects of his life. 'When was the last time you saw her?'

He leans forwards in his chair and rests his elbows on the table. He has a streak of dirt on his wrist and a smudge on his cheek. I wonder if he's come straight from the farm.

His hazel eyes darken. 'A few years ago, although I'd hear from her now and again, just to let me know she was safe. She fell out with my parents a long time ago. She always was a bit of a wild child.'

'I'm sorry, Drew. That sounds tough.'

'We used to be so close,' he says, and I sense he wants to get it off his chest. 'When we were kids. We're only two years apart. But it's my dad. You know he's not well, and I don't think he'll last the year. I'd like to find Sarah-Jane so they can say goodbye to each other.'

'When was the last time you heard from her?' I ask as I print off a leaflet about what he should do next.

He rubs at the stubble on his chin. 'Well, that's the thing. She'd never usually leave it too long in between getting in touch. Maybe every few weeks. She gave me her number for emergencies but when I didn't hear from her in three months, I rang it. It was dead.'

'Have you tried the police?'

'I have. But they haven't done much about it.' He shrugs. 'Because we haven't seen her in the last few years, I suppose. I did tell them it's unusual she hasn't been in touch, but they didn't seem particularly concerned.'

I take a notebook and pen from the desk drawer. I know this is beyond my role as an adviser, but I can't resist getting some more information so that I can help him, even if I have to do it in my spare time. 'Where was she living and working when you last heard from her?'

'I last spoke to her in April. She said she was still working in Reading but she didn't say what she was doing. She's had all kinds of jobs. She used to work at a clinic.'

I scribble this down. 'Do you remember the name of the company she worked for?'

'She's always so cagey. That's what's so frustrating and made me panic when I couldn't get hold of her. I know nothing about her life except that she was living in Reading and had worked as a receptionist for a clinic. Last time I spoke to her she said she'd left the clinic a few years ago, but I remembered the name, rang them and I did manage to find someone who was also working there at the same time. They now live in Bristol and they've agreed to meet me later, so you never know. They might have some information, although it's doubtful. I'm running out of options.'

I look up at him, pen in hand. 'Do you think she could still be in the Reading area?'

He shakes his head. 'Maybe, I dunno. She did say when I last spoke to her that she wanted to move on. That she didn't feel safe.'

'Safe?'

He hangs his head. 'I worry that she might have got involved with some dubious people.'

'What makes you say that?'

'Just reading between the lines. The things she didn't say. I don't think it was only falling out with my parents that kept her always moving on or never wanting to give me her address.' His shoulders sag and my heart goes out to him. 'I keep hoping she'll call, but she never does, and Dad's getting frailer by the day. And –' he sits back in his chair – 'I don't even know if she'd care. That's the thing. She hasn't bothered to speak to my dad for years, after all. But, I dunno, I feel it's only right that she gets the chance to say goodbye. Do you know what I mean? And, more than that, I just want to know that she's okay. That she's safe.'

It's gone four thirty by the time I arrive home. Rufus will be back from college soon. The house feels even emptier after a weekend of people, although my mum insisted on leaving after lunch yesterday afternoon. I was tempted to reveal all about the conversation I'd overheard between the Morgans, but something had stopped me. I'm still not sure what. Maybe I'm worried Mum will judge me for listening in on them because her prejudices are hard-wired, and I know that what she terms their 'good breeding' will always be at the forefront of her mind. She even back-tracked on the pram business when I pushed her on it, doubting herself, and I know it's because my working-class mother, who grew up on a council estate in Hatfield, believes the Morgans are somehow above her, so she has to be wrong. I hate that she thinks like that, but I can't change her.

After she left yesterday I went into the spare room and listened to the tape I'd left running overnight, but, just as I'd suspected, all it had picked up were the orchestral sounds of wildlife at night. My back gate remained bolted and nothing had been knocked over in my garden.

Phoenix jumps up at me as I let myself through the door and I grab his lead. 'Come on then, boy,' I say. 'Time for a walk.'

As I round the corner of the street and head towards Gloucester Road I'm thinking about Drew and his missing sister. I'd printed off a list of organizations for him and he said he'd contact them, but I wish I could do more to help him. I'm so deep in thought that I don't notice the couple up ahead until I'm almost right behind them. My heart picks up speed when I see it's Marielle and Henry. They're holding hands and every now and again Marielle rests her head on his shoulder before righting herself. I slow down to keep a discreet distance, telling myself I'm not going to follow them, per se.

We carry on along Gloucester Road, past the record shops and the tattoo parlour and the store selling expensive shoes. There is a festival vibe to the area today, thanks to the heat. I can hear an old Massive Attack song somewhere in the distance and smell something spicy and delicious wafting from one of the restaurants.

And then, ahead, they pause outside – of all places – Collette's café. I hover in the shadow of a florist's, trying to hide behind a potted lemon tree, while at the same time wondering if I've lost my mind. I see myself as though from above, a crazy middle-aged woman crouching behind a tree to spy on her neighbours. Collette is bent over a chalk-board in a patterned maxi dress and flat strappy sandals, her blonde hair scooped up in a topknot. Even the sight of her makes me relive all the stress and trauma from last year. I've managed to avoid her since I told her what I thought of her son. She exchanges a few words with the Morgans, then disappears inside, and I notice them greet another woman. She's about ten years younger than me, with curly dark hair, and she's carrying a tiny baby in white cotton dungarees. This must be the daughter-in-law,

Heidi. She passes the baby to Marielle, who coos over him and pats his back as she drapes him over her shoulder.

Marielle kisses Henry's cheek and takes a seat beside Heidi at one of the outside tables. Henry waves at them as he continues down the street. I wonder where he's going.

'Can I help you?' A woman wearing an apron and a patient smile looms over me. 'Are you looking for anything in particular? An indoor plant, perhaps?'

I straighten, embarrassed. 'I . . . um . . . sorry, thanks, but no, I was just looking,' I say, hurrying away, Phoenix trotting by my side. I cross the road so that Marielle doesn't see me. I'm on the same side of the street as Henry now and spot his white hair bobbing up and down, head and shoulders above most people. I trail him as Gloucester Road steepens, and then he turns right into Sommerville Road. My whole body feels clammy but Phoenix shows no sign of flagging and is pulling ahead. It looks as though Henry is walking towards St Andrew's Park so I follow him down a residential road. Yes, now he's going through the main gate. Phoenix and I enter the park. I let him off his lead and he bounds ahead happily. It's much cooler in the park, sheltered by trees, and people are sunbathing on the grass. Henry heads to the van that serves as a pop-up café and orders a can of Pepsi Max. Then he stops in a patch of sunshine to drink it, looking at his watch. I sit at the base of a tree in the shade, Phoenix sniffing the grass at my feet, and push the sunglasses further onto my nose. I pretend to read something on my phone but I've half an eye in Henry's direction. It looks like he's waiting for someone – I wonder who. He holds up his hand and waves to someone approaching. A man. I watch as he draws closer, taking in his familiar round-shouldered walk, his windswept hair, his heavy boots. I take a sharp breath.

It's Drew Mayhew.

Why is Henry meeting the man who, earlier today, told me he's looking for his missing sister?

13

HENRY

December 1986
London

Her name was Marielle Bishop-Smith and she was twenty-eight years old, worked in academia and was the daughter of a wealthy property tycoon. She must have recognized something in him because when their eyes locked at the Christmas party they'd started moving towards each other as though pulled by invisible magnets. When she reached him she whispered in his ear, in a beautiful, husky voice, 'Do you want to get out of here?'

'Very much,' he'd replied. It was suddenly the thing he wanted most in the world.

She'd giggled, hooked her arm through his and all the awkwardness had left him. He knew it was a cliché but there was no other way to put it: he felt as light as air, as though all his bad thoughts and feelings had dissipated. Every sense was on high alert as he helped her into her cream faux-fur coat, his fingers brushing against her soft, porcelain skin. He couldn't take his eyes off the silk of her dress shimmering over her curves.

'I don't normally do this kind of thing,' he'd murmured, as they hailed a cab outside the V&A. *But I recognized something in you. A kindred spirit.*

'Neither do I.' She'd smiled up at him in mock wide-eyed innocence and he couldn't tell if she was joking. It was the first time he'd felt his heart twist with an emotion he didn't understand. They chatted non-stop in the cab on the way to her place. Words that had failed him in the past now spilt from him as if a dam had been breached. By the end of that fifteen-minute journey she knew more about him than anyone he'd ever met. She told him about growing up in a huge but echoing manor house in the countryside, with a conveyor-belt of nannies, a disinterested stepmother and a father who was always away. He told her about a mother who had left him and a father who hated him and how he'd been desperate to leave home.

'Now,' she'd said sternly, as the cab pulled up in front of a red-brick mansion block of apartments near Regent's Park, 'I'm trusting you aren't a serial killer before I let you into my home.' Her green eyes flashed and she threw her arms around his neck and kissed him. He felt it in every fibre of his being.

If he'd known then about the darkness that lived beneath her glossy facade, would he have made the same decision? He knew, without a doubt, that he would.

14

LENA

I'm cross-legged on the grass, watching Henry and Drew as they sit at one of the round tables by the pop-up café. Henry has bought Drew a cup of tea, and he dunks the teabag in the way he does when he visits me at Citizens Advice. Drew's body is angled towards Henry so that I can't see his expression, but they look to be in deep discussion. Are they friends? It seems a very unlikely friendship, especially as Henry and Marielle haven't long lived in Bristol, but that's judgemental of me. They might go way back for all I know.

The grass is prickly on my legs but at least it's cool here, under the tree. Phoenix is curled up beside me, snoozing. I'm still pretending to be absorbed by my phone, with my sunglasses on, but my gaze doesn't leave the two men. After about fifteen minutes they get up and shake hands. Then Henry walks away, continuing past the playground, and exits the park through the entrance on the other side. Drew stays at the table. I contemplate following Henry as he's not heading in the direction that would take him home, but I'd also like to ask Drew what they were talking about.

I get up quickly, Phoenix suddenly alert, and make my way to the van to order a Sprite. Phoenix is busy lapping water from the bowl the van owner has left out for dogs. I amble past Drew's table, on the pretence of looking for one of my own, then fake a double-take.

'Drew! What a surprise. How are you?' I take a seat on the chair next to him, feeling like the hammiest actor in the world.

He looks up at me in surprise. 'Lena. Hello. Oh, and you've brought your dog. Hello, boy.' He bends down to pat Phoenix, who flops at his feet. 'I'm assuming he's a boy?'

'He is. We're just out for a walk. What are you doing here?'

'I was meeting someone who used to work with SJ, Henry Morgan.'

'Henry used to work with your sister?' I ask incredulously.

He frowns. 'Yes. A few years ago now. Remember I told you she used to work as a receptionist at that clinic in Reading? Well, Henry worked there too, around the same time. How do you know him?'

I cast my mind back to our conversation earlier. He did say he was meeting an ex-colleague of his sister's, but I never thought in a million years they would turn out to be Henry Morgan.

'He's my neighbour,' I say. 'Not long moved in. Does he know something about your sister?'

Drew looks downcast as he rubs at the tattoo on his bicep. 'Not really. He was one of the surgeons at the clinic and he said . . .' he gives a little cough '. . . it's a bit embarrassing really, but they had to let her go.'

'As in sack her?'

'Unfortunately, yes. Lateness, apparently, and some un-orthodox behaviour. He didn't say what and I was too mortified to ask. Our family have always had such a great work ethic – farmers, you know, you must understand that, Lena,' he says earnestly, his eyes not leaving mine. 'But Sarah-Jane was never like the rest of us and, as I said before, I have started to worry she might be involved with some unsavoury people.'

'And Henry hasn't seen her since she left?'

'That's what he said. Three years ago, apparently.'

'But you don't believe him?'

His expression sharpens. 'I didn't say that. Why? Do you know something?'

Shit, I've said too much. 'No, not at all. Sorry. It just sounded like you were unconvinced, that's all.'

'What do you know about Henry?'

'Um . . .' I can feel heat flooding my face. 'Not much, really.'

Marielle's voice breaks into my memory.

You promised me you'd take her. I've got everything ready. The room . . .

And then Henry saying, *I know . . . but . . . after what happened before . . . should we really try again?*

I remember the night in my living room with Jo and all the crazy theories we discussed. Kidnap had been one, of course, but neither of us really believed it. It was just light-hearted chat. Could there have been some truth behind it? No. It's ridiculous. I'm putting two and two together and making five, just because of my conversation with Drew and seeing him with Henry. His sister sounds flighty, that's all, and Henry worked with her.

It's not going to go away. And I'm not going to forget about it. This has to happen as we planned. It's the only way.

It's too risky . . . we could get caught . . .

Their voices crowd my mind. Have I dismissed their conversation too quickly because they seemed nice and polite and respectable? Am I no different from my mother?

My thoughts bounce, back and forth, back and forth. I don't know what to believe. I've never been very good at trusting my own judgement. I wish I'd listened to my instinct over what I suspected Simone was up to, but I hadn't wanted to believe it at first because I liked her. Because she was fun and pretty and respectable. And the same for the doctor who was part of the scandal. I'd always trusted doctors implicitly, so my foundations were shaken. I wanted to believe they were innocent so I said nothing. I regret it now and I can't let it happen again.

I concentrate on blocking my ping-ponging thoughts. 'I'm so sorry, Drew. I really am. I wish there was something I could do to help.'

He smiles sadly. 'Thank you, Lena. You've always been so kind to me. Do you have any brothers or sisters?'

I shake my head. 'Sadly not. I'd have loved siblings, but my parents split up when I was nine and neither married again. My dad has passed away now and my mum has a boyfriend, but she only met him a few years ago.'

'And do you like him? This boyfriend?'

I picture Mick, with his tufty hair, his big, bulbous nose and his love of hiking and rare birds. He's never had children of his own but has a menagerie on his smallholding:

pigs, goats, chickens and dogs. When she comes to stay, he always remains behind to 'look after the animals' and has never shown much interest in getting to know me or Rufus. When we've gone to visit Mum in Rye, he'll pop in and have a cup of tea before swiftly heading back to his own place. Mum says he prefers the company of animals to people, but he seems fond of her, at least. 'He makes my mum happy so that's good enough for me.' I stand up and dust down my dress. 'Well, I'd better get Phoenix home. It's too hot for him to be out this long.'

He nods, but doesn't move from his chair.

Drew looks so lost, sitting there, so forlorn, that my heart goes out to him. I sit down again. 'Here, take my phone number. Call me if you think of anything else that might help.'

He looks a bit taken aback and then he smiles. 'Thanks, Lena. That's really kind.' We exchange numbers and I get up to leave. I say goodbye, clip the lead to Phoenix's collar and head out of the park.

On the walk home it strikes me that Henry could have spoken to Drew over the phone. A courteous but brief call to say Sarah-Jane used to work for him, but he hasn't seen her in years. Instead he made the effort to meet him and sat there talking to Drew for fifteen minutes. Why?

15

I slow down as I pass the Morgans' immaculate house, with its shiny yellow front door, brass knocker and the freshly pruned window-boxes. It has taken me twenty minutes to walk back from the park and, as I retraced my steps down Gloucester Road, I saw that Marielle was still with Heidi at one of Collette's wooden tables. I glance up at the blank opaque windows as I pass, wondering what secrets lurk inside the house.

I continue on to my own front door and let myself in. I head straight for the kitchen and open the patio doors to let in some air. It's nearly six but Rufus still isn't home. Phoenix darts past me and into the garden. Straight away he scampers towards the hedge that separates my house from the Morgans'. I don't think much of it at first. Phoenix has never escaped from the garden despite the gap in the hedge that Rufus used to slide through so he could play with Joan's grandson when he visited. But today I'm shocked when I see Phoenix disappearing through it.

I get down on my hands and knees to poke my head through. And, yes, there's Phoenix, as bold as brass, standing on the Morgans' lawn, his head tilted. He has something in his mouth.

'Phoenix,' I hiss. 'Naughty dog.'

He continues to stare at me before dropping whatever was in his mouth onto the Morgans' immaculate lawn. It glints in the sunshine.

'Phoenix.' I crawl through the gap. 'Come here. Come here, boy.'

But Phoenix picks up the object with his mouth again and trots over to the Morgans' patio with it. For goodness' sake. What the hell has he found? He settles down, puts whatever it is between his paws and starts chewing it. I crawl through the gap. I have no other choice, I reason. The Morgans won't be impressed to find my dog in their garden.

I stand up, dusting the dry soil from my knees. The lawn has a slight slope down to their huge glass extension and from here I can see right into their beautiful hand-painted kitchen. An illicit thrill of being somewhere I shouldn't runs through me but it's quickly replaced by fear of getting caught. I dash over to Phoenix, who thinks this is a game, leaps to his feet and away from me. We have a cat-and-mouse chase across the lawn as I get more and more frustrated. 'Drop it. Drop it, boy,' I say, as he backs into a corner with the object in his mouth. It looks small, like a toy mouse with a charm dangling from it. But as I get closer I see that it's a key with a keyring attached – some kind of knitted pink thing. Phoenix drops it and I grab it before he can pick it up again. It's wet with his saliva and covered in bits of soil. On closer inspection I can see it's a small pink bear, its foot now slightly chewed, thanks to my dog. Something about it tugs at the edges of my memory but I can't place where I've seen it before. What was it doing in the hedge? I slip it into the pocket of my dress. The Morgans might have dropped it, or it could have been one of the developers, or even one of Joan's daughters. Who knows how long it's been there? I grab Phoenix's collar and encourage him back through the gap in the hedge. I'm going to have to get that filled in somehow. Now he's discovered it I'm sure he'll want to go through it again.

When I'm back in my garden, dusting soil from my knees, I spot Rufus by the sink in the kitchen. A guy is sitting at the table drinking a glass of water. I squint as I get closer. He looks early to mid-twenties and has foppish blond hair and a chiselled jaw. He's wearing a white T-shirt and jeans and has leather laces wrapped around one of his tanned wrists. He wouldn't look out of place in a 1990s boy band.

'Hi, Mum,' says Rufus, leaning back against the worktop. 'This is Kit.'

Kit?

'He's here to teach me guitar,' clarifies Rufus, when I look at him blankly. Of course, I remember Charlie saying he'd found him a teacher. I was expecting him to be older. There is something familiar about him.

'Oh, hi, Kit. Lovely to meet you. I'm Lena. Have we met before?'

'Hey, Lena.' A lazy grin spreads across his face. 'No, I don't think so, although you might have seen me at one of your husband's gigs.' Estranged husband, I want to say, but I fight the urge to correct him.

'You can use the living room, if you like,' I say. 'It's much cooler in there.'

'Great, thanks.' Kit stands up and reaches for his electric guitar, which is propped against the wall in a cushioned case. He's taller than Rufus and broader, instantly making my son look much younger, and I feel a surge of protectiveness towards him.

Rufus leads Kit into the living room, chatting away, and I swell with pride. The months at college have done him good. A few years ago he found it hard to look strangers in the eye, never mind talk to them, but he seems at ease with Kit. Before long I hear a guitar riff float through the house.

I head upstairs to my bedroom and take the bear from my pocket. There is only one key attached to it and it's a simple Yale. I sit on the edge of my bed staring at it for a while. It looks like a front-door key. I really should show it to the Morgans just in case they mislaid theirs when they were moving in.

As I stand up to go back downstairs I notice a movement outside. A man is pacing up and down on the other side of the street, his head lowered. I recognize his gait and when he looks up and glares towards the Morgans' house I realize who he is.

Drew.

What is he doing? He's crossing the street so that he's standing by the Morgans' classic Jaguar. I continue to watch as he runs a hand slowly over the bonnet, his brows knitted, his expression dark. He continues to stand there for a few more minutes and, just as I decide to go down and find out what's going on, I see Henry opening his front gate. Drew is now gesticulating towards the car. He looks upset and his voice is raised, but I can't make out what he's saying over the sound of Rufus butchering the electric guitar in the room below. I watch, mesmerized, as Henry reaches over and squeezes his shoulder. It seems a friendly action, but Drew shrinks back, his expression one of alarm. Then Henry leans over and says something in Drew's ear. Drew shakes his head and mutters a reply. Henry turns away from him to walk back into the house. Drew stares after him for a couple more seconds before he slopes off down the street with an air of dejection. What was all that about?

16

NATALIE

Natalie's eyes flicker open. Where is she? The light is dim and there is a pounding at the back of her head that runs all the way down her neck, through her arms and to her fingers. Her whole body feels sore and heavy, as if she's been hit by a bus. Is that what happened? Was she knocked over? Is she in hospital? She tries to prop herself up on her elbows but even this small movement takes every ounce of energy she has. She's on a narrow bed, tucked up tightly beneath a crisp white sheet overlaid with a knitted navy-blue blanket. It must be a private room. It's white-washed and clinical, like a hospital, and there is a slight citrus scent undercut with bleach. She surveys the bare walls, the stripped floorboards, the patterned rug that lies next to the window, which is covered with white venetian blinds. In the corner is a rocking chair and, perched on a gingham cushion, a grey rabbit with a matching gingham bow tie. She blinks again. That's odd. It looks too nice to be a hospital room. Maybe she's in some facility, like rehab. But why would she be? She doesn't have a drug problem. She doesn't drink too much.

She flops back against the pillow, drained.

Is it still Sunday? Images shift and resettle in her mind. Why does her brain feel so foggy and her memories scrambled? She tries to put them in some semblance of order. She can't remember much. And then a snippet of memory. Walking through a park. She was running from something. Did she fall and crack her head? That would explain the shooting pain at the base of her skull.

She jolts when the door opens and a woman walks in wearing blue scrubs and a disposable face mask. She must be a nurse, she thinks, with relief. So, she is in a hospital. A very nice one too, from her surroundings.

The nurse is pushing a trolley into the room. On it is a tray of food, which looks like fish fingers and mashed potato. The smell makes her feel nauseous. Why does she feel like she's got a hangover?

'Where am I?' she asks the nurse, as she approaches the bed. 'Which hospital?'

The nurse doesn't reply. She doesn't flinch or make any sign that she's even heard her.

'Excuse me?' Natalie wonders if any sound is actually coming out of her mouth. She feels like she's in a dream. Maybe she is dreaming. Maybe she's dying. Maybe she suffered a brain injury in the park and is lying there, right now, on the hot tarmac, bleeding out from a head wound, surrounded by concerned onlookers, and this is all some out-of-body, weird near-death experience.

She tries to prop herself up again but finds she can't. 'Please,' she rasps. Her voice sounds weak but she's surely making some sound, yet the nurse continues to ignore her. She wheels the trolley over to Natalie's bed, but she doesn't look her in the eye. Instead she busies herself with pouring Natalie a glass of water from a jug. Then she slowly unwraps a knife and fork from a white paper napkin and begins cutting up the fish fingers as though Natalie is a child. Natalie can feel her mouth gaping open as she watches the nurse arrange her knife and fork for her and place the glass next to her plate, just so. And then she looks at Natalie squarely in the eye for the first time.

'Eat up, there's a good girl,' she says, as though Natalie is five, her voice muffled behind the mask. She reaches over and Natalie flinches as the woman props pillows behind her and helps her sit up. She positions the trolley so that it's next to the bed. She picks up the glass of water and brings it to Natalie's lips. 'You need to drink,' she says. 'Drink it all. You are severely dehydrated.'

'Where am I?'

'Drink.'

'But what's happened to me?'

'I said drink,' she says, tipping it into Natalie's open mouth and making her splutter. The nurse tuts and tries again, and Natalie does as she's told.

'That's better,' says the nurse when Natalie swallows the water. Natalie can't tell if the nurse is smiling behind her mask. All she can see is her eyes, and they look empty. The nurse replaces the glass. 'Try to eat,' she says, handing Natalie the plastic fork. Not metal. Not something she could do any damage with.

'Can you please tell me what's ha—'

'Eat,' the nurse snaps. 'I'll be back in a bit.' She turns and leaves the room.

Natalie lets the food grow cold. She reaches up and touches her head, but finds no dressing or bandage, no stitches or anything that suggests she's been wounded.

What happened in the park?

She pulls back the sheet and blanket. She's wearing a hospital gown although she's still got her underwear on. She inspects her skin. Has she been drugged? She feels as if she has been. She reaches around to touch the soft skin on her upper arm. It's tender.

Natalie's gaze flickers towards the door. It doesn't look like the kind of door you'd see on a hospital ward, or even a private room like this one obviously is. The door is pine with a keyhole and there is no glass. And everything is quiet. Too quiet. There is no background cacophony of a busy hospital. No bleeps of machinery, ringing of telephones or hurried footsteps from the corridors outside.

She glances at the cut-up food and the mashed potato congealing on the plate and her stomach turns.

Something is wrong. She feels the kick of it deep in her gut and she trusts her instincts. She's been attuned to keeping herself safe for the last eight years, after all. Why can't she remember what happened? And where is her bag? She would have had it on her at the park: she never goes anywhere without it. She glances towards the rocking chair. The rabbit with the bow tie stares back at her with its beady eyes and something tugs in her memory. A rabbit with a tartan bow tie, its large head flopping over the side of an overnight bag. But just as quickly the memory vanishes.

17

LENA

Susi rings the next morning to say they can offer me some holiday cover to increase my hours. 'We'll see how it goes,' she says. I can't keep the euphoria from my voice as I thank her. 'You're a hard worker, Lena. And a great adviser. You care . . .' She lets the rest of her words hang in the air. She thinks I care too much, I know that. She's had to warn me before about getting too emotionally involved when I tried to help a woman leave her abusive husband. After I found her a place at a women's refuge she changed her mind at the eleventh hour and went back to him. Susi assured me there was nothing more I could have done but I still think about the woman. I worry about what her life is like and whether she's ended up in hospital.

I text Charlie the news that I have more hours, starting next week. He replies with a thumbs-up emoji. I stare at it, annoyed. I text back angrily, *Let me know how much extra you want me to pay per month towards the mortgage.*

He doesn't reply, and I worry he'll still say we need to sell the house.

It's early, and the sun is already bursting from the sky. While I'm out taking Phoenix for a walk I call Jo. She said she'll let me know when Paul can come over to install the camera for the back garden, but I haven't heard from her since Sunday, and it goes to voicemail. I end the call without leaving a message. I'd forgotten she's in chambers on a Tuesday. After witnessing whatever was going on between Henry and Drew yesterday, my suspicions are heightened and I've been tempted to call Drew. But then I remind myself that I don't really know him and he might not be the nice guy he appears. I also know that Susi wouldn't look favourably on me contacting him.

I walk around the block with Phoenix, and by the time I return home I've already decided to call Drew regardless.

He answers on the first ring. 'Lena! So lovely to hear from you. I was going to call you, actually.'

'Oh, yes. Any news on Sarah-Jane?'

A pulse of silence before he says, 'I could use your advice. Would it be okay to meet?'

'Um . . .' I'm not sure if meeting is a good idea. He was acting so strangely last night. 'It's my day off so I won't be at the office.'

'Ah . . . I'm at the farm. I can't leave it today. With Dad ill it's too much for Mum on her own. Is it possible you could come here?'

I don't like the thought of going to his farm by myself.

'My parents will be there,' he says, as though sensing my hesitation. 'Dad's upstairs in bed but Mum will be floating about.'

It's the only way I'll be able to meet him today so I agree.

'Perfect. Thanks, Lena. I'll text you the address.'

I end the call, and less than a minute later a text comes through from Drew. The farm is near Keynsham so not too far away. I try not to think about what Susi would say if she knew, and I'm breaking all sorts of ethical rules, but before I've had time to talk myself out of it, I'm kissing Phoenix's fluffy head goodbye and heading out of the door.

Henry's blue Jaguar isn't parked outside as I head to my red Fiat 500. I traded in my last car after Charlie left so Rufus could learn to drive in something smaller, but the waiting list for an instructor is so long it will be at least a few more months before he can begin lessons.

I'm thankful for the aircon as I head towards the A4. My satnav takes me through various winding single-track lanes where I have to keep reversing to let other vehicles pass until eventually I come to a smallholding in the middle of nowhere. The gate to the yard is open and a grey stone house stands proudly among a cluster of corrugated-iron-roofed low-level buildings. A rusty tractor and an old Volvo estate are parked in front of the house and different types of fowl are strutting across the concrete.

I pull up next to the Volvo, careful not to run over any of the chickens, and get out of the car. The ground is uneven under the flimsy soles of my flat sandals as I make my way to the front porch. Even from here I can smell the unique scent of their house: a combination of home-cooked food mixed with wet dog and damp clothes.

The door opens after my second knock and an elderly woman stands on the threshold. She's round-shouldered and tiny, like one of those peg dolls, with a mass of white-blonde hair. I'm assuming this must be Drew's mum, and she can't be that different in age from my own mum, even though she looks decades older.

'Hello,' I begin, wondering how best to explain my presence without upsetting her. I don't know what Drew's told her, if anything. 'I'm a . . . friend of Drew's. He's expecting me.'

She flashes me a knowing smile and I realize, too late, that she thinks we're a couple. 'Of course, come in. We love meeting Drew's friends. Not that he has many who come to the house any more, and none as pretty as you.' Despite myself I flush and follow her inside. The narrow hallway is cluttered with boxes, which we have to weave past as she leads me to a gloomy kitchen at the back of the house.

'Take a seat, my love, while I go and fetch Drew. Can I get you a cup of tea or anything?'

'Ah, no, thanks, I'm good.' I return her smile.

She disappears into the dark hallway, and I cast around for somewhere to sit, but the chairs are loaded with stacks of papers. I stand at the open doorway that leads to the garden and, beyond that, a huge field. Two black Labradors stroll over the patio towards me and I step outside, grateful for the fresh air, to stroke them. I head towards the fence that separates their garden from the field beyond. It's beautiful out here with more of a breeze than I'm used to in Bristol, thanks to the open landscape. I breathe in the air with its subtle smell of manure that has always been synonymous with the countryside and my childhood, living with Mum in Rye where I grew up.

A moment later, Drew appears in the doorway, his mother hovering just behind him, but she moves back into the kitchen as he strides across the garden to greet me. He's wearing a navy polo-shirt with the name of his farm across his left pec and his jeans are tucked into wellington boots. His arms look strong and toned and here, in his own domain, he seems more self-assured, which makes him more attractive.

'Lena, thanks for coming.' He beams at me. The two dogs come up to him, each pushing their noses into the palms of his hands. 'Do you mind if we go around the side? I haven't told my mother anything about this yet.'

'Sure.' I glance towards the house. In the gloom of the kitchen I spot his mother's pale hair. I let him lead me around the side of the house to one of the barns.

'The cows are in the field, so let's go in here,' he says, taking me into the stalls. It's even cooler in here and smells of straw with the faint whiff of ammonia. He sighs. 'This is a long shot, Lena. A complete long shot. And I could be so wrong about this. But your neighbour, Henry. Something didn't seem right about him, and when I spoke to you afterwards, I sensed you doubted him too. He told me that she was sacked. Sarah-Jane is many things. She's selfish and wilful and stubborn – God, she's stubborn – but she's bright. It didn't ring true, but then I figured, even though I still spoke to her regularly, I hadn't seen her for a long time so perhaps she'd changed, you know? So after I spoke to Henry I stayed in the park and rang the clinic she used to work for and they confirmed she hadn't been sacked. She'd just left one evening as usual and hadn't turned up the next day. The woman I spoke to said that the clinic was annoyed because she was supposed to give notice and she'd left them short-staffed.'

'So, wait. I'm confused. Your sister was working with Henry around three years ago, before he retired, and then abruptly left? But you've spoken to her since then?'

'Oh, yes, lots since then. Like I say, I spoke to her around three months ago. But the woman at the clinic was very helpful when I told her I was worried about Sarah-Jane and she gave me a number for a woman called Milly, who shared a flat with my sister. I rang Milly, who told me Sarah-Jane had moved away from Reading earlier this year but that she spoke to her last week.'

I reel in surprise. 'But that's good news, isn't it?'

'Milly said she sounded paranoid and upset. She also told Milly she was worried about being followed and that she kept seeing the same car everywhere.' He angles his body towards me. 'You'll understand why I was angry with Henry when I went to his house yesterday evening after I tell you the next bit.' He pauses. 'Milly told me that the car SJ kept seeing was a classic car. Blue.' He watches me intently, waiting for it to sink in.

'A Jag?'

'She didn't say what make. I went to ask Henry why he had lied about Sarah-Jane being sacked from the clinic, then saw the car and—'

'Wait! How did you know where they lived?' I doubt Henry would have told him. He met Drew in the park after all.

He hesitates, glancing at me, and it hits me that it's my address, not theirs, that he knew. I'd never given it to him, but I did tell him Henry was my neighbour. I feel a stab of discomfort. How does he know where I live unless he's followed me?

I forgot about the fucking dog.

Could that have been Drew? Yet he didn't know I had a dog . . . or had I told him when he came in to Citizens Advice?

I'm suddenly all too aware that we're here, in this isolated barn, alone.

He swallows, shame-faced, but doesn't answer my question. 'So, er, yeah, I saw Henry's car and was about to confront him to ask if he'd been following my sister or knew more about where she was, but then he came out of his house.' His face contorts. 'I was furious with him and asked him outright, but then . . .' He rubs his hand across his chin. 'Something weird happened. He was really calm. More than calm. Cold. And he told me, in a very quiet, steely voice, that my source was mistaken. Sarah-Jane *was* sacked three years ago and he hasn't seen her since. And, God, Lena, it was sinister. The way he spoke to me. I was . . . I was actually a bit scared.'

A chill washes over me that this man, this younger, fitter guy, is scared of Henry.

'What do you make of Henry?' he asks. 'You seem a bit freaked out by him too. Why?'

'I . . .' I shuffle and look down at my hands. I don't quite trust Drew. He still hasn't explained how he knows where I live. There's a brooding intensity behind his handsome face, which gives him a hard-man edge, like he could be in a Guy Ritchie film. But then he did say that Henry had scared him. I look up. His eyes bore into mine as he awaits an answer. 'I heard something, last Thursday night when I was recording sound for my son, and it made me . . . not suspicious exactly, but . . .'

'Like what? What did you hear?'

'Um. It wasn't much, to be honest. But he and his wife sounded as if they might have been talking about something illegal. They talked about taking someone and getting a room ready. They also said something about it being too risky but that they'd got away with it before.'

Drew pales. 'You think they were talking about kidnapping someone?'

'I don't know.' I grimace. 'They could have been talking about anything, but then you told me about Sarah-Jane and that she'd worked with Henry, who perhaps lied about her being sacked. And now her telling her friend she was being followed. The classic car . . . I don't know, Drew. Maybe she moved back here since you last spoke to her and Henry was following her for some reason, I . . . I don't know . . .'

'You think they were talking about kidnapping my sister?' His voice shakes.

My head swims. 'It's all so tenuous – you don't know exactly when your sister went missing but, according to her friend, Milly, she spoke to her last week. And whatever the Morgans did in the past, whatever they were talking about when I overheard them, they are planning to repeat soon. Maybe they've done it over the past few days.'

His dark brows knit together. He has a line between his eyes that makes him look angry even when he's not frowning. 'Did you record their conversation?'

'No, unfortunately, not all of it. And not the bit when they were talking about doing something risky, or their worry about getting caught. I did record the first bit, where Marielle says to Henry that he promised to "take her" but that in itself isn't enough to prove they were talking about kidnapping someone, is it?'

'God!' He buries his head in his hands, and I stand by his side awkwardly.

'They never actually said the word "kidnap",' I backtrack. 'We have to remember that, Drew.'

He groans in response, then lifts his head so that he's looking at me with pain in his eyes. 'All I know is that my sister left Reading for God knows where, was apparently worried about being followed, kept seeing the same blue classic car and Henry lied about her being sacked three years ago. Urgh!' He kicks the side of the stall in anger. 'If only SJ would get in touch with me. Milly gave me a different telephone number to try – the one she'd been speaking to her on – but that was also dead. Milly is worried too . . .'

'Could you . . . could you maybe go to the police again?'

'Based on a half-overheard conversation that might or might not allude to kidnap and something they've got away with before? A highly renowned surgeon who might, or might not, have been following her?' He throws up his arms, exasperated. 'Who would the police believe? Someone like him or . . .' his shoulders droop '. . . someone like me?'

18

HENRY

March 1987
London

'I can't tell Daddy about how serious we are,' Marielle said, snuggled up in his arms one Sunday morning while the wind and rain battered the windows of his tiny flat. 'He wants me to marry someone rich and important.' He could hear the veneration for her father in her voice and an uneasy feeling began to grow at the thought of losing her. With Marielle he didn't have to pretend. She never made him feel weird or small. She happily listened to his classical music, and took him seriously when he talked about the state of the world. She made him feel as though he was a proper person, someone who could be liked, admired, even loved. She didn't recoil in horror when he talked about his abusive father or his absent mother. She held him a bit tighter when he detailed the belt lashings his father had readily doled out after his mother left, as though he was taking out on Henry all the fury he felt towards his runaway wife.

'He doesn't think what I do is important? I'm saving lives.'

She sat up, propping herself on her elbow. 'I know and it's very worthwhile. Daddy knows you're ambitious. He just needs talking around, that's all.'

'But what if he doesn't ever come around? What if he insists you marry some City hotshot?'

'I don't want anyone else and I don't need his money.'

Henry fidgeted. It was easy for her to say that when she'd grown up with so much. She'd never known what it was to struggle, to heave yourself out of a life scraping around for every last penny. Going without food because your father had spent it all down the pub. Henry knew he was clever and was going places. He was determined to make something of his life. And Marielle had a degree in classics. She wanted to be a lecturer. And, okay, it was never going to earn her a massive income, but that didn't matter to him. He'd be happy here, in this tiny flat, with just her. For ever. But even as he thought it, he knew it wouldn't happen. A woman like Marielle Bishop-Smith couldn't be expected to live a life so small, so modest. Not after the way in which she had been brought up.

But he couldn't walk away from her. He needed her. She'd entered his life and made him feel whole for the first time. He couldn't go back to being that half-person. He just couldn't.

Marielle threw back the covers and stepped onto the cold floorboards while he marvelled at her naked body. She turned her head to look at him with a coy smile as she whipped on her peach silk dressing-gown, then made her way over to his record-player – one of the things he'd bought himself when he got his first wage packet – and put on a record. The hiss as the needle made contact with the vinyl sent shivers of happiness through his body as the exquisite notes of Vivaldi washed over him, instantly relaxing him.

'Come back to bed,' he said, watching her cross the room. She was wearing a frown now, which unsettled him. 'What is it?'

'The problem is my stepmother.' She climbed onto the bed.

'What about her?' He didn't know much about Violet, except that she was, according to Marielle, a 'vacant, pill-popping gold digger'. But she had been married to Marielle's father for many years, after the death of his first wife, Marielle's mother, Julia, when Marielle was five. Violet and Lawrence had a daughter together, the precocious (according to Marielle) Savannah, who was just seventeen.

'She doesn't like me much. She wants everything to go to her precious Savannah. And I'm worried.' He didn't like to ask her why she was worried when she'd just said that she could live without her father's money.

She slipped into bed beside him, the silk of her dressing-gown brushing his skin. 'She's been trying to get Daddy to disown me for years so that she and her sprog get everything when Daddy dies. It's no coincidence she married a man twenty years her senior.'

'Your father wouldn't do that, though, would he?' He had met Lawrence only a few times but it was obvious he adored his firstborn.

She rolled her eyes. 'Who knows? She's tried so many times to turn my father against me. It's never worked, but now, with you . . . If my father doesn't approve it could drive a wedge between us that Violet will exploit.' Her gaze met his. She looked so sad and lost that it tore at Henry's heart. He knew how much her father meant to her, especially with her mother gone.

He wrapped his arms around her. 'Then I'll just have to do what I can to get your father's approval, won't I?' She snuggled into the crook of his shoulder, and he kissed the top of her head. 'I'll do anything for you.'

19

LENA

I mull over my conversation with Drew as I'm driving home from his farm. I'm playing the soundtrack from John Carpenter's *The Fog*, which Rufus recommended, and I can't stop thinking about Drew's sister. Different theories drift through my head, not helped by the atmospheric music. When Sarah-Jane worked with Henry, did she discover something about him that he doesn't want getting out, and it's taken him this long to find her? Is that what all this is about? No, it's a ludicrous idea. I think of *The Vanishing*, which I saw years ago, and shudder when I remember how an unassuming chemistry professor, played by Jeff Bridges, carefully orchestrates a kidnapping and abducts Sandra Bullock's character from a service station.

Fifteen minutes later I've pulled up outside my house. Henry is running a soapy sponge over his car's windscreen, the pale blue bonnet gleaming in the sunshine. He looks the picture of respectability: a suburban retired grandfather happily going about his day. Look at him, for goodness' sake, with his neatly pressed linen shirt and his chino shorts, not a drip of perspiration on him. Yet just yesterday he'd made Drew feel threatened.

A cool customer. A surgeon. Not easily rattled.

I'm letting my imagination run away with me. All this stuff with Drew and his sister isn't helping and, more than that, I know, deep down, that this is a distraction for me. A distraction from feeling lonely, from worrying about my broken marriage, with Rufus about to leave home. It's my anxiety about the future that's causing all these increasingly dark thoughts.

Henry nods in acknowledgement when he sees me, but he looks serious as he continues washing the car. I remember the key that Phoenix found in the Morgans' garden.

'Excuse me, Henry,' I say, as I approach him. I reach into my bag where I'd put the keyring earlier in the hope I'd run into either Henry or Marielle. 'My dog found this in your garden. I'm so sorry, he got through the gap in the fence.' I smile in apology.

Just then Marielle walks briskly out of the house. She's wearing a gingham apron, which is at odds with her neatly coiffed hair, her immaculate make-up that hasn't sweated off, like mine has, and her well-cut dress. She's wearing kitten heels and looks as if she's about to go out for a champagne lunch. It's almost as though she's quickly thrown on the apron to give the impression of domestic bliss. Non-threatening.

Did she come out to see me?

'Lena. Lovely to see you again.' There's something in her tone that makes me wonder if she saw me tailing them yesterday. 'Henry, lunch is ready.' And then she glances down at my outstretched hand and frowns. 'What's this?'

'Lena found it in our garden,' says Henry.

'Well, my dog did,' I clarify, not wanting Marielle to think I've been snooping around her property. 'Sorry, the bear got a bit chewed. Just wondered if it belonged to you?'

'Oh, yes, that's –' begins Henry.

At the same time Marielle shakes her head, 'No, that's not ours.'

I glance from one to the other, trying to read their expressions. 'Are you sure?'

'It's not ours,' repeats Marielle, firmly. She shoots a glance at Henry. Is it my imagination or is that fear I can read in her eyes?

'No,' agrees Henry. 'No, I don't recognize it.'

'Okay.' I slip it into the pocket of my dress. 'Well, nice to see you both.'

When I get to my front door I look back to see Henry has stalked into the house, Marielle trailing after him. He's left the bucket on the pavement, his precious car half washed. I recall Drew's story about his sister being followed by someone in a blue classic car and, despite the blazing sunshine, goosebumps pop up on my arms.

I'm surprised to see Rufus and Kit in the kitchen. Rufus is strumming his guitar with an expression of intense concentration, his fringe falling into his eyes. I can see the nodules of his spine through his T-shirt and a surge of love threatens to overwhelm me. He's taller than me, basically a man, but he'll always be my little boy. I turn towards the sink to hide the tears that have filmed my eyes. This is ridiculous. He's growing up. It's normal. I just wish I'd appreciated every single minute, cherished it, because it's all so fleeting. Nearly eighteen years of my life gone, just like that. I wish I'd been more patient, less stressed, more grateful for the little moments, the moments that had felt insignificant, but now, under the magnifying-glass of passing time and regret, mean everything.

'Oh, hi, aren't you supposed to be in college?' I say, my voice thick. I fetch a glass from the cupboard and pour myself some water. Pull yourself together, Lena, for crying out loud.

'Lecturer is sick, so we have the afternoon off,' Rufus says, without looking up from his guitar as he plucks the strings with a plectrum.

'Hi, Mrs Fletcher.' Kit smiles kindly and, from his expression, I can tell he's noticed that I'm a bit wobbly. He runs a hand through his boy-band hair and there is something instantly recognizable about the way he does it. Again I get the feeling I've seen him somewhere before.

'Please, call me Lena. Can I get you a drink? I doubt Rufus has offered you one!'

'We were just finishing,' says Rufus. 'I'm trying to get this riff . . .'

'It's good,' I say. 'Is that "Seven Nation Army"?'

Rufus turns his face to me, eyes alight. 'Yes!'

'I'd love some water, please,' says Kit, getting out of his seat and coming towards me.

I reach for another glass and turn on the tap. 'I'm sorry it's not very cold,' I say, handing it to him. 'I wish I had one of those fridge water-dispenser things.'

Kit takes the glass with thanks. He has a pleasant face, I think. Smiley. 'I don't mind it room temperature,' he says, and takes a glug. He sits down again, placing his glass on the table, then slides his guitar into its case, which is plastered with stickers: WWF, Barnardo's, Amnesty International, as well as bands like Muse, Kings of Leon and Led Zeppelin. Rufus is still strumming.

'Are you in a band, Kit?' I ask.

'Yes, just me and some uni mates. We do a few local gigs, but we're not like Moderation or anything.' He sounds impressed by Charlie's band. 'To get a record deal would be the dream . . .' He shrugs, his cheeks pinkening. 'I know it's a long shot.'

'It's great to have dreams,' I say.

'Do you, Mrs . . . I mean, Lena?'

I jolt in surprise at the personal question. Kit's watching me carefully and I can't tell if he's just being polite or if he's really interested in knowing the answer. 'Well, I'm a bit long in the tooth for all that now,' I say, waving a hand dismissively.

'Nonsense. You're still young. Rufus told me you used to be a nurse.'

'Well, not quite. I was a student midwife and then . . . I realized it wasn't for me.' A whoosh of heat travels up my body when I remember everything that happened at the hospital where I did my training.

'Oh, that's a shame. Do you ever regret leaving?'

'Sometimes, yes.' It was a knee-jerk reaction. I'd lost faith in the hospital and the people I was working with. 'You know what they say about a few bad apples spoiling the pie, or whatever it is.' I laugh.

He raises his eyebrows. 'Absolutely.'

'Anyway, things happen for a reason. If I'd stayed I might not have met Charlie or had Rufus, so . . .' I lift my shoulders.

He grins and playfully punches Rufus's shoulder. 'With a bit more practice he'll be great.'

Rufus looks up eagerly, flushing with pride. 'Really?'

'Totally. You've got talent, mate. You'll pick it up in no time.' He lugs his guitar case onto his shoulder. 'Anyway, see you on Friday, Rufus.' He heads for the door.

I nudge Rufus and whisper under my breath, 'Go and show him out.'

Rufus hands me his guitar and leaps up. I can hear them talking by the front door. When five minutes pass and Rufus doesn't return, I go into the hallway. He's left the door open but he's not in the front garden. I pop my head out, glancing up and down the street. Henry is back to washing his car and Rufus is standing beside him, admiring the Jag. I shrink back into the hallway, but only enough so that I can still observe them without being seen.

There's no getting around it. Whatever the truth, I don't trust Henry. And I don't like him being friendly to my son.

'Thanks, Henry,' I hear Rufus saying. 'I'll take you up on that. Bye.' He strides back towards the house and I dart into the kitchen and start unloading the dishwasher. I hear the front door slam and Rufus reappears.

'I was just talking to Henry,' he says affably, sticking his hands into his pockets. 'He's got a cool car and said he'd take me out for a drive in it.'

I blanch. Over my dead body, I think, but I don't say as much to Rufus.

'But it reminds me,' he continues. 'The sounds you recorded for me the other day, well . . . I listened to the tapes at college earlier and I heard voices. Was it them next door?'

I'd forgotten to erase that part of the tape before I gave it back to Rufus. I explain how I'd accidentally picked up their conversation. 'But I stopped recording as soon as I discovered it.'

'I was in a rush to get my assignment completed so couldn't make it all out, but what were they on about? It sounded a bit odd.'

I reach for my phone. 'I can play it to you again – I recorded it from your tape. It's not great, as I only managed to get it by placing my phone next to the sound system's speaker.'

'Okay. Sure.'

I play it and shudder as their voices ring out, sounding tinny.

'. . . I don't know, Mari . . .'

'You promised me you'd take her. I've got everything ready. The room . . .'

'I know . . . but . . . after what happened before . . . should we really try again?'

A long pause. Rustling. '. . . we have no choice . . .'

I press stop on my phone and look at Rufus. He's staring at me questioningly.

He sits back in the chair and rests his ankle on the opposite knee. He's still got his trainers on.

'Don't tell me you think they're, like, spies or something? I agree it's a bit odd, but this isn't *Arlington Road*.' He chuckles at his own joke. We'd watched the film together a few months ago; it's about a college lecturer who specializes in terrorism and his growing paranoia that his neighbours are about to bomb a government building.

'All right. I know. I'm not saying that.'

'They could be talking about taking a relative somewhere.' He frowns.

'But what about the other stuff I heard? I didn't record it, but they talked about a plan and it being too risky and that they were worried about getting caught. That's not talking about a relative coming to stay, Ruf.'

'Shame you didn't record that bit,' he says, standing up, his attention already waning, his fingers no doubt itching to get back on his phone or strum the guitar. He goes to the fridge and grabs a carton of orange juice. 'Real life is more boring than the movies.' There's a mournful tone to his voice.

'Is everything okay?'

He turns to me, carton in hand. 'What? Apart from the fact we could have a couple of psychos living next door?' He grins. 'I'm just saying life isn't as exciting as a movie, that's all.'

Later Freddie calls for Rufus and the two of them head out to the cinema to watch some arthouse film recommended by one of their lecturers. He promises not to be back late. I try Jo again, but it goes straight to voicemail. I know it's a busy time for her at work, but I'm desperate to seek her advice about the Morgans and to fill her in on everything that's happened since I last spoke to her on Sunday. I'll also feel a lot better once Paul has installed the camera in the back garden. The gate, thankfully, has remained bolted.

As I sit down with some tea and toast I feel a stab to my thigh and realize I've still got the key I found in the pocket of my dress. I fish it out, staring at the little knitted bear with toothmarks in its foot, thanks to Phoenix, then open the kitchen drawer and dump it in there, along with a ball of elastic bands, an empty lighter, a box of matches, a pen, a couple of blue candles and two Argos pencils. I'm just about to close it when I see a metal keyring in the shape of a poppy. Joan's spare key. She gave it to me when she lived next door in case she ever locked herself out. It's cold between my fingers as I grasp it. The developers kept the original front door, but they might have changed the lock. My heart pounds as a plan takes hold. Could I . . . No, that's totally unethical. I can't just sneak into their house. What if they caught me? But if I did, I might find out what the Morgans are planning. There may be something inside their house that holds a clue as to what they're up to and whether they do know about Sarah-Jane's disappearance.

No. I can't. I absolutely can't. It's wrong. It's trespassing. What if someone saw me? How would I ever explain it?

I drop Joan's key back among the rest of the paraphernalia and slam the drawer shut.

But for the rest of the day I can't stop thinking about that key.

20

'We're just not set up for this heat,' says Kath the next morning, pulling at the neck of her dress and using the fan on her sunburnt chest. 'We need aircon.'

'Aircon is a germ spreader,' announces Susi, whisking in on a cloud of Jo Malone to go to the filing cabinet, then wafting out again, a folder tucked under her arm.

'I'm sure she's an alien,' whispers Kath with a roll of her eyes when Susi's left the room. 'She never gets hot or cold.'

In the winter the office is like a fridge, and when Kath and I are huddled around the radiator, swamped in scarves and thick jumpers, Susi continues to wear her trademark silk blouses.

I try to distract myself from thinking about the Morgans and Joan's spare key, which is burning a hole in my kitchen drawer, by keeping myself busy, volunteering to be the adviser every time someone walks through the door. I keep my head down and Susi seems pleased with me. I still haven't heard anything from Charlie, and I'm worried he's going to push for the house to be put on the market.

'So, we'll start with the holiday cover,' Susi says, when we're standing in the little kitchen making tea in a lull between clients. 'Anna is away for the next two weeks so it would be great if you could work the two extra days a week and cover as much of her load as possible. And if it works out we could see about maybe making it more permanent. I might be able to find some extra hours if the budget allows, but I can't promise. We'll see how it goes, okay?'

'Great,' I say, stirring my tea, all the while thinking, *I need to get into the Morgans' house. Find out what they're up to.* It goes around and around in my head like a chant.

I half expect Drew to come in today and I'm disappointed when four o'clock arrives and he hasn't. I remember how dejected he'd looked yesterday, how powerless when we were talking about him going to the police. I consider calling him, but it crosses a professional line, and now that Susi has given me some extra hours I need to keep her onside if I want it to be a more permanent arrangement.

Rufus asks me to pick him up from college on my way home because he's bringing back some heavy equipment. I wonder if it's the sound monitor and boom mic but when I get there he's carrying a tripod and a light ring. I help him load them into the boot. 'What's this for?' I ask, as we get back into the car.

'Freddie and I are filming a two-hander for our end-of-year project. We're going to take some footage of Dad's gig at the weekend. We've arranged to do a location recce tomorrow evening while the place is empty, for a before-and-after.'

Tomorrow is Thursday. Our movie night and a week since I overheard the Morgans. I try to keep my voice even. 'Oh, right. Does that mean we'll have to do our film night another time?'

'Maybe Friday this week. I'm thinking of *Rear Window*.' He turns to me with a glint in his eye.

'We've watched that loads of times . . . Oh, I see! Ha ha, very funny.'

'What about *Disturbia* then?'

'Not heard of that one.'

'A teenage boy under house arrest spies on the man next door and starts believing he's a murderer when a woman goes missing. Sound familiar?'

'Hey!' I protest. 'I'm not spying on the Morgans, okay? But I do like the sound of *Disturbia*. Let's watch that.'

'Cool. It's a date. And, talking of dates . . .' he glances shyly at me and I wonder if he's going to tell me he's met someone '. . . Dad's told me about Rosie.'

My heart sinks. 'Ah, yes.' I turn into our street.

'He says you've met her. Are you okay with it?'

I sigh. I don't want him to know how hurt I feel about it. 'Well, it's a bit weird, if I'm honest. But . . . I want Dad to be happy.'

I pull up outside our house. Henry is lifting a small suitcase into the boot of the Jaguar and Marielle is watching him with her arms crossed.

'Oh, look. Your favourite neighbours.' Rufus grins playfully. 'I wonder if they're off on a murder spree!'

I tut at him, then step out of the car. Henry waves, closes the boot lid and gets into the driver's seat.

'Hi,' calls Marielle. She looks as if she's about to get in on the passenger side but seems to think better of it. She walks over to me and lowers her voice. 'We're away tonight but we'll be back first thing tomorrow morning because

I'm looking after my grandson. But . . .' she hesitates '. . . would you mind just keeping an eye on the house?'

I can feel Rufus's breath on my neck. *'Oh, the irony!'* I can imagine him saying.

'Sure.' I frown. 'Is something wrong?'

'No. Not at all. It seems a very nice neighbourhood and everything. It's just . . . we've had a few incidents.'

'Incidents?'

'Yes. Since we moved in. Silly things. Stuff being moved around the garden. A stone thrown through our shed window. Probably just kids . . .'

'I've had the same with the back gate,' I say, in a rush, 'and I thought someone was in my garden. This is usually a safe area, but . . .'

'It is a city at the end of the day,' she says, reaching for an oversized pair of sunglasses from her pale-yellow Dior quilted handbag and slipping them on. I look at her handbag wistfully. I've got a weakness for bags. Unfortunately a designer one is beyond my budget.

A horn toots and we jump. Henry inclines his head at Marielle.

'Whoops, here's me chatting away. I'd better go, but thanks, Lena. And lovely to see you, Rufus,' she adds. She scuttles towards the car in her kitten heels. She waves as Henry pulls away from the kerb and we watch as he drives at a snail's pace down the street.

When they've gone Rufus turns to me, shaking his head, laughter in his eyes. 'I can't believe you think that old couple are up to something dodgy.' He blows his fringe out of his face and heads down the front path, leaving me to get his equipment from the boot.

Rufus goes up to bed early and I stay downstairs for a while longer, flopped onto the sofa with Phoenix curled up by my side, watching *Selling Sunset*. At least I can binge-watch reality TV now that Charlie doesn't live here any more. He only ever wanted to watch serious dramas about drug cartels or spies. I turn off the TV. The living-room window is open wide, and the night is still, with only the occasional drone of an aeroplane overhead, or a far-off vehicle.

I get up, about to turn the lights off, when I hear it.

A baby crying.

I move to the window. It sounds like it's coming from the Morgans' house. But it can't be. Marielle told me herself that they're away tonight.

The cries are louder now, more insistent. I pull aside the curtains and poke my head out of the window. The street is deserted. It's gone eleven. No, I'm not imagining it. The cries are definitely coming from next door. Perhaps, at the last minute, Marielle called her son and daughter-in-law and asked them to house-sit. Phoenix cocks his head at me, noticing my agitation, and I bend down to soothe him. Then I go to the front door, stepping out into the warm night air. There are no lights on next door. It looks deserted.

They asked you to keep an eye on the house, a little voice inside my head pipes up. *You're doing nothing wrong if you want to check*.

Before I can talk myself out of it I dart into the kitchen, grab Joan's spare key and my phone, then close the front door quietly behind me so as not to alert Rufus. Adrenaline surges through me as I hurry down their front path. They don't have a Ring doorbell and I can't see any cameras. They don't even have a security light, and I approach their front door in darkness. I hesitate. What should I do? They could have an alarm.

I decide to knock in case Heidi or the Morgans' son is there. When nobody comes to the door I knock again, my heart thudding. I peer through the semicircle of glass in their front door, but the hallway is in darkness. The house looks empty. I step back, peering at their upstairs windows. They are all closed. Surely if someone was in, the windows would be open. It's so muggy, even at this late hour.

I glance over my shoulder. Can the neighbours opposite see me? It's so dark in the Morgans' front garden that it's doubtful. Before I've had the chance to change my mind I fish in my pocket for Joan's key and put it into the lock. I hold my breath as I turn the key, half expecting it not to work. But the door opens. I brace myself for some kind of alarm system, planning to close the door and run back to my house if it suddenly goes off, but there's nothing. Gingerly, I step over the threshold and close the door behind me.

The hallway is wider and more impressive than mine, with high, ornate ceilings and original cornicing that was unfortunately stripped from my house by the previous owner. Overhead there is a huge glass chandelier, and a pair of Marielle's gold ballet pumps sits neatly by the old-school radiator along with a pair of highly polished brown leather lace-ups. The newly painted stone-coloured walls are bare, with no photos or any personal touches, like pictures or even mirrors. Shadows play upon the walls, and I pause, straining to hear the baby. But there is just silence. Did I imagine the crying baby? Perhaps it was coming from somewhere else after all. Now I'm here I don't know what to do. What am I hoping to achieve?

I should go home but curiosity takes over. I think of everything that's happened since the Morgans moved in: the conversation I overheard on the boom mic, the man caught on tape swearing about my dog, the fact Sarah-Jane was being followed by a blue classic car, Henry lying about her being sacked, his coldness towards Drew. But it's more than that. It's a feeling I've got deep in my gut, something unsettling, that makes me feel uneasy. Something about *him*. I have to trust my instinct this time. After all, look what happened during my training. I was only nineteen then. I knew nothing about the world, or about the people in it. I didn't know about the darkness that could lurk behind a respectable exterior. Behind a *doctor*. I was too scared to speak up. But I'm not that innocent young girl any more.

With resolve I push open the door to the left. It creaks on its hinges, sounding overly loud and creepy in the dark, empty house, like in a horror movie. I blink a few times, hoping my eyes will adjust. I don't want to turn on a main light so instead I use the torch on my phone. I sweep the triangle of light around the room, which is empty. And then it lands on the far wall, and I gasp. I step further into the room. At first I think it's some kind of trendy wallpaper, but as I get closer I can see that it's newspaper clippings, layered on top of each other, taking up nearly half the wall. What is this? I move my phone to see them better, but because of the way they are pinned together they are hard to make out.

BABY FOUND ON HOS . . .
. . . ORGANS FOR RESEARCH AT . . .
DRUGS LORD FOUND DEAD IN . . .
BRIGHT SPARKS WIN NATIONAL AWARD
. . . ADOPTION RACKET WITNESS SPEAKS . . .

This is seriously weird. I'm taking a few photos with my phone when a shrill cry makes me jump. It's the baby. The baby is crying again, and it sounds like it's coming from upstairs.

I freeze, listening intently. There are no other noises. No movement from upstairs. No sign that someone is in the house. Just the solitary sound of the baby crying. I move back into the hallway. The cries get louder. They are definitely coming from upstairs.

Surely Marielle and Henry wouldn't be cruel enough to leave a baby alone at home.

I've got to see for myself. I can't leave.

I head up the stairs, my heart pounding in my ears. The baby is still crying. I follow the sound, past the first door and along the landing to the next. The cries are louder now. I push the door open to reveal a nursery and the cries instantly stop. A pretty white cot sits in the middle of the room and I can just make out the dark, familiar shape of a baby in a Grobag, like I used to dress Rufus in at night.

There's no way Marielle would leave her grandson asleep alone in the house. And then a thought occurs to me. Unless she hasn't left the house and is here after all. I think of the shoes downstairs. Oh, my God. Have I got this completely wrong and she's here? But I saw them drive off in the car. She told me herself they were away for the night. The hairs on the back of my neck stand up and a cold feeling washes over me. I spin around, half expecting her to be standing on the landing, watching me. But nobody's there. The action makes me topple against the nursery door and it bangs against the wall. I flinch, imagining Marielle charging down the landing to see what the noise was. But there's nothing. I brace myself for the baby to start crying again but there is just silence. Gently I walk towards the cot. I can't believe she's left a baby here all alone. A cute, chubby-cheeked baby.

But there's something wrong.

The baby's eyes are open. Glassy.

My mouth goes dry as I reach over to touch the baby's cheek. It's cold and I recoil in horror. It's so lifelike, but it's not real. It's not real.

The baby is fake.

21

NATALIE

A loud bang wakes her and Natalie sits upright in bed. Is the nurse coming back to feed her? She's starving and she's desperate for the loo. There is a small, windowless en-suite, which she's been using, even though just walking across the room to the toilet is enough to shatter her. She doesn't understand why she has no energy. With every movement she feels like she's walked ten miles across a desert and she's never slept so much. The strange nurse has been in a few times but mostly Natalie's been too out of it to have a conversation with her, and any interaction has had a lucid-dream quality. Once she was sure she saw the rabbit move on the rocking chair. She'd only ever felt this way once before, when an old boyfriend had convinced her it would be a good idea to drop an acid tab at Glastonbury.

Natalie reaches underneath her to feel the mattress. To her shame it's wet and so is the back of her hospital gown.

She thinks she's been here two nights now. But it's hard to know exactly because for most of it she has been in a fug. Why won't the nurse talk to her and explain what she's in for? What happened at the park? So many questions swarm in her mind, and fear is creeping in as the blackness again wipes everything away, like an eraser to a pencil sketch.

In the early hours of the morning she was awake long enough to lug herself from the bed to the window. Not that she could see much, just the glimpse of a garden and a house opposite. And then the nurse had come in. The nurse who doesn't speak. She's always masked but there is something familiar about her eyes, which peer at her with such hostility. She's not seen any other nurses or staff since she arrived, and it adds to her impending panic.

'Eat up,' she always says, after unveiling another dish. Despite everything, Natalie finds she's unusually hungry so she does as she's told and then, straight afterwards, always feels ridiculously tired and heavy-limbed, but the fear has abated and the hours drift in a wash of darkness.

She has no idea what time it is now, but that bang: it sounds as if someone is right outside her door. If only she could drag herself out of bed. If only she didn't feel so tired.

The trolley by her bed is empty. The nurse hasn't come to collect it. Usually after she's woken from one of her heavy sleeps everything has been cleared away.

Natalie concentrates on trying to listen for sounds beyond her room. There is the creak of footsteps and a shadow moves along the narrow crack at the bottom of the door. With all the energy she can muster, Natalie swings her legs out of bed and crawls across to the door, not helped by the hospital gown she's been dressed in.

She tries the handle. It's locked. Why is she locked in?

She's all alone. The only patient.

And then, with a sickening moment of clarity she acknowledges that she's not a patient at all – but a prisoner.

22

LENA

The baby is fake.

I stare down at the doll in shock. It looks so real. It even cries like a baby. It must be on some kind of timer. Is this what Marielle pushes around in the pram? Does that mean she doesn't have a grandchild? But I saw her with a woman I assumed was her daughter-in-law, Heidi, and she was holding a baby. I don't understand.

Bile burns the back of my throat. I need to get out of here.

I sprint downstairs as though chased by ghosts, the echoes of the baby's eerie cries still ringing in my ears. The eyes are the only thing about it that don't look real. Everything else, those perfectly rounded cheeks, the tiny fingers ... God.

My hands are trembling as I let myself in at my front door.

'Where've you been?'

I jump. Rufus is sitting on the stairs in his pyjamas.

'I'm sorry, love. I heard something – from next door. I just wanted to go and investigate. You heard Marielle. She asked me to keep an eye on the place.'

His face darkens. 'You should have told me. It could have been dangerous if there'd been a burglar or something.'

He's right. 'I thought you were asleep.'

'Can you tell me next time?' He doesn't wait for me to answer as he strops up the stairs. I feel a tug of guilt. I follow him and watch as he climbs into bed.

'I'm really sorry, Ruf. I heard a baby crying.' I perch on the edge of his bed. I'm tempted to tell him that I let myself in with the spare key but stop myself. 'It was nothing. Anyway. My mistake.' I bend down and kiss the top of his head. He smells of my fruity shampoo.

'Fine,' he says, turning his back to me. I squeeze his shoulder and leave the room.

'And you didn't have a chance to look around their house?' Jo asks the next day. We're sitting outside a little café on the lower slopes of Park Street, not far from Jo's chambers. She texted me early this morning, asking if I'd meet her in her lunch hour and apologizing for taking so long to get back to me. The sky is bleached and shimmery. The area is busy with students and shoppers, all making the most of the heatwave. At one point I'm sure I see Kit on the other side of the street, his guitar case on his back, but he melts into the crowd.

'No,' I say, as I cut into my breaded chicken breast. 'I was freaked out after finding the fake baby. It was so creepy, Jo. So lifelike. More so than any toy doll I've ever seen. It was only the eyes that gave it away. But also . . . I dunno . . . it's kind of sad.'

'How so?'

My heart feels heavy. 'Like, why does she have it?'

Jo takes a mouthful of avocado and chews it silently.

'Sometimes it can be . . . after a loss.'

Jo swallows. 'You think she once lost a baby? Do you think she lied about having a son, then? And a grandson?'

'I really don't know. She could have a son but have lost another baby. Or maybe she's lonely. She wants something to love . . .'

'Then she should get a pet.'

'Jo!'

'I know, and I'm sorry for her if she did lose a baby, but she's nearly seventy, isn't she?'

'You'd never get over losing a baby.'

Jo's voice softens. 'I love how big your heart is, Lena, but you could be jumping to conclusions. You don't know that's the case. What about the conversation you over-heard? The stuff with the missing sister of one of your clients. And what about the man's voice on your tape? The garden gate being left wide open. Someone was in your garden. Oh, which reminds me, Paul says he'll pop over on Saturday to install the camera, if that's okay? I'm sorry we haven't done it before. He was away at the beginning of the week and we've both been manic at work.'

I wave away her apology. 'It's fine. I don't think anyone's been back in the garden. The gate has remained locked.' I put down my knife and fork. 'I know this sounds weird, and it's not like I've got much to go on, but I have this gut feeling I can't quite shake that maybe Marielle is a little scared of Henry. Intimidated by him, perhaps.'

'What makes you say that?'

'I don't know. It's just little things. Like when I saw them arguing in the front garden. She seemed rattled. And she's always friendly and he's, well, colder in a lot of ways. Like he'll wave and say hello, but it doesn't seem as authentic. Like I'm a nuisance.' I sigh. 'It's hard to explain. And when I was in their house I saw something else.' I bend down to reach into my bag for my phone and scroll to my latest photos. 'Look at these.' I slide my mobile across the table.

Jo puts down her knife and fork and pushes her reading glasses onto her nose, then picks up my phone. She frowns. 'What is this?'

'This is the wall in their downstairs room. I've taken a few – the first is of the whole wall and the next two are close-ups of a few different articles.'

'It's a bit blurry.'

'It was dark in there and I had to use the flash, but . . . Can you see what it is? Most of the wall is covered with newspaper clippings. Look at the headlines. There's one about an adoption racket.'

She narrows her eyes. 'Yes . . . I remember this, or a story like it, in Romania in the 1980s.' She looks up from the phone. 'Why would they have it?'

'I don't know. And then there was one about a drugs lord, although I didn't manage to take a photo of that. It's really odd. Really random.'

Jo hands me back the phone and pushes her glasses onto her hair. 'Your neighbours are obviously a bit weird, Lena.' She picks up her knife and fork and concern floods her face. 'Please be careful. You don't know what they're capable of. Promise me you won't go into their house again.'

'I promise. It's strange. I feel conflicted because I like Marielle. And I feel sorry for her. But Henry . . . I still think he knows more about Drew's sister. He's really cagey about it, according to Drew, and he was threatening when Drew asked him about it after realizing that Henry has a classic blue car and Sarah-Jane was being followed by one.'

'Leave it to Drew,' she says, through a mouthful of sourdough. 'It's not your business, hon.' She reaches across the table and takes my hand. I notice a new flower tattoo on her wrist. 'I know things are tough right now. Everything is up in the air, with Charlie. And Rufus. But, please, don't get involved.'

After our lunch we say goodbye and Jo walks up the hill to work. I continue past College Green and the central library.

The central library. I pause outside its impressive doors, remembering Marielle telling me about her daughter-in-law, Heidi, and how she worked there on a Thursday. It's Thursday today, and this morning when I woke up Henry's car was parked outside, so they must have travelled back especially to look after their grandson. Does Marielle use the fake baby when the real one is back with his mother? What does Henry make of it? He must know his wife has this – this *life-sized doll*. Is Marielle having some kind of mental breakdown? Is that why Henry lets her have the doll? On occasion I've noticed he's almost irritated by her, especially the way he reacted when I asked him about the key Phoenix had found in their garden.

The library is cavernous, but I might be able to find Heidi. I could just ask her a few innocent questions, that's all. No harm done. I know I promised Jo, but this will be the last thing. I need to find out, for my peace of mind. After all, I'm the one living next door to them. Not Jo.

I've always loved this library, but I haven't been inside since Rufus was younger. We used to wander around gazing in awe at the domed glass roof and the beautiful floor-to-ceiling bookshelves. It was like a museum. As soon as I step into the foyer and inhale the familiar scent of polished wood and dusty books I'm transported back in time and, once again, I feel the nostalgic pull deep within. The yearning to turn back the clock. I spend half an hour perusing the books while keeping my eye open for Heidi. I'd forgotten how long the library is and it takes me a while to get from one end to the other. I can't see her anywhere, and when I'm considering giving up, I spot her by the arts section. She's bent down, unloading a trolley, neatly slotting books back onto one of the lower shelves. Yes, it's definitely her. The same long dark curly hair and a similar bold-print maxi dress to the one she was wearing when I saw her with Marielle.

I steel myself. Then I head over to her on the pretence I'm looking for a book on architecture. She stands up, smiling pleasantly, and points me to a different section of the library. 'Thanks so much. It's Heidi, isn't it?'

Confusion flits across her features. 'No, I'm Lindy.'

'Oh,' I say, surprised and a bit embarrassed. 'Sorry. I saw you with my neighbour, Marielle, the other day. I assumed you were her daughter-in-law, Heidi. You were with your baby.'

Her eyes light up. 'Yes, I know Marielle. A lovely woman. She's my old university lecturer. That was the first time I've seen her, oh, in years. We've kept in touch sporadically, and when she told me she was moving to Bristol I suggested lunch. She was so excited to meet my baby daughter, Lily.'

'That's lovely,' I say. 'Do you know Heidi? Marielle said she worked here too.'

She frowns. 'No, there's no Heidi here. And Marielle never mentioned it when I told her this is where I work. Anyway, nice to meet you,' she says, turning back to her trolley of books. I say goodbye and walk away, wondering if Marielle lied about having a daughter-in-law. If so, does that mean that she's also lied about having a son and a grandson?

23

It's Friday, and I'm at Citizens Advice. I've just finished helping a client draft a legal letter to a supplier who has failed to pay their bill when I spot Drew sitting on a bench in the waiting area. He looks forlorn, his head dipped, his arms resting on his knees and his hands in prayer shape. He's got on heavy workboots and jeans and must be sweltering.

I feel sick when I remember I went to his house out of hours and we exchanged numbers. I've crossed a boundary with Drew and have become too involved. Susi could sack me if she finds out.

He looks up when I approach, and smiles.

'Drew,' I say brightly, whisking him into a side room before he says anything in front of Susi. 'How are you?' I indicate the seat facing my desk.

He sits down heavily. 'Not great, I'm afraid, Lena. My dad took a turn for the worse last night.' He rubs his shoulder. 'I can't stop thinking that SJ is in some kind of trouble.'

'If you have concerns, Drew, I really think you should go to the police. Just tell them everything you've told me.'

'I keep thinking Henry knows something. The classic car that was following her and the fact he knew her and lied about why she left the company so abruptly. And then the plan you heard them talking about. Did you say you had it on your phone?'

'Only the first bit.'

'Will you send it to me?'

I want to say no. I could be putting myself in danger. Not to mention how Susi will react if she finds out. I could lose my job and I need it more than ever if I want to keep the house. But if the police find out that Henry has done something criminal, he'll be arrested. So it won't matter that he knows I was the one who helped turn him in.

All of this gallops through my mind as I assess Drew sitting there, worry etched all over his handsome face. I'm concerned for him. Does he have many mates? Someone to go for a drink with? To vent to? A girlfriend, perhaps? He's never mentioned any, and I picture him at home on the farm with the boxes in the dark hallway and all the clutter, looking after his parents and their menagerie while worrying about a sister who may or may not be in danger. I wonder how he copes.

'Will you send me the recording?' he asks again. He sounds so desperate.

I can't stand by and do nothing.

Not like I did before.

'Okay,' I say. 'It's not much. And it's obviously out of context so it's doubtful the police will take it seriously.' I reach for my phone and text him the soundbite. 'Here we go.'

His phone pings and he exhales in relief. 'Thanks, Lena. I'll go back to the police. Like you say, it's not much to go on, but it's worth a shot.'

'It must be so tough, coping with it all by yourself.' I clear my throat. 'Listen, is there anyone you can talk to? Someone to help take the weight off?'

'I have you to talk to, Lena. You've helped me more than you know.'

'I'm here to help you professionally, but is there some-one you're . . . um . . . close to?'

Confusion shadows his eyes. 'I thought we were friends.'

An uneasy feeling begins to simmer. 'Well, I'm your adviser, Drew. And I'm worried about you, that's all. I'm worried you've got a lot on your plate and nobody to help you.'

'Why don't you come over for dinner tomorrow? My mum liked you.' His gaze grazes my wedding finger as he notices the absence of a ring.

'That sounds lovely, Drew, but I'm afraid I wouldn't be allowed to.'

'What do you mean, "not allowed"?'

'My boss. It's against the rules because you're a client.'

'I'm not exactly a client, am I? I'm not paying you for your services. I've just come in here to ask for advice, but I don't have to come again if it's mixing business with pleasure. You've been so kind to me, Lena, the way you've helped me.'

'That's . . . well, that's my job.'

He looks at me intently. 'Is it your job to come and find me in the park? Is it your job to come over to my house? I think all that goes above and beyond, don't you?'

The room shrinks in size and feels even more airless. 'I . . .' Is he right? Is there an attraction between us or is it just my obsession with the Morgans that propelled me to help him? I assess him sitting there, watching me. He *is* attractive, but I'm not ready to date anyone. How can I, when I'm still not over Charlie? And then another, less charitable, thought enters my mind. Drew has a hold over me now. Is he using it to get what he wants? 'I just really wanted to help you find your sister,' I say feebly.

Drew doesn't say anything for a moment or two and an awkward silence fills the room. Then he pushes back his chair and stands up. 'Right. Well,' he clears his throat, 'I'll let you know what happens.' All the warmth has left his voice. Wil he report me to Susi?

I stand up, ready to escort him out, but he leaves the room, closing the door firmly behind him.

24

HENRY

August 1987
London

Henry surveyed the downpour as he exited the tube station. He'd been in such a hurry to leave his flat that he'd forgotten his umbrella. Still, even the dull, wet bank-holiday Monday wasn't enough to dampen his spirits. He had a spring in his step for the first time in weeks. He was finally going to see Marielle again.

He'd missed her so much: her smell, her touch, her voice, her face. He'd ached for her in the time they had been apart. All sixteen days, thirteen hours and fifteen minutes to be exact. It had felt like a lifetime, and it had made all his anxieties and abandonment issues rise to the surface. He knew he'd lost weight in the time they'd been apart. He'd hardly eaten, barely slept. He was surprised he'd still managed to go to work in the morning, but that would be because of what his mother used to call his big brain, which meant that even when it was functioning at a quarter of its capacity it was more than most people's.

Marielle was standing at the entrance to Hyde Park, clutching a black umbrella and wearing sombre clothing, as if she'd just come from a funeral, not the South of France. Her burnished hair stood out against the monochrome backdrop and when she saw him her eyes lit up. Relief spread through his entire body. She didn't look as if she was about to finish with him.

'Henry,' she cried, planting a kiss on his lips and throwing her arms around his waist, the umbrella dragging on the ground as she buried her face in his damp wool blazer. He rested his chin on top of her head, not caring that the rain pummelled his hair and dripped down his chin. Everyone else melted away and it was just the two of them, standing in the rain in a wet embrace.

Before she had left for Nice more than two weeks ago he'd asked her to marry him and she'd thrust a dagger into his heart when she'd told him that she had to spend some time with her father, away from her stepmother. Her plan was to drip-feed him positive things about Henry, all the reasons why she loved him, before she was ready to accept his proposal. Their love affair had been so intense, so all-consuming that he assured her he understood. He'd heard enough from the snippets Marielle had given him after she returned from supper with her father, which she presented like leftovers in a doggy bag. She'd told him what her stepmother thought of him. Apparently he was only after Marielle because of her family name, or her – or, rather, her father's – money. This hurt Henry. He might be many things, ambitious being one, but he wasn't a gold-digger and he certainly wasn't with Marielle because of her wealth. He loved her unconditionally. 'I know Daddy would love you if his mind wasn't being poisoned by *her*,' Marielle had said, on more than one occasion, but just before the Nice trip was announced he'd noticed that she seemed more withdrawn when they were together and he'd sensed that she was somehow disappointed in him. She'd still said she loved him, but it had sounded unconvincing, as though if she uttered it often enough she'd start to believe it. He couldn't blame her, he supposed. He was used to disappointing people – they expected him to be confident, charming and gregarious, yet he knew he was gauche in social situations. It was only at work where he could shine. He thought Marielle had seen through all that. Yet here she was now, seemingly happy to see him and squeezing him so tightly she took his breath away.

'I was worried you were going off me,' he said, when she pulled away. He took the umbrella from her so he could hold it over them both.

'I'm so sorry I gave you that impression. You know I had to go on this trip. I had to spend some quality time with Daddy. Away from *her*. And it worked! He's happy for us, darling. He gives us his blessing.'

This surprised him. 'But what about your stepmother? You've always said your father is wrapped around her little finger.'

'Oh, well, that's the thing,' she said, looking up at him. 'My stepmother has been ill for weeks. All the time we were in France. And then, well, it's terribly sad in lots of ways, although' – she lowered her voice – 'not for us, but, Henry, she . . . well, she died yesterday.'

'She died?' The shock reverberated through him.

'Yes. The day after we got back. They think she was taking too many sleeping tablets. She'd been self-medicating for years, apparently. She was in the bath, and they think she must have passed out and drowned. I was the one who found her. She was only forty-six.'

He didn't know what to say.

She reached up and wiped away a drop of rain from his cheek. 'This means we can be together. Properly. Without her judging and turning Daddy against us.' She pressed her mouth against his ear, her breath soft against his skin. 'Now we can get married. It's me and you against the world, Henry Morgan.'

'Me and you against the world.'

She pulled away, tucking a strand of hair behind her ear demurely, and he wondered if he'd imagined the smile in her voice when she whispered in his ear.

'I've booked us a table at the Ritz for afternoon tea,' she said, linking her arm through his. 'We can celebrate our engagement.'

He should have told her then that it was in bad taste to celebrate so soon after her stepmother's death, despite how much Marielle had disliked her. Maybe if he had it would have stopped things escalating. He could have managed her expectations. But her excitement was infectious, and all he cared about, in that moment, was how pleased he was that he hadn't lost her.

25

LENA

When I get home from work I'm surprised to see Charlie's van parked outside my house. He's standing on the doorstep, looking flustered in his paint-splattered overalls, the sun highlighting the toffee tones of his hair.

'What are you doing here?' I brush past him to open the front door. He gave me back his key when he moved out. Phoenix charges out to greet us.

'Just here to pick up Rufus.'

'He's at college.'

Charlie's good-natured face looks momentarily confused. 'Oh, yes, of course. I thought they'd finished for the summer.'

'Not until next Wednesday. And, anyway, isn't Rufus staying over at yours tomorrow night?' He'd said we were watching a movie tonight.

He lifts his shoulders in a half-attempt at a shrug, then bends down to pat Phoenix's head gingerly. Phoenix side-eyes him before strutting into the house.

'That dog's never liked me.'

I roll my eyes. 'Don't take it personally. He doesn't really like men.'

'He likes Rufus.' Charlie straightens. 'We talked about him coming to a gig tonight. Rufus, that is.' He chuckles. 'He wanted to do some filming. Something to do with one of his media projects.'

'He said it was tomorrow night.'

'Ah, yes, sorry about that. My fault. The date was moved.'

The equipment Rufus had brought home from college for the two-hander. I remember now. I bite back my disappointment. We can always watch the movie tomorrow night.

Charlie stands there, taking up most of the doorway. Funny how in just seven months he looks so out of place in what was once his home. He pulls at the straps of his overalls while rolling back on his heels, the action so familiar that I feel a lurch of nostalgia.

'Do you . . . er . . . want to come in?' We still haven't talked about the house and he never answered my text about Susi offering me holiday cover.

His eyes widen in surprise. Then his expression relaxes. 'If you're sure?'

'Of course.'

He follows me into the kitchen. The bin bag needs changing and there is the faint aroma of rotten veg. I open the patio doors, pour us both some lemonade without asking – it was always his favourite soft drink – and then, because there is no shade in our garden, we sit at the kitchen table with Phoenix flopped at our feet.

'Doesn't look like the weather's going to break any time soon,' he says, sipping his drink and looking awkward. Sometimes I can't believe this is the man I shared my bed with for so many years, who was there at the birth of our son, who sang to my swollen belly when I was pregnant, who held my hair back when I was sick after a terrible bout of food poisoning, who wrote songs about me. He has seen me at my best and my worst. The person I thought knew me better than anyone. He's like a stranger now. A stranger who has to make small-talk about the weather. Suddenly I feel heavy with sadness and unsaid words. What happens to all the emotions, all the love, after you split up? Where does it all go?

'So,' I say, coughing to disguise the crack in my voice, 'you never texted me back about the mortgage. Susi has upped my hours to cover holiday leave. From next week I'll be full time for a couple of weeks and she said if it goes well she'll try to make it more permanent. Rufus is getting a summer job too, not that I'll take any money from him, but . . .'

He raises his eyebrows. 'That's great.' He looks down at his big hands, stroking his fingers across the wooden grain of the table. He'd bought it eight years ago from a reclamation yard and spent weeks sanding and revarnishing it so that it gleamed in all its honey-toned glory. He always did prefer to buy something pre-loved rather than brand new. He said he liked a piece of furniture to have a history. I feel a jolt of surprise when I see that he's still wearing his wedding band. I wonder what his new girlfriend, Rosie, thinks about that.

'So . . . you want to keep the house?' he asks without looking at me.

'Yes. Of course. I love it. This is where Rufus grew up. This was where . . .' I was about to say this was where we were at our happiest, but it would feel wrong under the circumstances. Because it was also where I was at my most miserable. He almost sounds disappointed. Was he using my lack of full-time paid employment as an excuse to sell up?

'Right.' His jaw tightens.

'I thought you'd be pleased.'

He sighs heavily, which makes his huge shoulders shake. 'I am. Of course I am. But, Lena, you won't be earning enough to allow us to keep the house for ever. We do need to sell it when Rufus is eighteen.'

'Do you need the capital from it?' I wonder if that's it. He's run out of money now he has a new girlfriend to woo.

'No, Lena. Like I said before, everything has gone up and running the flat and a three-bedroom house is expensive.'

We slip into another awkward silence. I can tell there is something on his mind, something he wants to say to me, but I know better than to probe. Charlie is a man of few words. That has always been part of the problem. For some-one so creative and passionate, who has written incredible, heartfelt songs, he's rubbish at having a proper conver-sation. He channels his feelings into his songwriting: I spent most of our marriage trying to work out how he was feeling by reading between the lines of his lyrics.

'I know you're attached to this house . . .' he begins.

My eyes well up.

'Lena?'

I sniff. 'I'm being sentimental, that's all. Ignore me. It's just . . . I keep thinking of when Rufus was little. I miss it. I miss it all and . . .' I falter.

'I understand.' He places his hand on top of mine where it rests on the table. 'I really do. But it's because you're looking at it all through rose-tinted glasses now Rufus is about to fly the nest. It was hard work at times. Do you remember that massive tantrum he threw in the middle of Tesco? You were so embarrassed. You thought everyone was judging you for being a bad mother because you snapped at him. Or when he was tiny and we were so sleep-deprived because he was suffering with reflux? It was horrendous.'

I laugh, guilty. 'It was. You're right.'

'Do you really want to go back to those days? Like, *really*?'

'Well . . . maybe not those *exact* days.'

He squeezes my hand and then removes his to pick up his lemonade. There is a pulse of silence, of shared memories, a life.

'He's a good kid,' he says.

'He is. And he's happy now he's left that school and those . . . bullies.'

Charlie doesn't say anything. Instead, he takes a sip of his lemonade. He never wants to talk about what happened last year. I wonder if it's because it marked the beginning of the end for us. I decide to change the subject. We're getting on so well, for a change.

'Did you know that the house next door was bought, in the end? Henry and Marielle moved in recently.'

He lifts his brows. 'And what are they like?'

'Ah, now, there's a story.'

He grins. 'Well, I'm all ears.'

It's a relief to be able to tell him everything, and his presence is comforting. He sits very still, his hands cupping his glass as I fill him in, beginning with the overheard conversation last Thursday. As I get to the bit about Drew and all the stuff with his missing sister, I notice his expression cloud with uncertainty, which makes me falter a bit, but I carry on regardless until he's totally up to speed.

'Right,' he says, with a frown, when I've finished. He scratches the stubble on his chin. 'So you're saying you suspect the new neighbours are, what, criminals? You do realize how that sounds?'

'Well, I don't know for definite what they're planning. That's the problem. But the creepy doll, the lying about having a daughter-in-law, the wall of newspaper clippings . . . it's all a bit weird, isn't it?'

'You should never have gone into their house. God, Lena, what were you thinking?'

'I knew they weren't there. And the baby crying, I had to check it out. You'd have done the same.'

He grimaces.

I chew the skin at the side of my thumb. Charlie's eyes are still on me and there is a sudden tension in the air. I break eye contact and turn away from him to take a tin of beans I don't need from the cupboard.

'Be careful, Lena.'

I swivel back to face him, still clutching the tin of beans. 'What do you mean?'

'Just keep out of it. It's none of your business.' He stands up, adjusting his overalls.

'You're such a pacifist,' I snap, hearing how resentful I sound. Things would have turned out differently between us if only he'd taken more action – if he'd stood up for Rufus more when he was being bullied. If he'd stood up for me.

He ignores the barb. 'You've got Rufus to think about. If these neighbours are dangerous, or whatever, you don't want to be in their firing line. I don't think you should have given Drew the recording.'

Feeling suddenly queasy, I put down the tin of beans. Charlie opens his mouth to say something else when we're interrupted by the buzz of my mobile. I pounce on it, hoping it might be Drew with news about his police visit. But it's Susi.

'Hello,' I say, moving away from Charlie to stand in the frame of the patio doors.

'Lena, hi. I'm sorry to be calling you at home but we need a word.' She sounds stern and I feel the first kick of unease.

'Okay. What about?'

'It's about Drew Mayhew. It's been brought to my attention that you've been visiting him at home. Is that correct?'

'I . . . well, yes, but . . .' How does she know? Have the police said something already or has Drew told her after I said no to dinner?

She sighs in disappointment. 'Lena, this is unethical. You know that.'

'But . . .' I can sense Charlie's eyes boring into my back and my body temperature goes into overdrive. 'It's a long story.'

'Well, then,' she says crisply, 'you should tell it.'

'I . . .' I flounder, not sure where to start.

'Not now,' she snaps. 'I want to see you first thing on Monday. And I have to warn you, Lena, your job is in jeopardy. If you can't keep a professional boundary as an adviser, this line of work may not be for you.'

'Listen, Susi, I . . .'

But she's ended the call.

26

The silence echoes around my small kitchen, and I squirm under Charlie's questioning gaze. A familiar heaviness presses down on me and I'm back to that day last winter and the conversation that ended our marriage. It had taken place right here in the kitchen too.

Why didn't you fight for us?

I notice a blush reddening Charlie's neck and he clears his throat. 'So . . . er, I'm assuming Susi's pissed off.'

I sigh as I place my phone face down on the worktop. 'Yep. Nothing new. You know what she's like.' I force a laugh. I don't tell him that my job is now at risk, although, from the look on his face, I can see he's guessed.

He takes a step towards me. 'Lena . . .'

Just then Rufus bounds in with Freddie, the two of them acting like excitable puppies as they chatter away about the gig tonight and how they're going to 'crash' at Charlie's flat afterwards. If Rufus is surprised to see Charlie and me standing so close together he doesn't say.

'You didn't tell me you were staying with your dad tonight,' I say to Rufus, trying to keep the peevishness from my voice.

Rufus's face falls. 'Sorry, Mum. I forgot we said we'd watch *Disturbia*. Can we do it tomorrow night instead?'

I plaster a smile over my face. 'Of course we can. Oh, but didn't you arrange with Kit to have a guitar lesson this evening?'

'Oh, yes, how's that going?' Charlie interjects. 'Kit seems like a nice lad.'

'Yeah. Good. Kit's great. A better teacher than you.' He elbows Charlie good-naturedly in the side. 'He had to cancel tonight. He said he might come over tomorrow when I get back. Anyway, come on, Fred, I'll just grab my stuff.' And then they disappear. I can hear their size tens charging up the stairs, and turn to Charlie with a half-hearted shrug.

He throws me a concerned look. 'You're welcome to come too? It's been a while since you were at one of our gigs.'

I try not to look horrified at the prospect of hanging out with Charlie's new girlfriend. 'Ah, thanks, but it's okay. I've . . . I can, erm, meet Jo or something. And I'm just glad he's happy. Especially after what happened last year at school.'

Charlie immediately clams up. Even after all this time he still doesn't want to talk about it.

'What is it?' I bark. 'You've always been so . . . *weird* whenever I've brought up Rufus's bullying. You can't always bury your head in the sand.'

'And you can't always poke yours above the parapet,' he retorts.

'What's that supposed to mean?'

He shakes his head. 'You haven't changed.'

'And neither have you.'

We glare at each other. How dare he? Why doesn't he ever want to face anything? I literally have to bite my tongue to stop all the things I've kept quiet about, all the resentments and his failings, spilling from my lips. We have to co-parent our son. We can't afford to fall out.

'Tell Rufus and Freddie I'll wait in the van,' he says coldly.

'It's too hot. You don't have to do that . . .'

'It's fine. I'll see you when I see you.' And then he stalks out.

This is exactly why we split up. *This*. His inability to discuss anything that makes him feel uncomfortable. Maybe he's different with his new woman.

Five minutes later Rufus rushes into the kitchen with his backpack to give me a kiss goodbye, Freddie hovering behind him with the tripod. 'See you tomorrow,' he calls.

'Bye, Mrs Fletcher,' adds Freddie. The front door bangs shut, and they're gone.

I feel bad for snapping at Charlie. For a moment at the kitchen table, sharing memories of Rufus, I'd felt close to him again. I'm also worried about what Susi is going to do with me on Monday. Charlie and Jo were right. I shouldn't have got involved with Drew and Henry, but now it's too late. I can't erase everything I've learnt about the Morgans in the last week. I can't unhear their conversation or unsee the strange things in their house.

I take Phoenix out for his evening walk. The air feels stuffy and polluted. A few others are also walking dogs, or ambling along alone, or in pairs, as I take a circuitous route around the residential streets, stopping every now and again for Phoenix to cock his leg against a lamppost. When I return I see Henry and Marielle in their car, pulling away from the kerb. Marielle waves at me as they pass, and I watch as they drive down the street. They must be going away again, and I'm relieved, although Marielle didn't ask me to keep an eye on their house this time.

It's nearly dark now, and when I get in I let Phoenix off his lead and slump onto the sofa. I keep thinking about Susi's phone call earlier and how annoyed she'd sounded. I can't afford to lose my job and I wonder again if Drew has dobbed me in.

I'm just about to turn on the TV to watch something I can sink into and not think too deeply about when my mobile buzzes on the coffee-table in front of me. Drew's name flashes up on the screen.

'Hello. Drew?' I answer cagily, wondering what kind of mood he's going to be in.

'Hi. Yes. Sorry, Lena. I hope it's okay to call, but I thought you'd want to know how I got on at the police station.'

'Oh. Yes, absolutely.'

He sounds fired up. 'Well, they didn't disregard me as readily as I thought they would. They took a statement and they listened to your recording. And they took it seriously when I told them what Milly said about her being followed by a cla– Oh, hold on. The officer I spoke to is trying to get through. Can I call you back?'

'Sure. Bye.'

He ends the call and disappointment rips through me that he's left me hanging.

I expect him to call me back but at least an hour passes and he still hasn't. I stop myself reaching for my phone to text him. I'm desperate to know what the police have said, and what they plan to do, but I can't look too eager because I've already given Drew the wrong impression and my job is in jeopardy.

I'm watching *The Traitors US*, but I can't concentrate. I get up, go to the window and look out onto the street. There is no sign of Henry's car. I doubt they'll be back tonight. I think of Joan's spare key sitting in my kitchen drawer.

I have to know what they're hiding. I have to find something, *anything*, that might shed light on what they're planning.

I wait until it's completely dark, when I'm as sure as I can be that Henry and Marielle aren't going to come home, before slipping out of the house with Joan's spare key. It's nearly eleven o'clock and the length of the street outside is quiet. Further down at the opposite end I can see a cluster of youths, but they are walking the other way, towards Gloucester Road. There is a light on in the house across the street, but the curtains are drawn. When I'm certain I won't be spotted, I creep down the Morgans' front path and let myself into their house. With trepidation I step over the threshold, taking in the familiar musky smell of their hallway. This time I head straight for their magnificent kitchen. It looks like it belongs in a high-end magazine. There are two suede sofas in the corner and a small TV on the wall. Everything is meticulously tidy, unlike my kitchen, where the tabletop is littered with Rufus's college work, or unopened post. I go to the sliding doors and turn the lock.

This time I'll plan my escape route and leave via these doors. If I slip through the gap in the hedge I'll have less chance of being spotted. Moonlight streams in from the Velux window above but I still need to use the torch on my phone to light the way, and it reflects back at me from the opaque glass. I must look like a burglar.

I rummage through their drawers, not even knowing what I'm looking for, but hoping something will stand out. Something that proves what they're up to.

And then I hear it.

A thud and a bang.

I freeze, my hand still in their cutlery drawer. I strain my ears, every nerve ending on high alert. *What the fuck was that?*

The noise came from above.

I stay where I am, too scared to move. I can hear the hum of the fridge, the creak of the pipes.

And then I hear it again. A loud crash. Like something's been knocked over.

Someone's upstairs.

27

NATALIE

She's a prisoner.

She's trying not to eat or drink anything that the nurse gives her, suspecting now that it's laced with drugs. Instead she uses the tap water from the little en suite bathroom. She can survive without food for a couple of days. She's never been a particularly big eater anyway. The nurse has helped her walk over to the tiny en-suite on a few occasions. At others she's managed to stumble and crawl. She's never even had the energy to scream at the nurse, or demand to know what's going on and why she's being held a prisoner.

Snippets from that day in the park have filtered through her drug-addled mind, like sunshine through cloud. There had been footsteps behind her. A car in front. A woman had got out of the passenger side and, at the same time, she'd felt a hand reach from behind her and cover her face with a cloth. Everything had gone black after that and the next thing she knew she was here, in this room.

Was this nurse the same woman who'd stepped out of the car?

Now that she's less woozy the memories are coming back to her.

She'd been in hiding for years. That's right. She remembers now. She talked to her brother occasionally to let him know she was safe but never where she was. She'd tried to keep her nose clean but somewhere along the way she'd fallen in with the wrong sort of people in an effort to make a quick buck. The temptation to rip them off had been too great and now here she was, living with the consequences.

Because all this, she now realizes, is linked to that gang.

Drug-dealing. That was always her weakness.

She'd received a phone call. When was that? Sunday? Monday? Someone from the gang had called her. They knew her real name. She'd been packing, fleeing her flat. This woman must be working for them. Is she keeping her here, drugged up, until someone from the gang arrives? And then what? What are they planning to do with her?

Yesterday afternoon the nurse had started asking her questions. She couldn't concentrate on what she was saying, and the nurse had given up. Now she wonders if they want information to pass on to the gang.

Natalie had hardly slept last night. She'd flushed her food down the toilet to make it look like she'd eaten it and, as she'd suspected, she'd felt more awake, more alert as a result. The drugs are still in her system, and she feels weaker than usual, but if she pretends to be sedated she can try to overpower the nurse, taking her by surprise. She plans to do it at night. The nurse might be taller than her, but Natalie is younger. And Natalie is desperate.

When the nurse came this morning Natalie pretended to be asleep. Then, after the nurse left, she flushed the cornflakes down the loo. She'd felt strong enough to walk to the en-suite, her legs less jelly-like, her mind sharper. If only she had some kind of weapon.

She casts about for something she could use, her eyes landing on the plastic cereal bowl, spoon and beaker on the trolley. She can't really do much damage with any of that. She just hopes the element of surprise is enough.

Natalie doesn't like to think of herself as a victim. She's always been in charge of her own destiny. And, yes, she's made mistakes. Big, life-changing ones. But she's never been given to reflecting nostalgically or regretfully on the past. It's the here and now that matters. Here and now, she's fired up. She won't let this sick individual hurt her or hand her over to the gang she ripped off. She'll do what she can to escape.

She's hit by a sudden bout of wooziness and stumbles back into the trolley, causing it to topple over with a crash. She freezes. Did the nurse hear? Natalie makes her way to the door and tries the handle. It's locked.

She slumps to the floor, exhausted. She needs to be patient. If she makes a move too soon she'll blow her cover.

Just as she's getting up she hears a noise outside the door. Is it her imagination or was someone calling a tentative 'Hello?' Footsteps on the landing. A cough. And she shrinks back when she sees the door handle jiggling.

Someone is outside. Maybe a suspicious neighbour. Her heart soars with a joy she hasn't felt in years.

This is it.

She's finally being rescued.

28

LENA

There's definitely someone upstairs. My heart lurches. Could it be . . . could it be Sarah-Jane? I have to check. I can't leave here if someone is being held against their will.

The stairs creak under my feet as I reach the top floor. There's a funny smell up here. Musty, unused. Dust motes sparkle in the slant of moonlight coming through the Velux above and I cough. For a newly refurbished house, this area feels unfinished. There is a single door on this floor. This must be the attic conversion. I approach slowly, my heart rate spiking as I reach for the door handle. This is it. Finally. The moment of truth.

The door doesn't budge. Of course it would be locked. It looks quite flimsy: maybe I could kick it in. I slam my shoulder against it and it bursts open.

I lurch into the room and gasp.

It's small and badly lit, but I can make out a single iron-framed bed under a sloped ceiling and freshly plastered walls. Apart from that, the attic is empty. Completely and utterly empty. It hasn't been converted into a bedroom, like I'd been expecting. I move further into the room, not quite able to believe what I'm seeing, as though I've stumbled through a door into an alternate universe. Cobwebs hang in the corners and a spider scuttles past, disappearing into a crack in the floorboards. It smells of damp plaster and rotting wood.

There's nobody here. No kidnapped woman. No Sarah-Jane Mayhew. No signs of life at all.

I move towards the bed, noting the stained, stripy mattress and the layer of dust on the top of the iron frame.

But I heard a crash and a thump. Where had it come from?

I can't hang around to find out. I need to go. Now.

With one last glance around the room, I leave, closing the door behind me. I note again how bare the walls are as I descend the stairs: no photos or personal effects, but they haven't long moved in. I can't stop thinking about the empty attic. As I move across the landing I notice the door to the master bedroom is open and, as I pass, I take in a double bed adorned with satin pillows in complementary shades of coffee and caramel, and a walnut dressing-table.

As I make my way down the three steps onto the half-landing I pause outside Henry's study. The door is closed. Is that where the noise was coming from? I slowly turn the handle, my heart in my mouth, and the door creaks open. I'm just about to step into the room when I'm knocked back by a sudden force. Something hard pushes against my chest and I fall flat against the wall, my heart racing. A streak of caramel and white flees past me and down the stairs. I put a trembling hand to my breastbone. It's just a cat. It must have been shut into Henry's study by mistake.

I can see it's knocked over a lamp. I swear under my breath, my legs wobbly.

I'm making my way down the remaining stairs when another sound makes me freeze.

A key in the lock.

29

I sprint back up the stairs, my chest hurting, and flatten myself against the wall on the landing. Oh God, oh God. What are they doing back? I thought they'd gone away for the weekend. Why did I think coming here tonight was a good idea?

I'm expecting the hall light to come on but when it doesn't I creep towards the banister and glance down. There's someone in the hallway. But it's not either of the Morgans. It looks like a man in dark clothes, a hoody pulled over his head. Is this a burglar? They aren't using a torch but are feeling their way in the dark towards the kitchen. I remember Marielle was concerned that someone had been going into their garden: the smashed shed window and things being moved about.

Then another thought pops into my head. Is this Drew looking for clues about his sister? Has he had the same idea as me? My mouth goes dry, and a cold sweat breaks out all over my body. I have no choice but to stay here, cowering in the shadows. Five minutes pass. Ten. My body aches with the effort of keeping stock still. I'm only shallow-breathing, worried the sound of an exhalation will cause the man to find me. I hear him below me, rustling through drawers and paperwork. And then I see him go into the little room at the bottom of the stairs. The room with the wall of newspaper clippings. He spends quite a bit of time in there and my mind races, trying to figure out possible exit routes if he decides to come upstairs. Perhaps I could hide in the attic. I find myself hoping the man is Drew. Yet if it is, how did he get in? Did he pick the lock?

The man reappears in the hallway. He doesn't look as tall as Drew, although it's hard to be certain in this light. I hold my breath. Just as I expect him to turn towards the stairs, he reaches for the front door and slips out, closing it softly behind him.

I exhale in relief, my legs giving way, and I crumple onto the floor. I don't move for a few more seconds, just in case the man comes back, but when I realize he's definitely gone I creep down the stairs. As I pass the room at the bottom, I look to see if he's taken any of the newspaper clippings from the wall. I notice a gap, but I can't tell which he's taken. I flee out of the sliding doors, scurrying through the gap in the hedge.

It's not until I'm in my own garden that I allow myself to relax, and my whole body starts trembling in delayed shock. That was so close. *So close.*

There is a light on in my kitchen and, from my vantage point, I can see right through to the front door. I think of the man I heard on the tape. *I forgot about the fucking dog.* How often has someone been in my back garden? I'd be totally unaware from inside the house. For the first time I wonder if I should get kitchen blinds. Thank goodness Paul is coming over tomorrow to install the camera at last.

I let myself in through my patio doors and lock them behind me, bending down to bury my head in Phoenix's fur, my heart still jumping about in my chest.

That's it. I'm done. I'm never sneaking into their house again. My nerves can't take it.

I go to the fridge, pour myself a glass of wine and down it in two gulps. Jo's right. She always is in that big-sisterly way of hers.

I pour more wine and go into the living room. I'll watch some comfort telly for a bit to calm my mind, I decide, as I sink into the sofa and turn on Netflix. Phoenix curls up next to me. I'm just about to scroll down to *Emily in Paris* when my phone buzzes. It's a text message. From Drew.

I know it's really late, so not sure if you're still awake. But if you are please call me. I have news about my sister.

I immediately call him. He answers on the first ring.

'I'm sorry I didn't have the chance to call you back earlier.' He sounds breathless. Excited. 'I've just driven back from St Albans.'

So it couldn't have been him in the neighbours' house. 'And Sarah-Jane?'

'It all happened so quickly when the police got involved. They located her in St Albans. It's all okay, Lena. She's fine. She didn't even realize we were looking for her and is embarrassed to have caused a fuss. She just went off radar for a bit, to clear her head, she said, after a bad break-up.'

'But . . .' my head spins '. . . she told her friend she was being followed. The blue classic car?'

'Yes. Her ex got a bit obsessive and started following her in his mate's car so she didn't recognize it. A midnight-blue Mercedes SL. Not a Jag. She's safe, Lena.' I can hear the relief in his voice. 'She's finally home.'

PART TWO

30

HENRY

April 1988
London

The wedding was planned for June: an extravagant, lavish affair that was costing more than he made in a year, but Lawrence Bishop-Smith was insistent on paying for everything, indulgently promising Marielle the earth.

'This wedding is helping to take my mind off poor Violet,' he'd said at dinner, one evening, in the type of restaurant where the waiters looked even more dapper than their customers. Henry was still wary of Marielle's father. He was too rich, too showy. He had people hanging off his every word, especially women, hopeful they might become the new Mrs Bishop-Smith. Secretly Henry felt Lawrence was a weak-willed man who, by all accounts, had allowed Violet to make financial decisions regarding his own daughters. Savannah, who had just turned eighteen, was off travelling the world, flying out the day after Violet's funeral with a fistful of travellers' cheques from her grieving father. Henry wondered if Marielle, too, had jumped at the chance to fleece her father while he was vulnerable by organizing a wedding before the funds started to dry up again.

Marielle now lectured four days a week at a university for the classics department. He liked that she was still ambitious despite her family money, even if he suspected the safety blanket meant she could do a job that wasn't particularly well paid. Henry had been lucky that he was an all-rounder at school, gifted in most subjects, and he'd funded himself through medical school with student loans and extra jobs. If money had been no object, he'd have been an academic, like Marielle, specializing in English literature, Victorian Gothic, not that he'd allowed himself to think about it too deeply because it was only ever a pipedream.

Marielle was already home when he got in, leaping up from the sofa and her latest bridal magazine to give him a hug. He'd practically moved in with her because her apartment was so much nicer than his shoebox in Marble Arch, but it didn't sit right with him. She'd persuaded him to take on more private work, which helped pay the bills, but although he earned a very good salary it was nothing to the money the Bishop-Smiths had.

'I've just had a lovely early dinner with Daddy,' she said, pulling him down so that he had no choice but to sit beside her. He hadn't even had time to put his briefcase down or take off his shoes. 'And he said we could have this apartment when we get married. He'd sign over the deeds to us.' The apartment was currently in her father's name.

The skin at the back of his neck prickled. 'I couldn't do that. It's my job to provide for us, not your father's.'

She scoffed. 'You're joking, right? You don't strike me as the kind of man to let his ego get in the way of good sense.' She shook her head in disbelief and narrowed her eyes. 'Unless I'm wrong about you, Henry Morgan?'

He fidgeted and pulled at his shirt collar. 'Maybe I can take on more private work . . .'

Disappointment was written all over her beautiful face. 'Don't be run-of-the-mill, Henry. That's not the man I fell in love with.'

'It's not run-of-the-mill to want to earn a good salary, to want to look after your wife,' he replied, offended.

'That's all very admirable, but that's not why I love you. I love you because you understand me.' Her eyes moved over his face as though she was taking in every inch of him. As though she was trying to work out if she'd been wrong to love him. This brilliant, confident, amazing woman. This woman who wanted to marry him. He couldn't bear to disappoint her. 'Don't let pride get in the way of our love. That's not what we're about. We're about defying conventions. We're about being true to ourselves and each other. I have told you things, Henry, I could never tell anyone else. And you've told me things. I thought we had an understanding.'

'We do,' he said, white-hot panic rising that she might start to see him in a different light.

She squeezed his hand. 'Good.' She smiled. 'Daddy did wonder if we'd need a bigger place. I know we've never discussed it, but he mentioned . . .' she took her hand from his '. . . children.'

He didn't want to share Marielle with anyone else. She had never talked about babies, never cooed over them if they walked past a pushchair. In fact, she'd once said, in passing, that she'd hate to be pregnant: it 'looked uncomfortable' and she'd feel as though she had an 'alien growing inside her'. 'Right,' he said, in alarm. 'I thought – assumed – you didn't want them.'

She sat rigid, her hands in her lap. 'I don't know how I feel, if I'm honest, Henry. I never thought I was destined to be a mother. Until . . . well, recently. I suppose it was falling in love with you.'

'I'd make an awful father,' he spluttered, thinking of his own dad. 'God, Marielle. Some people are meant to be parents, but we aren't those people.'

She'd treated him to a little smile, as though she had a secret he knew nothing about. 'Oh, I don't know, Henry. I think perhaps we could be those people after all.'

'You're . . . you're not pregnant, are you?'

She laughed. 'No. Of course not.'

'Good,' he said. 'Because I really don't want them, Mari.' His heart thudded and the air between them stilled. 'And I don't believe you really want them either.'

She patted his hand. 'Maybe you're right, Henry Morgan. But it's too soon to tell.' She got up and kissed him hard on the lips, but he continued to sit there, his stomach in knots. He loved Marielle with all his heart. He already knew he wanted never to be without her.

But he also knew, without a shadow of doubt, that he should never be a father.

31

LENA

I swallow my queasiness as I walk into the office on Monday. I arrive early, mainly to avoid the humiliation of Susi's wrath played out in front of mild-mannered Kath. I can't shake the awful dread that presses down on me that I might have lost my job.

Susi's office door is ajar and I can see her sitting at her desk, frowning at her computer screen, her half-moon glasses on a chain around her neck. I notice the tops of her arms are sunburnt, clashing with her yellow blouse and bringing out her freckles. I knock gently, my heart pounding.

She looks up, her mouth tensing when she sees me. 'Ah, Lena. Come in.' She's not smiling, but she hardly ever does. She indicates the chair and I slump into it.

Susi lifts her glasses to her face and blinks at me. 'Let's cut to the chase.'

My stomach lurches.

'As you know, we're here to talk about Drew Mayhew.' She's eyeing me sternly. 'It's been brought to my attention that you've been visiting Drew at home. That's totally overstepping the mark. What were you thinking?'

How does she know this? Has Drew complained about me? But he'd been so happy on the phone on Friday evening when he told me he'd found his sister. He'd thanked me for my help. He hadn't sounded cross with me.

'I – I only went to his house once. He really believed something terrible had happened to his sister and I wanted to help him.'

She clicks her tongue in exasperation. 'You know we aren't a missing-persons service and that it was beyond our remit. Yet you took it into your own hands. I don't know what's going on with you and Drew –'

'Nothing!' I blurt out. 'He's just a client.'

She purses her lips as though she doesn't believe me. 'In that case, you were acting as his adviser, and how you conducted yourself isn't the way an adviser should behave. We don't make home visits. We don't make empty promises and we don't do anything to make our clients' lives more upsetting and stressful.'

I look down at my hands folded in my lap. I swallow the lump in my throat.

'In light of all this, we should put a pin in this holiday cover. I'll give the hours to someone else. You're lucky, quite frankly, that you've still got your job. But consider this a verbal warning.'

When Rufus gets back from college I'm lying on the sofa in the front room with the curtains closed, my eyes puffy and red. Phoenix is curled up by my side, his head resting on my leg, his sorrowful eyes looking up at me when Rufus charges into the room in a cloud of Lynx and sweat. 'What's wrong?' he asks, in alarm, when he sees me.

I sit up, dislodging Phoenix, who jumps to the floor and nuzzles his nose in Rufus's hand. I decide to give a half-truth. 'I'm okay. I just . . . I was hoping to go full-time at work but they've decided to keep me on part-time.'

Rufus gently taps my legs to make room for him on the sofa. 'Why?'

'It's a long story.'

'What did you do?'

'Your mother got over-involved.' I force out a laugh.

'Oh, Mum!'

I bite my lip. 'It's okay.' I don't want to tell him I'm worried about Charlie selling the house, but Rufus isn't stupid.

'I finish college on Wednesday and then have some work experience. But after that I can get a summer job. That will help moneywise,' he says, and my heart swells with love for him.

I pat his knee and flash him a watery smile. 'Thanks, love, but I don't want you worrying about that. It will all be fine.'

He stands up. 'Drink?'

'I'll have a glass of water, thank you.'

He leaves the room and I swing my legs around, wiping under my eyes, and follow him into the kitchen. I sit at the table while he fetches me the water.

His T-shirt is clinging to him but despite the heat he's still wearing jeans. I haven't seen Rufus in a pair of shorts since he was little. He's always self-conscious about being too skinny. Not helped by those horrible kids from his school.

I survey my son, on the cusp of adulthood. I only want to protect him, especially since his father and I split up.

He'd been understandably upset: we'd blown his safe, ordered world apart. Whatever else had been happening in his life, all the other worries he had, home was always his safe space. But now I see I underestimated him. He's happier than he's ever been now he's at college with like-minded people, and away from that constricted school environment where everybody is put into boxes. He's thriving. Before he started college he always walked around as though he was trying to make himself smaller, invisible, back hunched, hands almost dragging, like an ape. But now he walks taller. He smiles more readily. He meets the eyes of strangers when they address him.

He takes a seat next to me. 'Has this got something to do with next door?'

'It's just . . .' I sigh. 'I don't trust them.'

He rolls his eyes. 'Mum. I think you should keep out of it.'

I flop back in the chair. 'I know.'

He gets up and gives me a hug. 'You care too much. But you're not always right, Mum. You jump to conclusions – you always have.'

Why do I feel he's not talking about the Morgans any more?

'What are you trying to say?'

He moves away and opens the fridge. 'Nothing. Is there anything to eat? I'm starving.'

'Ruf?'

'What?' He turns towards me, the slant of light from the fridge illuminating his profile.

'Is everything okay?'

'Yep. Can I have this Scotch egg?'

'Sure.'

He leaves the room with the egg and a Peperami, and I hear the thud of feet on the stairs. I know he'll be in his room for the next few hours, texting.

I stare around the empty kitchen, the clock on the wall ticking loudly as though it's goading me. Maybe Susi's right. Maybe working at Citizens Advice isn't for me. Perhaps it really is time to let go of the past and move on. Embrace the future. Selling the house would give me more money. I could retrain. Do something that makes me happy. Follow my own path instead of Charlie's. I need to forget about the Morgans now. And, okay, they're obviously odd and I'll never know why they have a fake baby, a possible made-up daughter-in-law and a wall of newspaper cuttings. Sarah-Jane is safe. I was wrong about the kidnapping. I've seen for myself that no woman is tied up in their attic. I have to accept that I will never know what they were talking about the day I overheard them.

32

NATALIE

Nobody has come to rescue her. She must have been mistaken when she thought she heard someone outside the door. An old house's creaks and groans: that was all it was. When she finally realized nobody was coming she flopped back into bed and cried tears of frustration and fear. The waiting is the worst part. Whatever they have planned for her she just wishes they'd get on with it and put an end to this awful, torturous misery.

She's feeling weaker now from lack of food. But she can't eat because she knows if she does she'll be groggy and brain-fogged again, and she needs to stay focused. She needs to escape.

She has no idea what time of day it is. The rabbit with the dead eyes stares at her, judging her, and she has the urge to throw it against the wall. *The rabbit*. She has the same memory of its head poking out of a bag. What does it mean?

A slant of sunshine is struggling to filter through the film of dust on the glass and she wonders why they haven't killed her yet. Why keep her here, locked up for days?

The sound of a key in the lock makes her jump and she sits up, gathering the sheet around her, as though for protection. The nurse is back, framed by the doorway, and this time she doesn't bring a trolley of food. Natalie's breath catches when she sees that the nurse isn't alone. A man hovers behind her, also wearing a mask. His eyes are bright and glaring and there is something about him that tugs at her memory, pulling her out of this nightmare and tumbling into the past.

'Please let me go!' she cries. 'If this is about the drugs, I promise to get the money I owe.' Her voice dies: the man is wearing scrubs, as though he's about to perform surgery. Her whole body goes cold with horror. What are they going to do to her?

The nurse comes towards her and perches on the edge of the bed. The man moves forward too. He is holding something. A syringe.

'I think it's about time you started giving us some answers, *Natalie*,' says the woman, her eyes hard. 'We've waited long enough.'

'What kind of answers? Please. I'll tell you everything I know. I promise. Just don't hurt me – *please* . . .'

The man steps forwards uttering a name, and instantly the rabbit's significance floods back and, along with it, everything else.

Now she knows exactly who they are and what they want.

33

LENA

Jo appears on my doorstep the next morning, armed with a big bunch of sunflowers, her top lip damp. She's slightly out of breath, which means she would have walked here. I'm so grateful to see her that, as soon as I open the door and she steps in to give me a hug, I have to blink back tears. I texted her yesterday afternoon to tell her I've been given a verbal warning and made to stay on part-time hours, but she was in chambers all day, so we haven't had the chance to speak properly yet. I was hoping Paul would come over at the weekend to install my garden camera but he's been called out to do a job in Manchester. Jo had been so apologetic when she rang to tell me on Saturday, and I had to assure her that it's fine, I'm grateful for the favour, and that, no, I don't think Paul is useless, but it had reminded me that he, like everyone around me, is busy with his life, trying to fit everything in: family, friends, work. How can I begrudge him that just because I've got time on my hands? If I get desperate I know I can ask Charlie, but it's not as though I've had any more late-night visitors in my garden.

'Oh, hon,' Jo says, as we pull apart. She hands me the sunflowers. 'Come on, let's put these in water. They're already wilting.'

I follow her into the kitchen and watch as she reaches up into the cupboard, selects one of my vases and fills it with water. 'There,' she says, as she arranges the flowers. She carries them over to the kitchen table. 'Sunflowers always cheer me up.'

'Me too.' I smile at her. 'Thanks, Jo.'

I make us both a cup of tea. Phoenix is lying in the shade of the kitchen table, his head between his paws. It's still early so the patio is in shade. But when Jo suggests we sit outside I shake my head. 'I can't trust that they won't be listening,' I say, indicating the Morgans' house. 'And there's so much I need to tell you.'

Jo grimaces and takes a seat at the table, careful not to disrupt Phoenix as she moves her chair. She puts down her mug and angles her body so that she's facing me. She's wearing a voluminous fuchsia sundress today. She gathers the fabric between her knees and fans herself with her hand. 'God, I tell you, this heat coupled with my hot flushes isn't a great combo.'

I pull out the chair next to her and fill her in on the latest.

'Lena! You promised you wouldn't let yourself into their house again,' she hisses. 'You could have been hurt.'

'Marielle told me her daughter-in-law, Heidi, worked at the library, but another employee there hadn't heard of her. Someone Marielle used to teach. It's weird, though, as I think she's tried to pass off this woman as her daughter-in-law. Marielle's got a baby doll that I'm sure she pushes around in a pram and is creepy as fuck.' I throw my hands up. 'It's bizarre. And don't even get me started on all the other stuff!'

'It *is* weird, you're right, but I'm worried about you getting involved.' She reaches for my hand. 'I don't want anything bad happening to you. If you'd got caught in the Morgans' house by that intruder, I dread to think . . .' She grimaces. 'You shouldn't feel responsible just because you overheard part of a conversation between them. You checked the house yourself. They aren't holding a woman hostage. Or a baby. And, no, before you say it, I'm sure they're not planning to steal anyone's baby. Look,' she lowers her voice, 'there's something going on with them, that's obvious. But, honestly, hon, I'd keep out of it. You nearly lost your job over this. Can you imagine what Susi would say if she knew the rest of it?' She makes a disbelieving noise and sips her drink, looking at me imploringly over the rim of her mug.

'You're right.' I sigh. 'I need to let it go. Especially now I know Drew's sister is safe. I just wish I didn't feel so . . .' I search for the words '. . . at sea. Everything's changing. My marriage ending. Charlie moving on. Rufus leaving next year. And me . . . where does this leave me? I've got no real job prospects. I'm only forty-four. I've got at least twenty years of working life ahead of me and I'm not qualified for anything.' I try to stem my panic. 'I've become too invested in this because . . . well, because . . .' *I'm lonely!* I want to shout. But it sticks in my throat.

'Because you've got too much time on your hands?'

'Well, yes. I thought I'd rectified that with moving to full-time, but now I've even messed that up!'

'Don't be disheartened. Maybe find something else to fill the gaps. Or another full-time job. You can do anything you want to, you know that, right?' Jo has always been my biggest champion, and I want to hug her. We've always said we're the sisters we never had, me an only child and Jo with three younger brothers.

'I'm sorry Paul hasn't put the camera up yet,' she says again. 'He's been so busy at work. But have you noticed if the gate was unlocked again?'

I picture the man riffling through the Morgans' drawers on Friday night and shake my head. Had it been the same man who had been in my garden the evening I overheard the Morgans' conversation? 'No. The gate's remained locked, thank God.'

'It's not your problem, remember?' She throws me a stern look.

I nod silently, remembering my vow to myself that I'd leave well alone, even though I already know that I won't be able to stick to it.

When Jo's gone I reach for my phone and scroll to the photos I'd taken of the newspaper clippings the first time I was in the Morgans' house. I study them again. I'd only managed to take three, one of which is blurry.

I zoom in on the partial headlines:

BABY FOUND ON HOS . . .
. . . ORGANS FOR RESEARCH AT . . .

DRUGS LORD FOUND DEAD IN . . .
BRIGHT SPARKS WIN NATIONAL AWARD

What does this wall mean? As far as I could make out, the cuttings looked totally random.

It's only lunchtime and Rufus won't be home until four so I turn on my laptop. The headline about a baby being found interests me but the accompanying story is impossible to make out because it's partly hidden by another article. I google 'BABY FOUND' anyway but too many entries pop up. I narrow it down to 'BABY FOUND ON HOSPITAL', assuming that's what the last word is, but again hundreds of entries flood my screen. It's difficult to refine the search when I don't know what I'm looking for and I can't ascertain anything from the actual article. I try the next one and get a similar outcome. When I reach the article about the BRIGHT SPARKS I can just make out the name of the local newspaper it came from, the *Salisbury Journal*. Again, the article below the headline is partly obscured so it's hard to read the story, and it looks like there's also a black-and-white photo, again partially obscured. I log on to the *Salisbury Journal* website and search for the BRIGHT SPARKS article instead. It immediately pops up onscreen and I scan the piece, puzzled. It's anodyne, about an electrical company in Salisbury that has won some industry award. Why would the Morgans have this? I scroll down and, at the bottom of the page, there is the same photograph, but this time in colour. It shows a group of electricians, all standing awkwardly, some smiling, some with their thumbs up, and a man in the middle holding aloft a glass trophy.

And then my attention is caught by a woman standing next to the trophy-wielding man. There's something about the way she's standing, the tilt of her head, the firm stance, that I instantly recognize.

Simone Harvey.

A rush of blood floods my face.

It can't be her, can it?

The hair is different and she's twenty-odd years older, but . . . there's a strong resemblance. There are no names under the photograph.

Simone Harvey. What are the chances that this could be her?

34

LENA

January 1999
London

It was a dull wet winter's day when I first met Simone
Harvey. The sky hung over the capital like a dirty grey
sheet, and I yearned for the crisp green East Sussex
countryside. My stomach was a mass of knots as the bus
ambled past dank building after dank building, warped
and surreal-looking through the rain-smudged windows.
Every time the doors to the bus pinged open they let in a
snap of cold air that wove around my ankles.

St Calvert's Maternity Hospital was in Hackney, a short
ride from my digs in Walthamstow, and I was on my way to
start my six-week placement on the dreaded labour ward.
I'd done most of my placements, last year, at St Calvert's,
which was part of a larger Trust, but on the post-natal ward
and the adjoining clinic. I'd heard horror stories about how
frantic the labour ward was, with all the pain and screaming
and blood, and I wasn't a fan of the sprawling Victorian
building that had once been a workhouse. I've since heard

it closed down and I can't say I'm surprised. It was about to collapse even back then.

The three-year course I was on was much more exhausting and time-consuming than I'd thought possible. While friends from school were getting pissed at the student union of their chosen university and staggering into lectures with a hangover, I was up early cleaning bedpans or mopping blood and mucus from the floors. I was in the second year and I preferred the lectures on campus to the placements, which often meant twelve-hour shifts three or four days a week. Lately I'd begun to doubt my choice to study midwifery. My mum had been a nurse, and it was assumed I'd follow in her footsteps. When I was growing up, Mum, Nanna and all my family often commented on how caring and interested I was in other people, not to mention how much I loved babies. But halfway through my second year I was already feeling jaded and burnt out.

Still, that Monday morning I was trying to put a brave face on it, bracing myself for what I already knew would be a long day ahead.

As soon as I walked through the familiar double doors of the hospital I was hit by the smell of disinfectant and sour milk, and queasiness gripped me. It was only 7.30 a.m. and I hadn't been able to face breakfast when I left home that morning. I went straight to Reception and explained who I was to a sleep-deprived midwife in a pink dress with a white pinafore, who told me, rather wearily, that she was just about to go off shift. There was a bit of a kerfuffle behind the desk when another midwife came in and also didn't know who I was or where I was supposed to be. I stood there feeling awkward, wondering if I'd been sent to the hospital by mistake, when a young woman bustled in wearing pale blue scrubs. This was in the days when scrubs were relatively new for midwives and a lot of the older staff preferred the traditional dress. This woman looked fresh-faced and wide-eyed, not weighed down and put-upon like the middle-aged women behind the reception desk. I was instantly drawn to her. She had a friendly face, clear blue eyes and brown hair, tied back, with two bleached stripes at the front. Later she would tell me the bleached stripes were inspired by Louise Wener from Sleeper, not Geri Halliwell, as everyone assumed.

'Elena Bull?' She was holding a folded pair of scrubs.

'Yes.'

She handed them to me. 'I'm Simone Harvey and I'll be your supervising midwife during your placement.'

I was surprised. I was nineteen and she didn't look that much older than me, although I'd later learn she was actually twenty-six and had been qualified for four and a half years.

'Nice to meet you,' I replied, feeling shy.

She grinned. 'Come. I'll show you where you can change.' She set off at a fast pace and I had to jog to keep up. I was taller than her by an inch or so but she walked as though she was six foot. She ushered me into a cubicle where I quickly slipped on my scrubs and dumped my bag in my designated locker. I'd already plaited my hair, which, back then, had been almost to my waist.

I recognized parts of the hospital from my time on the post-natal ward last year, but the labour ward was down endless corridors that led to a separate wing. I was already panicking about how I would find the ward tomorrow when I didn't have Simone with me. I couldn't even take mental notes because she was walking so fast.

'We're super-busy,' she said, as she swiped us in. 'We currently have mums in each of the three birthing pools.' She pointed towards one of the corridors. 'All six labour rooms are occupied and two are in theatre, one an emergency C-section. But you'll be down here, helping look after mums in beds three to six.'

I tried not to balk at the thought of being responsible for four labouring women. 'What stages?'

'Early. One or two centimetres dilated. Low-risk births. All waiting for their own room.'

I was grateful for that, at least.

She stopped and patted my shoulder. 'You'll be fine, and you won't be on your own. Janice and Maeve will be around, both very experienced. Dr Laura Barnard is on shift today if there are any problems. Which there won't be. Like I say, all early stages and low risk.'

She started walking again and didn't speak until we arrived at the ward. It wasn't the most inspiring of rooms. Long, thin and dark, despite the overhead light, and the windows looked out over the car park and grey skies. There were six beds in a row, four of which had heavily pregnant women lying on them, all with a grey-faced man at their sides, holding their hand. The other two were leaning over the beds while their partners rubbed their backs. They ranged in age from early twenties to late thirties. Some had monitors strapped to their bellies and every now and again one would moan in pain.

With one last reassuring smile, Simone left me, saying she'd be back to check up on me in an hour. Maeve and Janice, both in their early forties, seemed kind and introduced me to the women I'd be looking after. One woman, Grace, who was the youngest on the ward, suddenly went from being two centimetres dilated to eight and was quickly whisked off to a labour room within an hour of me being there. But it wasn't long before she was replaced by another woman in labour. I had to hold one woman's hand when she asked for an epidural because she was in so much pain, and I sat with her on the edge of the bed, trying to make sure she stayed completely still between contractions while Dr Barnard administered the drugs and the woman's husband looked as if he might pass out at the sight of the huge needle.

The shift went surprisingly quickly, and I really didn't have much time to think or to dwell on whether I was doing something wrong. I remembered all the information I'd learnt in lectures, and was relieved to be working with the experienced midwives.

Just as I was about to clock off Simone came to find me and we walked to the changing room together.

'You did well today, Elena. Well done.'

'Thanks. But please call me Lena.'

She smiled in response. 'Maeve said you're a hard worker who uses her own initiative. That's great.' She looked less fresh-faced twelve hours later, the soft skin under her eyes a bruised pink, and she had what I suspect was blood on the front of her tunic. She tucked a blonde strand behind her ear. 'Where do you live?'

'Walthamstow.'

'Oh, me too. Are you getting the bus?'

I nodded as I retrieved the bag from my locker.

'Great. We can travel back together.'

I was relieved to have someone to walk with to the bus stop. It turned out we lived just a few streets from each other, in identikit Victorian terrace house-shares. I laughed as Simone told me about her housemates and the tricks she played on them when they stole her food. 'Every time I go to make a sandwich there's hardly any bread left so I got one of those fake bread rolls from the joke shop. I wish I'd seen Carl's face when he tried to bite into it.' She didn't sound annoyed, and her eyes twinkled as she said it. 'I have a crush on him, so I forgive him. I suspect he knows and he takes advantage.' She blew one of her blonde streaks away from her face. 'If you ever fancy going for a drink, let me know. Shift work can be lonely.'

'Thanks,' I said, genuinely touched. On my last placement I'd had a horrible supervisor who enjoyed looking down her nose at me. Simone seemed respectful. Someone I could trust.

Some people enter your life and set you on a completely different trajectory. It turned out Simone Harvey was one of those people.

35

HENRY

July 2024
Bristol

The front door slams, echoing through the house and setting every nerve in Henry's body on edge. She's back. And who knows what mood she'll be in? He stays seated at his desk in the study that smells of dust mites and old, yellowing books, mostly early editions of his favourite classics for which he'd scoured little independent bookshops, auctions and specialist dealers. People are always surprised when he tells them of his hobby. As though it's an oxymoron that someone medical or scientific should be interested in fiction. Over the years he's carted those books around with him from house to house and from town to town.

When they moved here he'd been drawn to this room. The house was smaller than the country pile they'd lived in before, but he knew why Marielle had wanted it so badly. It was Fate, she'd said. Yet this room with its built-in bookshelves had sold it for him. He'd be happy to spend all his time in this room, buried within its musty walls and escaping into the pages of his familiar stories.

He can hear Marielle's heels clattering on the geometric black-and-burgundy tiles in the hallway. It sounds like she's pacing. Up and down. Up and down. Never a good sign. It means she'll be over-thinking, getting herself all riled up, and then she'll start obsessing again. He should have known, when he first met her all those years ago, that she wasn't the type to let anything go. He'd fallen in love with her tenacity after all. But now he's approaching seventy, he's exhausted.

Does he sometimes wish he'd never met her? Sometimes, if he's honest. He hadn't known then what kind of collision course they were heading for. But he can't imagine living without her either. She came into his life, shook it up and made it a hell of a lot more interesting than it would have been. Of that he has no doubt. And he loved her, oh, how he'd loved her. He'd been so blinded by love those first few years that she could have told him anything and he'd have forgiven her.

'Henry!' Her voice cuts right through him. 'Are you up in your study again?' Where else would he be?

He braces himself as he hears her climbing the stairs. When she enters the room he spins in his chair to face her, setting his expression to neutral.

She's framed in the doorway, looking immaculate as always in a vivid blue summer dress that brings out the violet in her grey-green eyes. Not a hair out of place, even in this heat. And despite everything, he feels a twinge of desire for her that hasn't let up in the forty years they've been together. If anything, he desires her more than ever. Is it even possible to love and hate someone at the same time? To desire someone and be repulsed by them?

'What have you been doing?' She raises a perfectly sculpted eyebrow. She'd plucked them too much back in the 1980s and now she has to draw them on every morning. Before he's had the chance to reply, her gaze flickers to the mobile that sits beside his keyboard, then lands on him again, pinning him to the chair. Those eyes. Glistening and beautiful, perceptive and challenging. He opens his mouth to speak but she charges on. 'The locksmith is downstairs.'

'Already?'

'Yes. I don't understand why you called them, Henry. It's totally unnecessary.' Marielle folds her arms under her full breasts.

'I just think it's best. We don't know who has a spare key.'

'You're being paranoid.' She throws him a stern look.

He glances towards the window, which is open. From here he can see into Lena Fletcher's garden. She's out there now with her son, a lanky teenager with Bob Dylan hair. Henry always notices other men's hair now he's started to lose his own. Lena is attractive, petite, with dark eyes that seem too big for her face. He watches them for a minute: Lena watering her tubs and her son throwing a football. He's talking, although Henry can't hear what he's saying, and every now and again Lena throws back her head and laughs, exposing her smooth, alabaster neck.

He turns back to Marielle, who is watching him intently. She sighs. 'Well, come on, then. Get up. What are you doing just sitting there anyway? We've got things to do. Plans to make.'

'Marielle . . .' he begins.

'Not this again, Henry. I won't have you bailing out on me. You promised me that we're going to do this. What's wrong with you? Are you getting weak in your old age? You don't have the stomach for it any more?'

'It's not that, it's just . . .'

'Don't you love me any more? Is that it? You used to do anything for me, Henry. Anything. And now you won't do this one thing. This one thing for me. After everything I've been through. After everything that's happened.' Her voice is rising, her features twisted with pain and fury.

He continues to press his nails into the flesh of his palm. 'Of course I love you. I'll always love you.'

'Then do this. For me. Like we planned. Like we've always planned.' She stands in the middle of the room and starts pulling at her hair, her fiery red hair, just like her temper. It was the beautiful red hair that had first caught his eye across a crowded room all those years ago. 'Don't let me down, Henry.' Her voice wobbles. He can't bear to see her cry.

He gets up and goes to her, circling her waist. She lays her head against his chest. He can feel the tears seeping into his linen shirt.

'I won't. Of course I won't,' he says softly. 'I'll do anything for you, you know that. Anything.'

'You and me against the world,' she murmurs into his chest, her breath hot against his sternum.

'You and me against the world,' he repeats dutifully.

He might as well do as she asks. He's running out of excuses and, really, why not appease her? Why not make her happy by doing this one thing? After all, they've already got blood on their hands.

36

LENA

I keep thinking about that photograph of Simone, now apparently an electrician. Why would the Morgans have that article pinned to their wall? I'd gone down a rabbit hole searching for Simone online, but there was nothing. No social-media accounts whatsoever. I'd googled her name and could find only a couple of newspaper reports from the old trial. There was a website for the electrical company with testimonials and reviews, but no names of their electricians.

'Mum, are you listening?'

I'm standing in the garden watering the plants with Rufus, who's back from college early. He's half-heartedly throwing a deflated football for Phoenix and he's been telling me about his latest short film, something about two friends trying to cover up a crime inspired, apparently, by Hitchcock's *Rope*, but my mind had wandered to Simone.

'Sorry, love. Miles away.'

'You're not worrying about money, are you?' His deep brown eyes fill with concern.

'Not at all. It'll be fine, don't worry.' I flash him what I hope is a reassuring smile, but he seems unconvinced. If anything, I probably look deranged. 'Sorry, you were saying about college . . .'

He perks up. 'Andy, my lecturer, has got me two weeks' work experience on a film set in Bath.'

'What will you be doing?'

'A runner. Unpaid. But it will be great experience. It starts next week. Can I do it?'

'Of course you can. How will you get there?'

'It's only twelve minutes by train from Temple Meads. Freddie's doing it too so we can travel in together.'

'That's perfect.'

Phoenix drops the ball at Rufus's feet, and he bends down to pick it up. He throws the ball over-arm and Phoenix catches it in his mouth.

'I'm glad you've got a nice group of friends now. After . . . well, you know. School.'

'Mum, you have to let it go. I played my part too.'

I stare at him. 'What do you mean?'

A blush creeps up his neck and to his cheeks. 'Nothing. It's all over with now.'

'Jackson was a little shit,' I spit. My anger about the way Rufus was treated sits just below the surface and it doesn't take much to make it boil over.

'Mum . . .' He glances at me and takes a deep breath. 'What?'

His unsaid words hover between us. 'Nothing.'

He throws the ball one last time for Phoenix, then goes back into the house.

I spend the rest of the afternoon scrolling through *Indeed* to find zero-hours contract work that would fit in around my current job. I'm not fussy, and by the time I've finished I've applied for ten different vacancies ranging from barista to shop assistant. I have to bite back my disappointment and anger with myself every time I think about how I messed up the chance to work full-time at Citizens Advice. I notice that Collette's café is looking for staff, not that I'll be applying.

As I close my laptop I wonder if I'd ever have qualified as a midwife if I hadn't met Simone or done my placement at St Calvert's. It would have been a difficult job to do around Charlie and his band, not to mention Rufus, but maybe I wouldn't have left London if all that hadn't happened. I wouldn't have met Charlie. But then I'd never have had Rufus and that's something I can't bear to think about.

Rufus is in his bedroom and I shout up the stairs that I'm taking Phoenix for a walk. As I leave I spot Marielle and Henry in their front garden. They're with a middle-aged man in overalls, his bald head shiny. By the look of the van parked behind Henry's Jaguar, he's a locksmith. Pinpricks of fear pop up all over my body. Do they know I've been letting myself into their house? Did a neighbour spot me and say something to them?

'Here are your new keys,' he's saying, in a broad Bristolian accent, as he drops them into Henry's hands.

'Thanks so much,' Henry replies, as he folds his fingers around them.

I walk towards my gate, Phoenix straining on his lead. If I turn right I won't have to pass their house. Yes, that's what I'll do. I'll pretend I can't see them and hopefully they won't notice me.

The stupid gate creaks as I open it and my heart falls when I hear Marielle saying my name. Fuck it.

She trots over. She doesn't look angry, or as if she knows I've been in her house. I'm thankful that Henry has gone inside.

'Marielle,' I say false-brightly, my heart hammering. 'How are you?'

'All good. I hope you are too?' She's still smiling and I begin to relax. 'Not working today?'

'No, not on a Tuesday. I work three days a week. What about you? You don't have your grandson today?' The image of the fake baby flashes through my mind, turning me cold. Does she even have a grandson? Now that I've been in her house and seen the fake baby and the wall of newspaper articles, I view her in a new light. I try to pick up every nuance in her words and her body language, but she's acting very naturally. There isn't even a flicker in her face as she goes on to tell me about Arthur and how much she loves looking after him.

'Oh, yes. You said your daughter-in-law works at the library? Is that the one in the centre?'

'Oh, no, in Yate,' she says, without a beat, the same placid smile on her face.

'And your son?'

'A lawyer.' Her smile widens. 'I'm so proud of him. Such a clever boy. Takes after Henry.' She lowers her voice conspiratorially. 'Henry would have liked Peter to follow in his footsteps and do a medical degree, but you know what kids are like. Is it the same with your son?'

'Well, he wants to work in film. He's very creative, like my husband.'

'And you, dear? Are you following your dreams? I gave up mine for my husband. I was a lecturer, only part-time, but before I had Peter I wanted to be an archaeologist somewhere like Delphi or Athens.'

I glance down at my feet, a strange heat flooding my body. 'Well, I sort of did the same. It was the right thing to do, for my family. But now, it's kind of left me . . .'

'In limbo?'

I look into her face and understanding passes between us. 'Yes, that's it. Exactly that.'

'We never imagine what our lives will be like when they grow up and leave us,' she says wistfully, her gaze still holding mine.

'I suppose I never had a dream, per se. Not like Charlie. Or Rufus. So I didn't mind. But . . .'

She looks at me intently. 'You never had a dream? A career you were desperate to pursue?'

I think of my midwifery training. That was the closest I'd ever got to fulfilling a dream career, but it didn't work out as I'd planned. I can't admit to Marielle why I left so I just shake my head.

She reaches out and pats my shoulder gently. 'It's not too late,' she says. She looks as if she's about to say something else when Henry calls her name. We turn in the direction of his voice. He's standing on their front step, his body rigid, his arms folded across his chest. He's so tall his head is almost touching the top of the doorway.

'Better go,' she says, taking her hand from my shoulder. 'Lovely to talk to you, Lena.'

I watch as she scuttles back into the house and Henry closes the door firmly behind them without acknowledging me.

As I walk around the park I can't stop thinking about Marielle. I'm so conflicted: I like her. I find her caring and understanding. Yet it doesn't tally with the other things I've discovered about her. The fake baby. That weird wall of newspaper clippings. The conversation I overheard between her and Henry. Henry's brooding presence. I thought she was lying about a grandson but after hearing her talking about her son, Peter, I now believe her. I'd assumed Lindy was Heidi, but now I know Heidi works at a different library it makes sense. Maybe Marielle has the fake baby for some innocent reason, like using it as a tool to practise with before taking on the responsibility of looking after a newborn baby again, thirty-odd years after having her son. It could be something as simple as that.

But what about the other stuff? a little voice in my head pipes up. *How do you explain that?*

As I'm making my way back down the street towards home half an hour later, I see Henry leaning against his car. When he sees me he moves so that he's obstructing my path. Has he been waiting for me?

'Henry,' I say, slowing down. 'Is everything okay?' Phoenix plonks himself at my feet.

'You tell me, Lena.' His blue eyes are penetrating, as though he can read my mind. He comes closer and lowers his voice. There is a chill in his tone. 'I know you let yourself into our house.'

I stiffen. 'I can explain.'

'Please don't insult my intelligence by coming up with an excuse. I don't know what you're playing at, and I haven't told Marielle because she likes you. She likes you a lot. So, I'm keeping this between us.' He leans closer, engulfing me in the scent of his washing powder and aftershave, and says, so quietly I have to strain to hear him, 'Amateur hour is over, Lena. You have no idea who you're dealing with. Keep away from us.'

And then he straightens and walks back into his house, leaving me staring after him in shock.

37

Rufus is sprawled along the sofa, with the blinds closed, watching a movie when I come in. He glances up and does a comical double-take at my appearance. I imagine my face is bright red and sweaty. My legs are still trembling, and I slump onto the chair. His brow puckers in concern. 'Are you okay?' He pauses the TV on a young Lauren Hutton's face.

'Just hot. What's this?' I indicate the TV. I don't want to worry him by telling him what Henry just said to me.

'*Someone's Watching Me!* My lecturer lent it to me. It's a 1970s made-for-TV movie by John Carpenter. Have you seen it?'

'About a woman in a high-rise flat being stalked? A long time ago.'

'Yes, that's it. Very Hitchcock and De Palma. Andy says it's one of Carpenter's underrated works. Do you want to watch it too?'

'Sure.'

Rufus presses play. It's only five minutes in and Lauren Hutton's character is just moving into a flat after a break-up. She's lonely, and witnessing her drifting around her apartment all by herself resonates within me. As the plot unfolds I try to concentrate, but I can't stop thinking about the confrontation with Henry. I already feel frazzled and unnerved, and this thriller isn't helping. We watched *Disturbia* together on Saturday night, and the film about a teenager's fascination with his neighbour whom he suspects of being a serial killer was a bit too close to home for me.

'Why won't anyone believe her?' I burst out, after Lauren Hutton's character is fobbed off yet again by the detective. 'They're treating her like she's just highly strung and irrational.'

Rufus doesn't answer. He's in his element, the TV screen reflecting in his wide brown eyes. I mutter an excuse about needing the loo and leave.

You have no idea who you're dealing with. Keep away from us.

Henry must suspect I've overheard their conversation. Maybe he saw me with the boom microphone. Maybe it was him in the garden and who I caught on tape that same night. I don't know what he's up to, or what he's planning, but he's obviously up to no good. And judging by the conversation I overheard, Marielle is in on it too. Is she being coerced into it by him? It didn't sound that way, but at times her demeanour around him suggests that he scares her.

I, on the other hand, don't bow down to bullies.

I walk into the kitchen and freeze in shock.

Someone is standing at my patio doors.

Phoenix, who had been in the living room with Rufus, is suddenly by my side, leaping into action and barking wildly.

The evening sun has cast the figure in shadow. Manshaped. *Henry.* My heart jumps but, no, this man isn't tall enough. Could this be the same person who was in my garden the night I overheard the Morgans? My gate was locked so how did he get in?

He raps his knuckles on the glass and gives a little wave, causing Phoenix to bark even louder. But this gesture reassures me. I must know him.

I move closer to the door, a shaft of sunlight nearly blinding me, and shield my eyes with my hand. Then I see who it is.

Drew.

An uneasy feeling creeps up on me. Why is he here, and why has he come to the back like a fugitive not wanting to be seen?

He must notice my reticence as he calls through the glass, 'Sorry, Lena, I was trying to avoid Henry.'

I instruct Phoenix to be quiet and unlock the patio doors, opening them a fraction. 'What's going on, Drew?'

I'm relieved when he doesn't try to come into the kitchen but stands on the patio, his hands clasped in front of him. He's in his work clothes. 'I just wanted to thank you,' he says earnestly, a lock of his hair falling into his eyes, 'for everything you did for me. For listening.' His eyes are hazel in the sunshine. He's handsome, and at a different time in my life, I might have been attracted to him.

'That's okay. I'm just so pleased you found her.'

'Yeah, cheers. Feel a bit bad that I blamed it on Henry but there were a few things that made him look a bit sus.' He shuffles his feet. He must be sweltering in those heavy boots. My gaze goes to the hedge that separates our gardens, imagining Henry lurking behind it.

'Come in.' I open the door wider and Drew steps into the kitchen. He bends to pat Phoenix, who sniffs around his ankles. I fetch Drew a glass of water and then we sit at the table.

'Thanks,' he says, taking the glass. He downs half of it in one go.

'So, you said Sarah-Jane was in St Albans?'

'Yes. For the last month or so. She was staying with a friend, apparently, trying to escape this obsessive boy-friend.'

'And you picked her up on Friday from St Albans. What time did you get home?'

'Late evening. I called you when I got back, remember? Must have been around midnight?'

I can't ask him if he was in the Morgans' house on Friday night without giving away that I was there. I'm going to have to trust that he's telling the truth about when he returned home.

He grimaces. 'She should have told me she'd moved from Reading. She was never sacked, though, she told me that much. So I don't know why Henry lied. Maybe he was confusing her with someone else. She said she didn't know him that well and that he left before she did. He retired to a place in Salisbury, apparently. At least, that's what he told the clinic.'

'Salisbury?'

'Yes. That's what SJ said anyway.' He twirls his glass and pours the rest of the water into his mouth. He puts the glass down. 'I still think Henry is odd. His reaction when I came to his house to ask about her was way over the top.'

I picture the article pinned on the Morgans' wall from the *Salisbury Journal*. The photo of the female electrician who could be Simone.

'Like, why act like that when he must have known he'd had nothing to do with SJ's disappearance?' He shrugs. 'Anyway, whatever. She's home now. Safe. That's all that matters.'

The sound of screaming emanates from the living room and Drew's eyes widen in alarm.

'Oh, it's just the TV. My son's watching a thriller. Homework for college, apparently.'

He laughs. 'Phew.'

I shift on my chair. 'Um, Drew, I hope you don't mind me asking, but . . . did you tell Susi, my boss, that I came to your house?'

His brows arch in surprise. 'No. Of course not. I would never do anything to get you into trouble. Why do you ask?'

'It's just . . . she gave me a verbal warning for doing it. And she probably wouldn't like the fact you're here now.'

'Hey. I'm here as a friend. Not a client. If it helps, I won't come into the office again. Although . . .' a flush creeps up his neck '. . . you must have guessed that I came in as often as I did just to see you.'

My body flashes hot. 'Oh . . . I . . .' I don't know what to say.

'If you ever fancy going for a drink or . . . on a date, maybe?'

'Thanks, Drew.' I smile kindly at him, flattered. 'I'm actually not ready to get into anything new right now. Relationship-wise. Charlie, you know? It's still quite raw.'

'I understand. I felt the same after my marriage collapsed.'

'But I'd like to be friends.'

He smiles at me and it softens his face. 'I'd like that too.' After a few beats he adds, 'I hope you know I'd never have told Susi about you helping me.'

I nod. 'I do now, thanks, Drew.'

His eyes cloud. 'Maybe it was Henry. I really don't like the guy.'

'Me neither,' I say in relief. 'There's just something about him, isn't there?' I find myself confiding in him about Henry's threat.

He looks appalled when I've finished. 'That's exactly the way he spoke to me. I know he might have been offended that I'd accused him of following her so I can understand if he was a bit snippy. But he was so cold. And threatening.'

Henry's words flash in my mind.

You don't know who you're dealing with.

Well, maybe it's time I found out.

38

LENA

January 1999
London

At first things were great between me and Simone. She was the perfect supervisor, somebody I aspired to be, and I looked up to her in a way I never had on my previous placements, although, to my disappointment, initially we didn't have the chance to chat much, even at 'lunchtime', which was really any time I had a spare five minutes to scoff a sandwich and a lukewarm coffee from the machine. Even though our shifts began and ended at the same time, I didn't always catch her coming out of the hospital and I was too shy to ask her if I should wait.

But, as luck would have it, at the end of my first week I was gathering my stuff from my locker, admittedly taking my time in the hope she might come in, when she appeared next to me. My heart did a funny little skip at the sight of her.

'Oh, I'm glad I caught you,' she said, peering around my locker door. 'I've been trying to catch up with you all afternoon to see how it's going but I got called into theatre to assist Dr Harris with an emergency C-section. I wanted to make sure you'd had a good first week. Janice said you're doing great and that you're a hard worker.' She beamed at me and I felt myself blush in response. 'So?' she asked earnestly. 'How do you feel it's gone so far?'

'Oh, great. Really great,' I replied. I tried to hide my burning cheeks by poking my head further into the locker and pretended to rummage through my bag.

'Phew.' She laughed and turned back to her own locker, pulling out a corduroy bag and stuffing her scrubs inside. She was wearing a Rage Against the Machine T-shirt with baggy jeans and, out of the corner of my eye, I could see her applying thick black kohl to her lids, peering at the little mirror stuck to the inside of her locker door. 'Do you fancy going for a drink?' she asked, not looking at me but at her reflection as she applied the pencil to her lower lids.

'What . . . um, now?'

'Why not? It's Friday night. I'm not working now until Sunday. Have you got any plans?'

I'd half-heartedly arranged to go to the pub with my housemates but I already knew I was going to bin that. 'No,' I said. 'No plans.'

'That's settled, then.' She slammed the door of her locker and grinned. We walked to the bus stop together. I was already looking forward to the night ahead and getting to know her better.

234

'Shall we go straight into town? I know this great club in Camden that plays alternative music. Do you fancy it?'

I glanced down at my boring burgundy baggy jumper and black jeans. 'I don't know if I'm dressed for it.'

'Oh, it's very casual. Do you have a T-shirt on underneath your jumper?'

'Yes.' Although it was a shabby grey Fruit of the Loom one. If I'd known we were going out I would have worn something better.

'That's good. It gets hot in there.'

I wasn't sure why we didn't just go to a pub in Walthamstow and was already starting to feel out of my comfort zone. Trendy alternative nightclubs weren't really my scene. I preferred the familiarity of our local old-man's pub. I glanced at my reflection as we passed one of the hospital buildings. I looked about twelve with my hair braided away from my face and my long black wool coat making me look shorter. Simone had on a black leather jacket, her straight hair bobbed around her face. I pulled the bands from the ends of my plaits and paused in front of the window to run my fingers through my dark hair. Already I looked older. Simone stopped too, and whistled. 'Very Catherine Zeta-Jones.'

'Ha, thanks. I wish.'

'Trust me. My mate Dan will go wild when he sees you. Are you single?'

'Um . . . yeah . . .' I'd just come out of a relationship and wasn't ready to start dating again. Chris had been my childhood sweetheart and we'd been together for nearly three years, but with us being away for long periods of time at different unis we'd grown apart. Still, I missed him, even though it had been four months since we mutually decided to end things.

'God, I hate January,' said Simone, linking her arm through mine. 'I hate the dark evenings, the rain. Just the greyness of it, you know. The weeks and weeks of dull monotony. Of knowing it's not going to improve for at least three months until we see a glimpse of spring. It's such an anticlimax after Christmas, isn't it?'

By now the bus had arrived and I followed her onto it.

She sat down, dumping her corduroy bag on her lap and hugging it. 'And the job,' she continued. 'So exhausting. I need to let my hair down on my days off. Forget about everything. Do you know what I mean?'

I nodded. I started to feel nervous again that we were going so far away from what was familiar to me. Would she get off her face and leave me alone in a part of London I wasn't very familiar with? I'd been to Camden Town only a few times with my housemate Kerrie, and that was to look around the second-hand shops for 1970s cord flares and retro jackets. My mates were all as vanilla as I was.

I could already tell that Simone wasn't like my friends. She was a lot older, more confident and experienced. And she talked, a lot. On that forty-five-minute bus journey I learnt that she'd grown up in Muswell Hill, in a four-bedroom 1930s detached where her parents still lived. She had one younger brother, Oliver, she'd done her degree in Reading, she loved all kinds of heavy rock, punk and metal, and she'd wanted to be a midwife because she loved babies. But she also dreamt of having money and travelling the world. She was single but had had two serious relationships ('and a lot of flings'), planned to marry a successful musician or an investment banker ('someone who earns a lot of money as I'm never going to be rich working as a midwife') and wanted either two or four children ('so one doesn't get left out').

As I followed her into that cavernous dingy club, to the thud of some heavy metal band I'd never heard of, I thought she was fascinating. Even when I realized, too late, that she was probably on something, that she kept sneaking off to the loo, leaving me with her mate Dan, a large, lumbering guy with dyed black hair and too much beard who kept telling me how his band were going to be famous.

When Simone had disappeared to the toilet for the umpteenth time, Dan leaned towards me in a cloud of stale beer and fags and said, 'Just be careful of Simone. She's a great girl and everything, but she's on a quest.'

'What do you mean?'

He tapped his nose in an infuriating manner. 'What you see isn't always what you get with her.'

I didn't like where this conversation was headed. I was enjoying the music, even if it was heavier than the bands I usually listened to, and I liked how unpretentious the club was, how unglitzy, how raw. I was happy that I'd made a new friend and already envisaging introducing her to my other mates, how they'd look up to her too. I didn't want to hear anything negative about her. 'She seems great to me.'

'Oh, she is,' he shouted, above the music. 'She really is. But she's also ruthlessly ambitious.'

I laughed. 'She's a midwife.'

'Yeah. For now. Look, I've known Simone for years. She's a hard worker, I'll give her that. And she likes babies. Who doesn't? But being a midwife isn't her passion. She fell into it.'

That sounded like me and I perked up. 'Not everyone is lucky enough to know what they want to do with their life.'

'Look, you seem like a nice girl. I don't want her to drag you down.'

'How is she going to drag me down?'

He lit a cigarette, then offered me one. I shook my head.

'Let's just say she's not afraid to get involved in anything illegal if it means she can make a quick buck.'

I laughed. 'What? Like drugs? Yeah, I'd kind of noticed her going off to the bogs every five minutes.'

'That's purely recreational.'

I felt uncomfortable and wanted the conversation to end. 'It's none of my business.'

He didn't listen. He leaned into me, his hot, rancid breath on my ear. 'She's involved in something at the hospital where she works. She told me once when she was drunk.'

A chill settled over my skin. 'What?'

'Just be careful is all I'm saying. When it comes to money her morals go out the window.'

I stared at him in disbelief.

He raised his eyebrows at me and carried on puffing at his cigarette, looking smug. I wanted to punch him in the face.

I didn't want my illusion of Simone to be shattered.

But I should have listened to him. I should have asked what he meant, asked exactly what Simone was involved in.

Instead I found out the hard way.

39

LENA

It's awkward at work on Wednesday. Susi stays in her office most of the day and I get the impression she's deliberately avoiding me. Every now and again Kath glances up from her desk on the other side of the room and smiles at me in sympathy. She knows Susi is angry with me but not the reason why. I'm tempted to ask Susi how she found out I'd visited Drew at his home, but I'm too embarrassed to bring it up again. So I keep my head down and hope that Drew sticks to his promise and doesn't come in. It was good to talk to someone who agreed with me about Henry Morgan. Jo was supportive, as she always is, but I know she thinks I'm paranoid. But Drew has witnessed Henry's dark side and his lies.

When I get home that evening I google Simone Harvey again, hoping that something might have popped up since yesterday, all the while knowing how unlikely it is. I'm not surprised when I don't find anything. The relentless sunshine streams through the patio doors, picking out every smudge on the stainless-steel cooker and my ivory cabinets. From the living room I can hear the faint strains of a guitar. When I got home Kit was already here giving Rufus a lesson. He's finished college now for the summer and starts his work experience next week.

I sit back in my chair with a sigh. I'm not getting anywhere with looking up Simone. But if there *is* a link between her and the Morgans, the only way to find out is to call the electrical company and ask to speak to her. My mouth goes dry at the thought of talking to Simone again after all these years. She tried to reach out to me once, after the court case, but I had already left London and, wanting to put the past behind me, I never returned her call. The jury might have found her not guilty, but I know very well that she was. And there is no coming back from that. Our friendship couldn't be saved. If I ring her now she might hang up, but the possibility of discovering something about the Morgans is too tantalizing a prospect to pass up.

Before I can change my mind I find the number of the electrical company and call it. A woman with a singsong voice answers after two rings: 'Herman, Hardy and Sullivans.'

I clear my throat. 'Hi, I was wondering if I could speak to one of your electricians, Simone Harvey.'

'I'm sorry,' she says smoothly. 'We don't have a Simone Harvey working here.'

'Ah, okay. I'm wondering, have you ever . . . um . . . had a Simone Harvey working for you?'

'No, my love, at least not in the fifteen years I've been with the company. We're a small family firm so I would know if we had anyone of that name here. Can I help you with anything else?'

'I'm looking for a female electrician,' I say, thinking quickly. 'And I think you've got one working for you?'

'I'm very sorry. We did have a woman electrician here, but she left last year.'

'Can you tell me her name?'

A pause. When she speaks again there is a new frostiness to her tone. 'No, I'm afraid not. What is this concerning?'

'Sorry. I'm only asking as I'd love to find her because my . . . um, mother is very elderly and she'd feel more comfortable with a woman electrician . . .' I falter, my face flaming at the lie.

'Oh, I see.' I sense her softening. 'Of course. I'm so sorry I can't help you.'

'Perhaps if you gave me her name I could see if she's gone to another firm.'

'She hasn't. She left very suddenly. I think she's no longer in the field. I'm sure there are other companies who employ women electricians. I suggest you look around.'

'But I . . .'

'Sorry I couldn't help. Goodbye,' she says firmly, and ends the call.

'For fuck's sake,' I mutter, under my breath, staring down at my mobile.

'What's up?' Rufus lumbers into the room, closely followed by Kit. He flops onto one of the kitchen chairs and Kit stands awkwardly by the patio doors.

'Oh, it's nothing,' I say, not wanting to get into it, especially in front of Kit. 'I'm just trying to find someone I used to work with, that's all.'

'Why's that?' Rufus pushes his fringe from his eyes. His hair needs cutting.

'It's a long story.'

Rufus eyes me suspiciously. 'Is this to do with the neighbours again?' He turns to Kit and rolls his eyes. 'Mum thinks the neighbours are a couple of psychos . . .'

'Hey! I've never said that.'

Kit takes a seat next to Rufus, his blue eyes brightening with interest. 'Really? What, like serial killers?'

'Yeah,' says Rufus. 'She's been watching too many thrillers with me.'

'I don't think they're serial killers,' I say, with a laugh, pushing the patio doors shut with my foot. 'And keep your voice down. They might hear you.'

'Mum's suspicious of them, then,' he says to Kit, 'because she overheard them talking about something illegal.'

Kit straightens, his eyes widening. 'Really?'

'No! Rufus,' I admonish. 'Stop it.'

'Oh, come on,' he says, warming to his theme and I can tell he's enjoying this, showing off in front of someone older, like Kit.

'It was nothing, really,' I say firmly.

'So why are you looking up your old work colleague?' asks Kit.

'I've just been, um, thinking a lot about the past, that's all, and decided it would be nice to get in touch. We were good friends once, back when we were both midwives.'

'And this has nothing to do with the Morgans?' says Rufus, doubtfully.

'Who are the Morgans?' asks Kit.

'The neighbours,' I explain. 'Marielle and Henry. And, no, this has nothing to do with them, Ruf.'

I notice Rufus throwing Kit a look of disbelief, but Kit is too polite to say anything further. Instead he glances at his watch and stands up. 'Anyway, I'd better go. I've got another lesson to teach at six. Nice seeing you again, Lena.'

Rufus jumps up to show him out and I immediately go back to my laptop. Maybe I should try searching Marielle again. I'm not convinced I'll turn up anything as I couldn't find any social-media accounts for her when I looked before, but it's worth another try and I don't have anything better to do right now.

I type in 'Marielle Morgan' and 'university lecturer London' and nothing comes up. There are a few Professor Morgans, each with an accompanying photo, but no matches to Marielle. I try again, this time typing just Marielle Morgan. Again, a few come up, scattered around the world, but none of them is her. I know she's retired but I'm surprised I can't find which university she worked for. There is no trace of her. I try again, this time adding 'Marielle and Henry Morgan' to the search. After scrolling down a few pages I spot an old *Times* wedding announcement from April 1988. My heart thumps with excitement as I click on the link. It's attached to a main piece about property tycoon Lawrence Bishop-Smith, who, according to the article, was Marielle's father and died about five years ago at the age of ninety-five after suffering with Alzheimer's for a long time. I'm more interested in the wedding announcement so I click on the photograph of Marielle and Henry, with the original write-up underneath. It mentions the 'very sudden' death of her stepmother, Violet. The photo is in black and white, stylish and shot in a studio. They're seated, both wearing formal clothes, Marielle's hand (with the large diamond on her finger) rests on top of Henry's, and I'm taken aback by how young they look, like two film stars from the 1950s. The piece gives little away so, instead, I decide to search for Violet Bishop-Smith. After a while I find a small newspaper article dated October 1987, which I read with interest.

SOCIALITE'S SUDDEN DEATH RULED TO BE ACCIDENTAL DROWNING

THE SHOCKING DEATH of the socialite wife of a wealthy property tycoon was today ruled as accidental drowning, an inquest heard.

Violet Bishop-Smith, 46, was found unconscious in the bathtub of her luxury home that she shared in north London with her husband, Lawrence Bishop-Smith, 64, and their daughter Savannah, 17. Toxicology reports showed a cocktail of barbiturates in her system and prescription Valium was found in her bathroom cabinet.

Mrs Bishop-Smith was found unresponsive by her stepdaughter, Marielle, 29, at around 2 p.m. on 30 August. Miss Bishop-Smith told the inquest, 'My stepmother had been ill for a while and she usually had at least one maid in the house with her. I called Violet's name but there was no answer, so I went to her bedroom and was surprised when she wasn't in her bed.

I knocked on her en-suite bathroom door and, thankfully, it wasn't locked. That's when I found her.'

Miss Bishop-Smith explained how she tried to revive her stepmother, but to no avail. There was no suicide note and Violet Bishop-Smith had not been diagnosed with depression. As a result, coroner Samantha Payne ruled Violet Bishop-Smith died from accidental drowning.

I read it twice, imagining a young Marielle's horror at finding her stepmother dead and feel a twinge of pity for her.

'I'm going to my room!' Rufus calls, from the hallway, and I hear him charging up the stairs.

'Okay. I'll make dinner soon,' I shout, not sure he's heard me. I go back to my laptop and, on a whim, I look up her stepsister, Savannah Bishop-Smith. Immediately an osteopath clinic's website pops up. I click on the link and a photograph of Savannah appears onscreen. She looks to be in her mid-fifties with short blonde hair and the same greeny-grey eyes as Marielle. This must be her: the ages match the article, with Savannah being twelve or so years Marielle's junior, and it's an unusual name. I scan the description under her photograph. She's a trained osteopath and acupuncturist based in Marlborough, and before I've had time to think about what I'm doing I've clicked on the booking form and made an appointment for tomorrow at 11.30 a.m.

Next I do something I haven't allowed myself to do for a long time. I bring up Facebook and search for Oliver

Harvey, Simone's brother and my ex-boyfriend. I can't think about Simone without remembering him and how much I'd once loved him. He was the first man to break my heart.

His profile comes up immediately and I click on it, pleased that his settings are lax. My tummy plunges when I see that he's more handsome than I remember, with still-thick brown hair, although he's broader, more tanned and rugged than when I knew him as the skinny, pale-faced twenty-two-year-old Cure fan. From his photos and posts, he's now married with two cute kids and loves surfing and hiking. I scroll through his photos, wondering why there aren't any of him and Simone. And then I see one, taken about sixteen years ago. They stare blurry-eyed into the camera with their arms around each other and Oliver has a pint in his hand. They look like they're at a party. Simone is wearing an olive sleeveless dress, a belt cinching in her slim waist. I click on more photos, obsessively scanning each one for the little signs that tell me about Oliver's life. About Simone's – even though she's only in that one photograph.

And then I freeze, my blood draining to my feet, as a photo of Oliver next to a white pick-up truck fills my screen. It's not Oliver who has caught my attention. Or the truck. But the set of keys he's holding because, dangling from it, is a little blue knitted bear and, apart from the colour, it's exactly like the one Phoenix found in the gap in my hedge.

40

The clinic where Savannah works is on the second floor of a Victorian building and I'm out of breath by the time I reach the top. There is no receptionist, just a tiny area with two chairs where, I assume, I'm expected to wait. I can hear voices coming from behind the door with the word 'Osteopath' on it. I take a seat and wait, my foot tapping impatiently and my blood pressure rising. Am I doing the right thing? What the hell am I going to say?

Before I can change my mind the door opens and a woman in a clinical white smock top and trousers appears with a middle-aged man. 'See you in a few weeks' time,' she's saying to him. 'And don't forget to do your stretches.' When he disappears down the stairs she turns to me with a wide smile. She's very attractive. The short hair in the photograph is now longer and swept up in a claw clip. She looks a lot younger than Marielle and I can't really see any family resemblance, apart from the eyes.

'Elena Fletcher?'

I stand up. 'Yes.'

'Please come in.' She ushers me into a small room that smells of incense, with ambient music tinkling away in the background. I'm thankful it's cool in here, and she guides me to a seat next to her desk while she busies herself removing the tissue paper from the white leather bed and spraying it, then comes over to me and sits down. 'So,' she says, in her soft, calming voice, 'what can I do for you?'

I tell her my lower back has been playing up and she takes a few details from me and inputs them into her computer. When I made the appointment I considered lying about my name but then decided to be honest. It's not like she's going to tell Marielle I'm a client. Why would that even come up? Then she asks me to take off my dress and lie face down on the bed in my underwear.

She asks me questions while she manipulates my back and tells me my problem is actually between my shoulder-blades and neck. 'You're very tense,' she says, and I want to laugh when I think about everything that's happened. Not surprised I'm tense. She asks me questions about my family and I find myself telling her about Rufus. 'I wanted a big family,' I admit. 'That's all I ever really wanted. Lots of kids. A house full of them. It was only ever me and my mum, growing up. But it hasn't turned out that way. I know in reality it probably wouldn't have been practical having loads of kids, as my husband is a musician so was always off gigging. Now I'm separated from him and my son will be going off to university next year and I'm at that stage in my life when I'm not sure what happens next. My son, Rufus, wants to do film studies at King's . . . He's so into his films and the house is going to seem so quiet without him. I wish I could just enjoy this time, you know, but I can't because all I keep thinking about is that he's going to leave . . .' I realize I'm over-sharing and stop talking, biting my lip so hard it draws blood. I'm thankful I'm lying on my front, my face in the hole, looking down at her white trainers so she can't see my flaming cheeks.

'I understand,' she says softly, her hands warm on my back. 'It's just me and my son too, although he's twenty-four now and is living at home after finishing uni. So don't be too despondent. He'll be back more often than you think.' She chuckles. Carefully, she guides me onto my side and I glance at the clock. Fifteen minutes have gone by already and I haven't even asked her about the Morgans. 'Do you have family around you?' she asks, in the same soothing tone. I wonder if she talks that way out of the clinic. 'Looking after my father took my mind off my son leaving home. He was an older father so needed a lot of care towards the end.'

'No. My mum doesn't live near me, but I have a very good friend,' I say, thinking of Jo. 'She's got the perfect family. A husband who adores her, two amazingly gifted, sporty, clever, popular kids. She's got a proper career, un-like me. She's like a sister to me. The sister I never had.' I pause, hoping this prompts her to mention siblings, but she doesn't.

'That's lovely,' she says instead. 'Friends are really important.'

'Do you have . . . any family near you?'

She moves on to my neck. 'No. My mother died when I was in my teens. I have a half-sister, but she's a lot older so we're not particularly close.' I try to nod and then realize I can't because she's turned me onto my back and is clamping my head between her hands. 'You've a lot of tension through your neck,' she's saying, and I try to think of ways to get the conversation back on track.

'Your son has never been close to any of his cousins?'
I blurt out clumsily, cringing inside. She doesn't notice
my discomfort as she walks around the bed and clasps my
ankles, asking me to bend my legs. Then she pushes my
heels towards my bottom.

'He has a cousin on my ex's side, but she's a lot younger.
And it never worked out for my sister, sadly. What about
your son?'

'I . . . um, no.' My mind is swimming. What did she
mean about it never working out for Marielle? Was I
right when I suspected Marielle of lying about a son and
daughter-in-law? 'Charlie has a brother, but he doesn't
have any children either.'

She straightens my legs gently. 'Right, well, that's all
done. You can put your clothes back on.' She sits at her
desk while I hop off the bed. As I'm getting dressed she
asks about my diet and whether I drink enough water. I
answer mechanically, but inwardly I'm reeling with confusion. 'Do you want to make another appointment?' she's
asking me, as I get out my purse and try to concentrate on
what she's saying.

'Um, well, I'm just visiting a friend in Marlborough. But
I definitely will if I'm visiting again. My muscles already
feel more relaxed.'

'Okay, great. I would suggest a couple more visits to an
osteopath. It's very tight through your back.'

'Okay.' I hand her my card and try not to blanch at the
fifty-five pounds I can't afford coming out of my bank
account.

'And don't worry about your son,' she says kindly. 'It
will all be fine when he's at uni. He'll be back before you

know it, dragging with him a sackful of washing. That's what Artie did, anyway.'

'Artie?'

'Yes. Arthur. It was my paternal grandfather's name. Thanks again for coming. It was lovely to meet you.' She's already turning to her next client, a young woman with tattoos down both arms who is sitting waiting for her, but as I walk down the stairs all I can think about are the times I've seen Marielle pushing a baby in the pram. A grandson she said was called Arthur.

There never was a grandson. Or a daughter-in-law called Heidi who works in a library. Or a son called Peter who's a lawyer. It's all made up. All of it. The image of that grotesque fake baby flashes through my mind and repulsion rips through me.

Why did Marielle lie?

As I drive home my horror at the extent of Marielle's lies twists and moulds like Play-doh so it resembles something else. Pity. There must be a reason why she's pretending to have a grandson. Yes, it's warped and weird, but I can't help feeling some strange affinity with her. Maybe she wanted children and couldn't have them. Perhaps this silicone baby makes her feel happy. Wanted. Loved. Who am I to judge her? Isn't that what we all want at the end of the day? To feel loved. To feel like we belong.

What must Henry make of it?

I remember their conversation:

'. . . I don't know, Mari . . .'

'You promised me you'd take her. I've got everything ready. The room . . .'

'I know . . . but . . . after what happened before . . . should we really try again?'

The thought re-enters my head that they could be planning to kidnap a baby. Why? To pass off as their grandchild? But why would they plan to kidnap a baby girl when Marielle has told me she has a grandson?

And none of this explains Henry's behaviour and his threats to me that day outside my house.

When I get home I log on to Facebook and click on Oliver's profile page again. I can't get over the fact that a keyring almost identical to his ended up in the Morgans' garden. I don't understand it, but it must be linked to the newspaper article I found in the Morgans' house. The receptionist at the electrical company said no Simone Harvey had ever worked there, but now, having seen that keyring, I'm wondering if Simone changed her name. The keyring Phoenix found is too similar to Oliver's to be a coincidence. The bear is knitted. Perhaps home-made. I've never seen one like it in the shops. The only way I'll be able to get answers is through her brother. My ex-boyfriend. We were so close, once, although we didn't exactly finish on amicable terms. But it's been twenty-five years and he's married now, with kids.

I type out a quick message.

Hi Oliver,
I know it's been a long time, and I hope you're well. I was wondering if you know how I could get in touch with Simone? I would love to catch up with her.
Lena

I deliberate over whether to put a kiss, decide against it and press send before I lose my nerve.

I go to the kitchen drawer where I'd put the key with the pink bear as well as Joan's spare. I find the pink bear straight away. But Joan's key, the metal poppy, isn't there. I rake through the detritus frantically. I definitely put it in here after I last went to the Morgans' house. It would be useless now the locks have been changed, but even so, where has it gone?

41

HENRY

June 1990
London

They'd been married for two years when Marielle mentioned children again.

He'd thought, *hoped*, that she'd forgotten all about it. Or, like him, realized that parenthood wasn't for them. But then she appeared before him, bright-eyed and excitable, telling him they needed 'to talk about something' and his heart had thudded to his feet.

By now they were living in a townhouse at 'the wrong end' of Islington, according to Marielle's father, who'd said sniffily, 'It's practically the East End,' when they told him they'd made an offer. But Henry had stood his ground, insisting to Marielle in private that he wasn't happy to live off her father and, to his surprise, Marielle had agreed with him. Although the area had already been gentrified, it was still a far cry from the manicured parks and white stucco-fronted houses that Marielle was used to.

Henry had recently had a great promotion at the private hospital where he worked, helped, he suspected – although the thought didn't sit well with him – by the fact he'd married into such a prominent family. Marielle was brilliant at entertaining his bosses: she made up for his awkwardness. People liked him a lot more when she was at his side. He was earning more than he had ever thought possible, and even though he had relented and let Marielle use some of her trust fund to renovate the house, he felt a sense of pride that he could meet the mortgage payments with his salary and bonuses alone.

It was a Saturday morning, warm for early June, and peaceful: he loved their small garden, and he could hear the birds singing and the tinkle of water from the fountain. The French windows were ajar and a gentle breeze reached where he sat at the table of their recently refurbished kitchen, which was always awash with light. In that moment he felt truly happy. He had everything he'd always dreamed of. He couldn't believe how his life had turned out, especially considering the way it had started. He was a lucky man. A lucky, lucky man. And then Marielle, the beautiful, intelligent, complex wife he adored, had had to come in and ruin it with a single sentence.

'So, I've been thinking,' she continued. Words that struck the fear of God into him. She sauntered over to where he sat. She was wearing a silk shirt dress and her feet were bare, her toenails painted the same shell-pink they always were. She pulled out a chair and lowered herself onto it gracefully. She was beaming at him and he tried to push down his unease.

'What have you been thinking, my love?' he said, closing his paper. Marielle got annoyed if he didn't give her his undivided attention.

'I think we should have a baby.'

His jaw hurt with the effort of trying to keep a neutral expression. 'We've talked about this and decided that's not what we want.'

She hesitated, her smile wavering. 'I think it's what I want, Henry. I'm nearly thirty-two now.'

He tried to keep the emotion out of his voice. 'You know how I feel about children. I don't want the past repeating itself.' He didn't want to share her with a child either. He didn't want their lives to change. But, more than that, he didn't believe he was capable of loving a child.

She tipped her head to one side, her eyes flashing. 'I know you didn't have a great childhood, Henry, but we have so much to give a child. It would be different for us. We would be good parents.'

He studied her face, shocked that she could lie to herself so easily. 'No, we wouldn't. You know we wouldn't. We're not the same as other people. *I*'m not the same. I'm damaged.' He added silently, *We're damaged.*

She gave a little laugh. 'What are you talking about, Henry? Of course we're the same as other people. Lots of people have tough childhoods but they go on to be amazing parents. Look how much we love each other. Did you ever think it would be possible to love someone else as much as we love one another? I certainly didn't. So, imagine how we'd feel about a baby. *Our* baby, Henry.'

He wanted to scream and shout and shake that nonsense out of her. But he did what he always did. He sat there, his face impassive, hiding his true feelings. He was good at that. He'd spent most of his childhood and adolescence doing the exact same thing. 'You know I don't want children.'

She got up and went to him, perching on his lap, her arms around his neck.

'We agreed . . .'

'I never agreed.' She pouted and removed her arms from around him. 'You were the one who said you didn't want them.'

'And you married me knowing that.'

'But you'd do it for me, wouldn't you, Henry? You always said you'd do anything for me.'

'Not this.'

She stood up abruptly, her eyes stony. 'Then we have a real problem, Henry,' she said.

42

LENA

Jo and I are sitting on a crowded terrace at a bar in Clifton, having a drink – non-alcoholic for me because I have to pick up Rufus from Freddie's house later. She's cross, as I knew she'd be, when I tell the latest about the Morgans. It's nine thirty and still light, warm enough not to wear a cardigan, and there's a joyous holiday vibe, which makes me feel nostalgic for all the city breaks I used to have with Charlie and Rufus, sitting in pavement cafés, just the three of us. Although the scent of body odour and sickly perfume that occasionally wafts our way quickly dispels this. On the table behind us a woman cackles loudly, which seems at odds with the serious conversation Jo and I are having.

'You need to be careful, Lena,' Jo is saying, prodding the ice in her mojito forcefully with a straw. 'That's sinister as hell what Henry said to you!'

'I don't know how he knew I'd gone into their house.'

She shakes her head and mutters under her breath.

'What?'

'It was reckless of you. You should never have gone in there.'

'I know.' I sip my nosecco.

'And now you've opened another can of worms with this Oliver guy. You told me before you were heartbroken over that split.'

Why do I feel as though I'm being cross-examined? 'I was. But it was a long time ago.'

She twists her bracelet around her wrist without looking at me. 'I just wish you didn't feel you had to get involved.'

'I can't help it. They live next door.'

She glances up at me. 'So? It's not your business. I don't know what my neighbours are up to and, frankly, I don't care.' Jo lives in a detached townhouse on one of Redland's premier streets where everyone keeps to themselves.

'Look, I know you're only saying all this because you're worried, but it became my business the night I overheard them.'

'Lena. You keep saying you'll drop it and then you don't!'

I put my glass down. 'That was before I found a keyring that looks very much like Oliver's in the Morgans' garden. And it was before I saw the photograph of her pinned to their wall. They've changed their locks now, so I won't be able to get back into the house, even if I wanted to, and I've misplaced Joan's key.'

She runs her hand through her dyed red hair. 'When you do get hold of Simone, what are you going to ask her? How is any of this going to help you solve whatever you think you're trying to solve?' She throws her arms into the air, exasperated.

'I just want to ask her how she knows the Morgans. Or if she knows something about them.'

'Just because the keyring is similar to Oliver's it might not be hers. And the newspaper clipping isn't just about her. It's about an electrical company winning an award. They might have that for any number of reasons. And you said yourself it might not even be her.'

'It certainly looks like her. I don't know what all this means, Jo, but I can't let it go. Please don't ask me to.'

'It's your life. You're a grown woman. Just be careful.'

I offer to drive Jo home and we make a detour to Freddie's house. I pull up across his driveway and text Rufus to say I'm outside.

Jo is in the front passenger seat fiddling with the vents. Even with the air-conditioning there is still a sheen to her skin. She sits back in her seat, the aircon on full blast and directed onto her face. 'That's bliss.' She sighs. 'God, I can't remember what it's like to feel cold. Oh, that reminds me.' She turns to me. 'There might be a full-time job coming up at my chambers. How good is your typing? Are you fast?'

I sit up straighter. 'I think so. I mean, I can touch-type.'

'It's just admin stuff, but Betty, who works there now, is retiring soon. I could put in a good word . . .'

'Oh, my God, Jo, that would be amazing! Thank you.'

She beams at me. She wants to keep an eye on me, which is lovely in one way but also quite mortifying.

'Where's my child?' I say, looking down at my phone. I'm just about to text Rufus again when Jo nudges me. I glance up to see him walking around the side of Freddie's house. But he's not with Freddie. He's with Jackson.

I gasp.

'What is it?' asks Jo.

'That's Jackson, Collette's son. The boy who bullied Rufus.' What is he doing with Jackson? And how does Jackson know Freddie? Freddie is a new friend from college. He didn't go to Rufus's school. Panic travels through me, making me feel even hotter. Is this some kind of set-up to hurt Rufus? I lean forwards so that the edge of the steering wheel is pressing against my chest. But, no, it looks like Jackson and Rufus are chatting amicably. Freddie is nowhere to be seen. 'What is going on?' I mutter, more to myself.

'Maybe they've made up.'

'I don't understand how. He's the reason why Rufus left that school.'

'You know what kids are like. So fickle.'

Unease spreads through me. I watch intently, trying to gauge their body language. Rufus is standing with his head bent towards Jackson, as though listening intently. Jackson is the one doing the talking. And then he steps forwards and, to my surprise, embraces Rufus. I exhale in relief. I still don't trust Jackson but at least it looks friendly. He disappears around the side of the house and Rufus walks towards the car. He's smiling.

'Hi, Jo,' he says, as he gets into the back seat.

'All right, Ruf?' says Jo, but I don't speak. Instead I watch as Rufus fastens his seat belt. When he still doesn't say anything I clear my throat.

'What?' He looks up.

'You? And Jackson? I thought you hated each other. Why is he at Freddie's house?'

'Oh,' he waves a hand dismissively, 'long story. But it's all fine between us now. Can we go?'

I continue to sit there, my body contorted so that I can see him in the rear seat. He's avoiding eye contact. 'You can't just leave it at that. I fell out with Collette. I handed in my notice on a job I enjoyed. I did all those things because of the way you were being treated.'

Rufus's expression closes. 'I didn't ask you to do all that,' he mumbles, still refusing to look at me.

Jo grimaces. I'm making her feel awkward. I turn to the front. 'Fine,' I snap. 'We'll talk about this when we get home.' I put the car into gear and pull away too fast from the kerb.

43

There is a heavy silence in the car on the way home. Jo
tries to break it with the odd chirpy remark but I don't
have the energy to force a smile. I snatch quick glances at
Rufus in the rear-view mirror. He's acting exactly as he
used to in year eleven, before he admitted he was being
bullied. All brooding and sulky. He'd matured so much in
the last eighteen months and we've never been closer,
despite Charlie moving out. But now it's like we've reverted
back two years.

I pull up outside Jo's house. 'I'll text you later,' she says,
as she gets out of the car, flashing me a sympathetic smile.
'Bye, Ruf.'

'Yeah, bye,' utters Rufus, half-heartedly, without looking
up from his phone.

When we get home Rufus heads straight upstairs without a word and I slam around the kitchen in frustration,
not wanting to charge up there after him and say something I might regret. When I've calmed down I ask myself
why I'm so annoyed he's made up with Jackson. I should
be pleased. It shows maturity that he can forgive someone who tormented him. I'm the one holding on to all
that bad feeling. Yet I can't let it go. The whole thing had
caused so many disagreements between me and Charlie
– it was the catalyst for our separation. And what was it

all for if Rufus just forgives Jackson? If Rufus acts like it never happened?

By the time I go upstairs it's dark and I perch on the edge of Rufus's bed. He's lying on top of the quilt in a T-shirt and the checked shorts he wears in bed, the flickering phone screen casting eerie shadows across his face. I take in his strong brow and straight nose, the way he brushes his hair away from his eyes automatically, just like he used to do when he was small, and I glimpse the little boy he used to be underneath the gruff teenage exterior. The little boy who used to clamber onto my lap when he was two, sucking his thumb, wanting me to read him a story.

'Ruf . . .'

He looks up with a sigh. 'Mum, listen . . . I can't talk about it tonight. I'm tired and I just want to go to sleep.'

It's only eleven and Rufus doesn't have to get up for college tomorrow. He's spending the next three days with Charlie so I won't have the chance to talk to him about it until Sunday and on Monday he starts his work experience in Bath.

'I'm sorry I was cross about Jackson,' I begin. 'I just want you to be happy. If you've forgiven him, that's great.'

'Mum . . .'

'Okay. We can talk about it another day.'

He grunts in response, but there's a barrier between us. I just don't understand why.

I get up reluctantly. 'Love you,' I say, as I go to leave the room.

'Love you too,' he replies automatically, without looking at me.

*

At breakfast the next morning Rufus doesn't mention last night and neither do I. Instead he talks about the film he's making with Freddie, his voice rising in excitement as he explains how he's going to set up a particular shot through an arched window at Freddie's house. 'We hope to enter it into a short-films competition for under-eighteens,' he says, his eyes lighting up as they always do when he talks about movies. As Rufus explains about atmosphere and plot, I listen in admiration, loving how creative he is when I've always been more practical, relieved that he has found his passion.

I'd booked today off work as holiday before Charlie and I split up because it's our wedding anniversary, and I'd forgotten to cancel it. I wonder if Charlie has remembered. Our first wedding anniversary as an estranged couple. I'd expected to hear from him after the way we left things last time, hoping he still cared enough about me to check in and make sure I hadn't lost my job, but there has been no word from him. It was Rufus who told me his dad was picking him up this morning and that he was staying with Charlie until Sunday. The three-day weekend stretches ahead of me, empty, and I contemplate asking my mum if I can go and stay with her in Rye. Anything is a better prospect than spending three days alone in this house with whatever Henry's planning next door. But I can't because her dogs wouldn't like Phoenix being there and I can't ask Jo to look after him because her daughter is allergic.

Voices from the street filter in through my open window. Rufus is upstairs packing a weekend bag. I move to the window, and recoil when I see Charlie leaning against the wall talking to Henry. It looks as though Henry is doing most of the talking and Charlie nods every now and again. Is he complaining to Charlie about me letting myself into their house?

Five minutes later the doorbell rings. 'I'll get it,' I shout up the stairs to Rufus before answering the door to Charlie. I can't tell by his expression if Henry has said anything to him about me.

'Hi,' he says, stepping into the hallway and closing the door.

'Saw you talking to Henry,' I say, going into the kitchen. He follows me.

'Yep. He saw my van and was asking about my availability. He wants a room painted.'

I think back to their immaculately decorated house. The only room that needs painting is the attic.

'He seems like a nice guy.'

I spin around to face him. 'You're kidding, right? After everything I've told you?'

'What? Like you letting yourself into his house?' He shakes his head in disbelief. 'I heard from Rufus that you're no longer going to be working full-time at Citizens Advice.'

'Something else might have come up . . . at Jo's chambers.'

He stares at me.

'And I told you about the fake baby, the wall of newspaper clippings and the conversation I overheard. God, Charlie, why, for once, can't you be more supportive? You're just like my mother.'

He opens his mouth to say something but closes it again. Rufus is standing in the doorway with his backpack.

'Right, well, we'll see you on Sunday,' says Charlie, his voice thick.

I kiss Rufus's forehead. 'Have a great weekend. Love you.'

'Love you too,' he says, flashing me a smile and I watch in silence as they trudge down the hallway.

Happy anniversary, I think, as Charlie follows Rufus out of the door.

I'd wanted to talk to Charlie about Rufus, but what would be the point? I used to love how optimistic Charlie was about life. That was one of the things that first attracted me to him. But as the years have gone by I've realized it isn't optimism: it's plain ignorance. Charlie never wants to hear anything negative. He wants to live in a world that smells of roses, where everyone gets along, where there are no gripes or anger or resentment. I tried to talk to him about Rufus at the time but he refused to believe anything was wrong. Just like he doesn't want to hear anything negative about the Morgans. Psycho kidnappers disguised as respectable Boomers have no place in Charlie Fletcher's life, not when he's living his very own version of *The Truman Show*.

I refuse to spend the day brooding or thinking about our wedding. I apply for some more jobs and check my emails, delighted when I see I have an interview next week for a retail-assistant role at a trendy clothes shop in Cabot Circus. I haven't worked in retail for a long time but it could be a good way of supplementing my income and meeting new people. I need to broaden my circle of friends, and stop letting what happened in the past with Simone prevent me from trusting people.

I log on to Facebook and my heart picks up speed when I notice that Oliver has replied. I click on his message. I can see he's signed off as Ol, which was what I always called him. And two kisses. Two.

Then I read the message with growing unease.

Hi, Lena
It's lovely to hear from you. Thank you for getting in touch.
You're probably not aware but nobody has seen Simone for
a while. We are all worried about her, as you can imagine.
Please call me on this number as I would love to talk to you
further about this.
Best wishes
Ol xx

Simone is missing.

44

LENA

January 1999
London

Of course I didn't want to believe Dan. I wanted Simone to be everything I first thought her to be. So I ignored the warning signs, which were small at first. The odd white lie here and there, silly things mostly, things that could be overlooked, like pretending she'd watched a programme on TV when it later transpired that she hadn't. Or saying she'd seen a band and backtracking in front of Dan. To begin with I found it endearing that she was trying to impress me. I already had imposter syndrome and felt like a small fish in a very large pond. I had to think on my feet: the labour ward was so fast-paced and every day was different. My placement was for six weeks but by the end of the first week, despite it being more exhausting than any placement I'd had before, I found I enjoyed the hectic atmosphere, thrived on it even. It gave me a buzz and the days sped by. Simone told me she'd been a midwife on the labour ward now for two years. It was only later I wondered if it was another lie.

By the third week Simone and I were becoming insepar-able, spending all our time off together. I didn't question why a more senior midwife – my supervisor, no less – wanted to hang out regularly with a nineteen-year-old trainee. I was at that stage in life where I was trying to work out who I was, while Simone was cocksure and con-fident. I hoped some of her vivacity would rub off on me. Not that I got the chance to see her much at work. She would come and check on me during the day, but she had her own duties to perform and I was mainly doing dogs-body stuff: running around after the more experienced midwives. I did get to assist on a few of the 'easier' la-bours, if there is such a thing. I rarely had to work weekends but Simone usually had a shift either on a Saturday or a Sunday. That didn't stop her going out a lot and I won-dered where she found the energy, until I saw her pop a pill on the bus on the way to work one morning. She'd winked at me as she did it, called it her 'pick-me-up', and I didn't ask any questions, refusing one when she offered it. I was never interested in dabbling with drugs.

Even though we tried out many different bars and clubs together, her favourite was always the humid Camden venue with its sticky floor, sweat-covered walls and dry ice that made my eyes water. She seemed to know so many people there and, usually, I was stuck talking to Dan at the bar while she went off to some badly lit corner with a random guy. One night I saw her deep in conversation with a man I hadn't seen before. He didn't look the type to hang out at dingy Camden clubs. He was older, late thirties, handsome in that clean-cut way and, instead of the ubiquitous band T-shirts and dark jeans everyone else wore, he had on a smart shirt and chinos.

'Who's that guy?' I asked Dan.

'Her dealer?' His large-set shoulders lifted half-heartedly, and his eyes, like two currants, wouldn't meet mine. 'I dunno, do I!' But something about the way he avoided looking at me made me think he did know who the guy was and probably regretted what he'd told me on the night I first met him. He'd tried to backtrack since, by telling me he'd been drunk and that I mustn't say anything to Simone. He'd looked scared as he'd said it, which made me wonder if he'd just been trying to make trouble. Or that he was bitter and jealous, and maybe wanted Simone for himself.

Simone chatted to the smartly dressed man for a good forty-five minutes or so and I was starting to get fed up with Dan. We'd already run out of conversation and both had stood at the bar, moodily nursing our drinks, for twenty minutes. For the first time I'd begun to wonder if I should refuse to come back to the club next time Simone asked. I felt out of my depth with her, as if I was walking a tightrope of danger, which was simultaneously exhilarating and terrifying. My feet were aching and the cheap beer was starting to wear off. I pictured Kerrie and my other housemates in our cosy living room, with the ripped sofas and the ugly carpet, lounging around watching a film on the telly, tucking into a takeaway and gossiping about different people on their respective courses. I missed them and I wanted to go home.

Just as I was contemplating leaving, even if it did mean having to trek back to Walthamstow on my own, Simone came over to me, smiling proudly. The older man she had been talking to had been replaced by a younger, more attractive guy with an unruly mop of shaggy black hair, tight black jeans and facial piercings. 'Lena, meet Oliver. My little brother.'

'Hey.' He elbowed her in the ribs good-naturedly. 'You make me sound like I'm twelve!'

I instantly perked up. I couldn't really see a family resemblance. Oliver sidled over to me and offered to buy me a drink. Over more cheap beer he told me he was in his final year at Manchester University studying politics and was just back for the weekend. Simone wandered off again, but this time I didn't care. I was enraptured by Oliver. He had a public-school accent, much like Simone's (even if she tried to hide it with Mockney), yet he talked like he was anti-establishment and had a piercing in his eyebrow that I found extremely sexy. When the club closed at 2 a.m. and we couldn't find Simone he offered me the sofa at his place in Muswell Hill.

'Shouldn't we try to find your sister? Something might have happened to her.'

He laughed, as though the prospect of anything bad ever happening to Simone was ludicrous. 'She's a lone wolf. She might end up back with Jasper.'

'Jasper?'

'Her on–off boyfriend. She sometimes stays with him in Walthamstow.'

She'd told me when we first met that she lived in Walthamstow, near me. And that she had a group of housemates, one who kept stealing her food and whom she had a crush on. Carl, or something like that. Not Jasper. 'She doesn't live in Walthamstow herself, then?'

'No, she lives at home, with our parents in Muswell Hill. She's saving up, she said. To buy her own flat.'

Another lie.

I agreed to go home with him. He told me his parents would be 'chilled' and I could sleep on the sofa. I didn't usually go home with men I'd only just met. I'd never had a one-night stand. In fact, I'd only ever had one boyfriend, but I told myself Oliver wasn't a stranger: I knew his sister. And his parents would be at home.

'I love my sister and everything,' he said, later that night as we sat chatting on the sofa in the dim light of his parents' living room, 'but she treats men like shit. Like Jasper. The poor guy is utterly loved up but she won't commit to him. She's nearly twenty-seven but likes to act like she's seventeen! She only uses him when she wants to stay in Walthamstow because it's closer to the hospital. She's a bit fucked up, to tell you the truth. But then' – he grinned at me in the half-light – 'aren't we all?'

Even then I jumped to defend her, telling him Simone had been good to me. 'She's kind, which not all my past supervisors have been.'

He tipped the remnants of the can of beer he'd been drinking into his mouth but didn't agree.

'She must be caring,' I protested, irritated by his silence. 'She works with babies.'

'Oh, she fell into that.' He pulled back the sleeve and showed me his wrist. 'See that scar? She did that when I was four. She was ten and should have known better.'

'So, you're not close? I don't have brothers or sisters. I don't get this whole sibling thing.'

He put an arm around my shoulders and pulled me in closer, as though my words had endeared me to him. 'We get on well now. But I wouldn't cross her.' He sounded flippant so I didn't take him seriously, and we started talking about ourselves and our music tastes and our desires for the future, and the whole time he made me feel like I was the most interesting creature ever to cross his path. We talked until the sun came up, and Oliver made me a bacon sandwich and a strong cup of tea. As we sat at the kitchen table, our thighs touching, grinning stupidly at each other over our breakfast, I knew I wanted this time together never to end. We were inseparable for the rest of the weekend, and when he went back to university on the Monday, we promised we'd keep in touch.

On Tuesday, my next shift, I couldn't help but watch Simone closely. She was kind and attentive to the expectant mothers, organized and efficient. Totally different, in fact, from the pill-popping, beer-swigging party girl I socialized with. I decided that Oliver was just being an annoying little brother, and that Dan had been drunk and, perhaps, jealous when he told me those things. Simone might party hard, but she worked hard too.

I didn't have the chance to talk to Simone much during the day, but as I was changing out of my scrubs at the end of my shift I heard two colleagues come in. I'd worked with one of the girls, Becky someone or other: she'd qualified two years ahead of me. The other woman was older, a junior doctor. I realized they couldn't see me behind my locker door and they were already midway through a conversation.

'She's just another in a long line of women he's shagged,' Becky was saying. I could hear the rustle of coats and scarves being taken off. They must have been there for the night shift. 'He's got a wife and three little kids at home as well.'

'Hugh Warrington is such a player,' the junior doctor replied. She had a Scouse accent but I couldn't remember her name and I'd only seen her from afar. 'Doesn't she know he'll never leave his wife?'

'Simone's a smart cookie.'

I stiffened at Simone's name.

'They're always together lately. Have you noticed? They're not being discreet. I find him so arrogant. I don't get what Simone sees in him.'

'He *is* a good doctor, but his morals are questionable. His wife has only recently had a baby . . .'

More rustling and the banging of locker doors. I didn't know what to do, so I stayed quiet, hidden by my locker, and their voices faded as they left the room.

I hadn't yet met a doctor called Hugh Warrington but I'd have put money on him being the well-dressed, older man I'd seen Simone with on Saturday night.

45

LENA

July 2024

The town is pretty with cobbled streets and colourful bunting fluttering between buildings. As I wander past the cathedral and bijou boutiques I imagine what it would be like to live here. Start afresh. Is that what Simone had thought too?

When I arrive Oliver is already seated at a table by the window. I can see him from where I hover on the street, his long fingers tapping against his cup. I hesitate, remembering the last time I saw him and the anger in his eyes. It was his idea to meet in Salisbury. It was roughly halfway, he said, between Bristol and Southampton, where he lived, but I wonder if it's because this is where Simone worked. Was this her last known address?

It had been strange to hear Oliver on the phone yesterday. We had been inseparable after that first night together. Our relationship lasted only a few months but our love – or lust – had burned bright until it was extinguished by the truth about Simone. It had taken a long time to get over him and, until I'd met Charlie, Oliver had been the love of my life.

He hadn't revealed much on the phone and had seemed surprised that I was free to meet him at such short notice – I didn't tell him this was my eighteenth wedding anniversary and that I'd forgotten to cancel the day off I'd booked before I split with my husband. I wonder what his own story is and why he, too, was free to meet on a Friday morning at the end of July. There are photos of him on Facebook: him, handsome and gym-toned, his wife petite and smiley and, for a wistful moment, I wondered what our life would have been like if we'd stayed together. I discounted it just as quickly. It might not have worked out with Charlie, but I'll never regret meeting him or having Rufus.

Even at 10 a.m. my sleeveless white cotton dress is sticking to me. I'd carefully selected what to wear this morning and I know it's because I want Oliver to think I haven't let myself go. The café is fairly empty and I'm thankful for the fans set up in every corner of the room. Oliver glances up when I come in, goes back to his drink and does a comical double-take when he realizes it's me. I rarely post photographs of myself on social media.

He stands up. He's wearing denim cut-off shorts and a white T-shirt that brings out his tan. His dark wavy hair is pushed back by sunglasses and there are no signs of the piercings he used to have. He looks like a sporty middle-aged dad. 'Lena? Oh, my God, long time no see.' We share an awkward moment when we're not sure how to greet each other. He shakes my hand and we laugh at the formality before he pulls me into a hug. I breathe in his scent of musky aftershave, soap and shampoo, as I hug him back. He's a lot taller than I remember, and obviously a lot older, but there is still that same twinkle in his dark eyes. We break apart and sit opposite each other. Straight away a waitress comes over to take my order.

'Thanks for meeting me,' he says, when the waitress has gone. 'I didn't want to have to explain it all over the phone and thought it would be better face to face.' He sighs, surveying me, and I immediately feel shy under his scrutiny, knowing that every moment of the last twenty-five years since we've seen each other is evident on my face. 'God, isn't it mad it's been so long? Where has the time gone?' He hesitates. 'I'm sorry you got caught up in it all, Lena.' His face flushes. 'And I'm sorry I didn't believe you when you told me what you suspected.'

'It was a long time ago . . .'

'I know. But I'm not proud of my behaviour and how we ended. I wanted to pick up the phone so many times. Stupid male pride. I'm sorry about what my sister did too.'

The waitress comes back with my iced latte and I take a gulp. My mouth has gone dry.

He narrows his eyes. 'Did you hear about Hugh Warrington?'

'Only that he went to prison. He didn't serve that long in the end, did he?'

'Three years, I think. But, no, not that. He died.' He sips his drink as I let the information sink in. 'Suicide. Last July. He was found in his bed surrounded by pills. Ironic, really.'

Horror inches up my throat. 'Oh, God. I didn't know that.'

'Good riddance, I say. I'll never forgive him for dragging Simone into it all.'

The long-buried anxiety from that time resurfaces and I swallow painfully. 'You said you think Simone is missing.'

He casts his eyes to the trail of granulated sugar on the oilcloth and begins dabbing at it. 'Yes. Nobody's heard from her.'

I'm reminded of Drew and his sister. 'Could she have just run off somewhere? You know what she's like. You used to call her a lone wolf.'

He scratches his stubble thoughtfully. 'That's what we thought at first. After the court case Simone left nursing. We tried to support her as best we could. The hospital left her job open – she wasn't sacked. And, as you know, she was found not guilty, not enough proof that she was involved, apparently. I think she got lucky with her defence lawyer. Dad paid for the best. Anyway, after the court case she got in with a bad crowd, typical Simone.'

I remember how defensive he was when I first told him my suspicions about what Simone was up to. We'd ended almost a year before the court case. Months before she was even charged.

'Drugs. Again.' He rolls his eyes. 'You know Simone. She's impatient. I guess she got bored waiting for what-ever new career she'd decided on to take off.'

'She was always such a hard worker,' I say.

He nods in agreement. 'But she loves money and she felt she never earned enough. She wasn't particularly academic at school – wasn't great with numbers, found science hard. She felt a high-earning career was out of reach for her and so, I suppose, she was always finding ways to supplement her income.'

'You'd think after everything that happened at St Calvert's she'd have learnt her lesson,' I mutter.

'True.' He shakes his head. 'It gets worse. About eight years ago she got involved with this county-lines drugs gang and went on the run when they threatened her.'

'And you haven't seen her since then?'

'Well, I have, on and off and in secret. Our mum died about twenty-odd years ago now, but Simone kept in touch with me and our dad, so we knew she was safe. She was happy, she said. I think she'd faced up to her mistakes at last and was trying to turn over a new leaf. And then her communication stopped. I tracked her down to here . . .' He throws his arms wide. 'She'd been living in Salisbury for the last few years. I even found out she'd been renting a flat over a kebab shop. I spoke to her landlord, who said she'd just vanished.'

I remember the keyring I'd brought with me to show Oliver. I reach into my bag for it and slide it across the table. 'Do you recognize this?'

He picks up the key and lightly touches the faded pink teddy bear, his brown eyes glistening. 'This is Simone's. My mum made them. I've got one too. A blue one.' He looks up at me. 'Where did you get it?'

My chest constricts. 'My next-door neighbours' garden. Do you know a Henry and Marielle Morgan?'

He shakes his head, his expression full of confusion and concern. He continues to stroke the teddy bear, his eyes not leaving mine. 'Why would your neighbours have Simone's key?'

'That's what I'm trying to figure out. The landlord told you about Simone vanishing. When was it? Two weeks ago?' I ask, thinking of the Morgans and the plan I overheard them talking about.

He swallows. 'No. It was last August.'

46

LENA

February 1999
London

The smartly dressed man I spotted with Simone at the Camden club was indeed Hugh Warrington. Suave, with slick dark hair brushed back over a handsome, if slightly arrogant, face.

'Don't you think Dr Warrington's a bit of all right?' I'd said to her, one evening, a few days after I heard Becky and the junior doctor gossiping. We were travelling back on the bus to Walthamstow together and she still hadn't told me she lived at home with her parents in the other direction. Oliver and I had agreed to continue our romance, promising to visit each other when we could. Simone had seemed happy for us when I told her about it and joked how she'd love me as her sister-in-law one day.

'What?' She'd laughed, too loudly. 'Hugh? He's, like, forty! Way too old for me!'

But she'd shifted in her seat and looked uneasy. It was another lie, I was sure.

After that, I watched them closely, but they always appeared professional when they were together. I did notice that they were mostly working the same shift, but I wasn't sure who organized the rota and it could have been a coincidence.

One day I saw them coming out of the walk-in cabinet where the medications were kept under lock and key. They were obviously arguing under their breath. I watched as she angrily thrust a large box into his arms and they stalked off in opposite directions. When Simone saw me hovering by the medical waste bins she smiled as though nothing had happened and continued briskly down the corridor.

One day, a week or so later, Janice asked me to assist Simone with a birth. 'The woman has been in early labour for hours,' she explained. 'She's young, a first pregnancy, thirty-nine weeks' gestation. She's becoming very tired. Birthing Suite Two.'

The woman in labour didn't look that much older than me and her pale face was contorted in pain. I was taken aback by how childlike in proportion she was. Even her bump was small and neat. She couldn't have been more than five foot. There was nobody in the room with her apart from Simone, who was standing by the foot of the bed with the chart in her hands. She glanced up in surprise when I walked in. 'Oh, where's Janice?'

'She sent me.'

She didn't say anything more, but I was sure I saw annoyance in her face. Instead she read out the information on her chart. 'Natalie Grant. Six centimetres dilated. Twenty-two years old. Weighs forty-eight kilos. I've prescribed her two five-milligram shots of diamorphine, but she's still in a lot of pain. It's been a long early labour. Dr Warrington is coming in to give her a third dose and a further anti-emetic.'

Midwives were forbidden to administer the third dose of opioids at this hospital. It had to be done by a doctor.

'Does she have a partner or someone with her?' I whispered. My heart immediately went out to the girl on the bed, who was panting through a contraction, her dark hair hanging either side of her pale face.

Simone guided me away from the bed so Natalie couldn't hear us. 'Partner not on the scene. Her mother is with her, but I sent her to the canteen to get some refreshments. She'll be back soon.' She was talking in an urgent way and her gaze kept sliding towards the door.

'What do you want me to do?'

'Sit with Natalie until her mum returns. Reassure her. She's refused an epidural, but she's tired. The baby isn't in any distress and the heartbeat is good, so it's just about managing Natalie's pain right now.'

'Okay.' I went to the bed and held Natalie's hand, talking gently to her, telling her my name and reiterating how well she was doing. Simone was standing at the foot of the bed writing something on the chart.

'You're doing great,' I said to Natalie again, as a contraction took hold, but I was worried about how pale she was. Simone didn't seem concerned although there was a strange energy coming from her and she kept throwing glances towards the door.

'Where's my mum?'

'She's just getting a cup of tea and a bite to eat. She'll be right back.'

'Oh, okay, thank you.' Natalie smiled up at me through her pain and then her face contorted again as another contraction ripped through her. She squeezed my hand tightly. I always felt useless at this stage, wishing I could do more to help rather than just assist. Janice had allowed me to deliver a few babies, making sure she was there to help if I needed it.

Simone clipped the chart back on to the end of the bed as Dr Hugh Warrington swept in. Immediately her face lit up. His smile faded as soon as he saw me sitting in the corner, Natalie's hand in mine.

'You can go, Lena,' Simone said. 'It's all okay now Dr Warrington is here.'

I was about to get up when Natalie squeezed my hand. 'No!' she cried. 'Not until my mum gets back.'

Simone and Dr Warrington exchanged glances, but they kept quiet. I watched as he talked gently to Natalie about how he was going to administer the diamorphine. Then he and Simone walked to the trolley in the corner, their backs to us. They were conferring, but I couldn't hear what they were saying. Dr Warrington approached the bed with a syringe and explained to Natalie that he was going to inject it into her thigh. She gripped my hand as he stuck the needle into her flesh.

'Ten milligrams,' he said to Simone, who picked up the chart from the end of the bed and scribbled on it.

I was confused. Ten milligrams was a lot, especially for Natalie, who was tiny. And I was sure I saw him administer a five-milligram dose. But I didn't feel I was in any position to contradict a doctor. He left without further acknowledging me and, when Natalie's mum returned with drinks and snacks and Simone was filling her in on what had happened while she was away, I sneaked a quick glance at the chart.

Three doses of diamorphine had been administered to Natalie, one every three hours. And, according to Simone's records, all were ten-milligram injections. Yet Simone had told me herself that she'd administered five milligrams. Natalie's weight on the chart was also noted as being 58 kilos, not 48, as Simone had said to me. Why would Simone record Natalie's weight as much heavier? Was it a simple mistake?

When Natalie was distracted by another contraction, her mother rubbing her back, I took Simone aside and pointed out the mistake. Instead of being grateful she just looked irritated. 'Oh, slip of the pen. I'll sort it. Just leave it for now,' she said.

Something else was bothering me too. 'Her hands look swollen to me,' I began, thinking of pre-eclampsia. 'Have you checked her blood pressure?'

'She's got carpal tunnel syndrome,' Simone said, without looking up from her chart. 'The swelling is fluid, and her blood pressure is normal.' She was talking to me like my supervising midwife, with authority, yet doubt still flickered in my mind.

'She's been in early labour a long time,' I insisted. 'And the baby has hardly moved down the birth canal. Shouldn't she be assessed for a possible emergency C-section?'

Simone looked up from the chart and for the first time I saw uncertainty in her face. 'I'll call Hu– Dr Warrington back,' she said. 'Always worth checking with a doctor.'

Less than a couple of minutes later Dr Warrington was back and I watched as he did a number of checks. 'You can leave now, Lena,' he said, his back to me. 'It's all under control.'

I left the room, an uneasy feeling gnawing away at me. My instinct was telling me that something was wrong with Natalie, but Simone was much more experienced and Hugh Warrington was a doctor. I had no choice but to trust them.

My shift ended before Simone's so I couldn't travel home with her. But when I returned to my student digs I went straight up to my room and grabbed my notepad from my desk. I turned to a page from a recent lecture about pain relief and diamorphine. And, yes, there it was, scribbled in my handwriting: *Consider a reduced dose in women who weigh less than 50kg.*

Had Simone lied about Natalie's weight deliberately to validate her reasons for the supposedly higher dose? But I had seen that Dr Warrington had administered five milligrams. What were they doing?

47

LENA

Oliver stares down at the pink teddy bear. 'I remember when my mum knitted these. She was in hospital, before she got really sick. We were too old for them, but . . .' He strokes the ear tenderly, then looks up at me. 'You found this in your neighbours' garden?'

'Well, in the hedge between their garden and mine. The weird thing is . . . you say Simone went missing last August but my neighbours only moved in a few weeks ago. I'm not sure why they'd have her key.' I remember Marielle's expression when I showed it to her. She was insistent it was theirs while Henry contradicted her. 'What did Simone retrain as? Was it an electrician by any chance?'

'Yes! How did you know?'

I tell him about the wall of newspaper clippings I found in the Morgans' home. 'And this one was from the *Salisbury Journal*. Look.' I bring up the photo on my phone and hand it to him across the table. 'Is this Simone? At the front of the photo?'

His eyes narrow, his face turning ashen. 'Yes. That's her.'

'So that's two things that link them to Simone.'

'Could they be part of this drugs gang that Simone was running from?' he asks. He's still dabbing at the grains of sugar on the table. I remember this about him, how he could never sit still. How he fizzed with pent-up energy.

'I don't know. But something isn't right about them.' I tell him everything, from the very beginning, leaving nothing out. I haven't told anyone else the whole story without sanitizing it so they wouldn't worry, or leaving parts out that cast me in a bad light. But with Oliver, a man I was once so close to but who is now almost a stranger, it's cathartic. We order another coffee, Oliver becoming more manic as the conversation progresses, not helped by the caffeine. When I've finished he's silent. And for a few moments he's actually still.

'Do you think you should go to the police?' I ask, when he doesn't say anything.

His eyes are anguished. 'I can't. This is the frustrating thing! She made us promise that whatever happened we wouldn't go to the police. She was terrified that if we did the gang would know where she was.'

'But she could be in danger. I don't know what the Morgans have to do with it but there must be some connection.'

'Do you think they knew Hugh Warrington? Perhaps they were part of what was going on at the hospital. You said Henry was a surgeon?'

I consider this. 'He was, but in neurology and, according to my online research, never worked at St Calvert's or any maternity hospital. Unless they knew each other from training or from working at a previous hospital together?' Is that what this is all about? That Henry was involved in what Hugh and Simone were up to back in 1999?

Oliver taps his nails against the floral oilcloth. 'Shit, Lena, I actually don't know what to do for the best. If I go to the police about this and she's just hiding from the gang I could put her in danger. They might still be looking for her. But if she is actually missing, properly missing, and she's in danger . . . God.' He buries his face in his hands and I stare at him helplessly. I don't know what to suggest either.

He looks up at me, his fingers pressed into his cheeks. 'What do you think I should do?'

'I'm not sure. But I have a bad feeling, Ol.'

His face softens at the shortened version of his name. He reaches across the table, the tips of his fingers lightly touch mine. 'Me too.' Then he retracts his hand and clears his throat. 'You know, I did have a phone call earlier this year, February, March time. From some guy who said he was a reporter.'

I sit up straighter.

'He was asking me about St Calvert's. Said he was doing a piece about it being twenty-five years since a baby was found on the steps of the hospital. I remember you and Simone telling me about it.'

'Oh, my God! Yes! I haven't thought about that for a long time.' It had been a few days before I left my training and just before I ended up confronting Simone with my suspicions over the drugs fraud. Finding the newborn baby had been overshadowed by everything that came after. Less than a year later I'd read about the court case and realized with relief that someone else must have blown the whistle on them.

It was Simone who found the baby on the steps of the hospital. It was around 6 a.m. and still dark. I'd been on a night shift. I was just leaving and Simone was arriving. She said someone had abandoned the newborn. We headed into the hospital together with the baby to report it, and to get confirmation that the baby hadn't been born to any patients from St Calvert's. I remember, years later when I first held Rufus in my arms, thinking of how desperate the mother must have been to abandon her baby and I'd cuddled Rufus even tighter.

'This reporter seemed to know it was Simone who'd found the baby,' muses Oliver. 'I'm not sure how.'

'There would have been a record, although good sleuthing on their part as the hospital has been closed for years. My name might have been there too, as we reported it together.'

He frowns and rubs the back of his neck. 'They didn't mention your name. They seemed only to be interested in Simone. Now I'm wondering if it was a ploy to try to find out where she was.' His mouth is set in a grim line. 'And she's never tried to get in touch with you?'

'Never. While I was trying to find her I contacted the electrical company from the clipping and they'd never heard of Simone. But judging by the photograph in the *Salisbury Journal*, it's obvious she'd worked there. You said she was using a different name?'

'Ah, yes. Natalie.'

'Natalie?'

'Yes. Natalie Grant?' His eyes narrow as a small noise escapes my lips. 'Why, does it mean anything to you?'

I haven't allowed myself to think of that pale-faced girl in a long time. A lump forms in my throat and I can feel tears stinging my eyes. 'Yes. Natalie Grant was a patient. At the hospital. Simone delivered her baby and . . . it was so sad. Natalie . . . died.'

48

HENRY

November 1994
London

Marielle was seated next to him on a park bench, wrapped up in a long houndstooth coat, a purple beret and matching scarf. Her cheeks were stung pink by the cold and her eyelashes spiky with tears. They had just come from the hospital where they'd sat with their hands clasped, while a grave-faced specialist had told them that the odds of them conceiving a baby naturally were very low. They'd had a bunch of tests in the preceding months to check his sperm, her eggs and reproductive organs. Tests he hated having but knew were necessary if he wanted to stay married to her. It was Fate, he realized. That was why they were unable to conceive. He'd always known they shouldn't be parents and he was right. Not that he'd said any of this to Marielle. He hated seeing her like this but he had to stop the corners of his lips curling up with relief when the doctor told them the news.

Henry had had to make a decision that day when Marielle told him she wanted a baby. Marielle had given

299

him an ultimatum. No baby, no marriage. And he couldn't face losing her. He didn't know who he would become without her, so he'd agreed, and secretly hoped and prayed nothing would happen. His prayers were answered when nothing did. After the first eighteen months Marielle had wanted to go to the GP for tests and he had persuaded her not to. 'These things can take a while,' he'd said, trying to sound as if he knew what he was talking about. But as she hit thirty-five, then thirty-six, she told him she was going to seek out a specialist, and he had no choice but to go along with it. He had even considered getting a secret vasectomy but he knew the specialist would be able to tell, so instead he had to hope there was something fundamentally wrong with one or both of them to stop them reproducing.

'They did say there's still a slim chance,' she said, looking up at him with big, hopeful eyes, taking out a cotton hanky and dabbing at her face. 'There is no reason why it couldn't happen apart from your sperm being a bit sluggish, and he said IVF might work.'

He didn't want to try IVF. He didn't want any more tests or interference or small, stifling rooms with adult magazines and plastic cups. But he knew Marielle would try to convince him, and he loved her so much that of course he felt bad for her and hated seeing her upset. He couldn't pretend to be disappointed, though. This obviously annoyed her because she snapped, 'This has worked out exactly how you wanted it, hasn't it, Henry? You never wanted a baby . . .' The tears started again and he could do nothing but wrap his arms around her while she cried into his scarf.

He knew that Marielle felt the same deep down. A baby would be catastrophic. She only wanted one because she couldn't have one, just like she behaved if a dress she liked wasn't available in her size: it made her want it all the more.

But she wouldn't give up on the IVF idea until, in desperation, he found someone who could help him: a doctor friend was willing to convince Marielle that IVF wouldn't work for them. She'd sat, dead-eyed and stock still, as the doctor explained how limited their options were.

Eventually she gave up talking about babies, instead throwing herself into work at the university.

And then, just as he began to relax and to believe they could get on with their lives blissfully baby free, she came to him with the worst possible news.

49

LENA

The sky is limpid and the sun creates a dreamlike shimmer on the horizon as I drive home from meeting Oliver. By the sound of it, Simone hasn't changed. Oliver and I had spent several hours talking over what her radio silence might mean, and when we left things, he still wasn't sure whether going to the police might put her in more danger. He hugged me goodbye as he said he'd let me know what he plans to do and made me promise to leave it to him.

I'm sickened to hear that she's using Natalie Grant's name. That poor girl. Her terrified face will be etched in my memory for ever. The day she died was the beginning of the end for my midwifery career. It was when I first suspected what Simone and Hugh Warrington were up to, but even they couldn't have known that Natalie had an undiagnosed heart condition. She suffered a cardiac arrest just hours after giving birth. I wasn't in the room when it happened, but I was devastated when I heard about it. Natalie's mum was left to care for the little boy, and even now, all these years later, and especially since having a child of my own, the thought of it brings me to tears. Natalie's death wasn't enough to put them off, though, and I can just imagine them trying to convince themselves that they weren't at fault because they hadn't known about her heart condition. Yet if they'd paid more attention to Natalie and her vital signs, instead of wondering how they could siphon off the medication, if they'd been watching her more closely, seen her unnatural pallor, her breathlessness and long early labour, the swelling in her hands, they might have been able to save her. Simone was an experienced midwife and Hugh Warrington a doctor with nearly fifteen years' experience. I never forgave them. I read in the newspapers that he was also found guilty of prescription fraud. My biggest regret is not having informed a senior member of staff when I first spotted it, but I was terrified I wouldn't be believed over someone as eminent as the godlike Dr Hugh Warrington.

I'd started watching them more closely after Natalie died, but they were clever and secretive, and I noticed that I was rarely put on a shift with them. I think Simone suspected I knew something because she continued to keep me close, hanging out with me in our spare time whenever she could. Dan's comments about her being involved in some hospital scam kept running through my mind. I was convinced about the drug fraud but I had no proof.

I remember the night I told Oliver my suspicions about Simone. We were spending the weekend together in Manchester. By this time, I was detaching myself from Simone. Every time she tried to arrange a night out I'd say

I was busy, and I tried to avoid her at the end of our shift so that I could get the bus back on my own.

It was a Sunday in the middle of February when the grey days and dark nights blended into one another. I'd been putting off telling Oliver all weekend, but it had weighed so heavily on me that he'd asked me a number of times what was wrong. We were in his room and I was packing my bag, ready to catch the train home, when I eventually told him. I'll never forget the look on his face. Utter disbelief and judgement. 'Why would you say that about my sister?' he'd snapped. 'There's no way she'd do that! It's illegal. You can't go around accusing her of stealing drugs from the ward and neglecting her patients. You'll ruin her career. She could go to prison.' I'd never seen him so angry. His eyes were like pools of black ink in his colourless face. He called me a troublemaker. A liar. He kicked a chair over and thumped his fist on his desk. One of his housemates knocked on the door to make sure everything was okay. I'd taken that opportunity to grab my coat and bag and leave. He'd never tried to call me after that. Not even when, six months later, Simone and Hugh Warrington were charged with various offences relating to theft, possession and intent to supply controlled substances. I'd been glad to leave London and get away from both of them, despite my heartbreak over Oliver. I spent a few aimless years in East Sussex working in retail and learning to touch-type, which I hated. I eventually moved to Bristol after visiting my old housemate Kerrie, who was doing a PhD at the university and falling in love with the city. I was working in a shop when I met Charlie and was happy to give it all up to follow him and his career. After all, it wasn't like I had one of my own.

When I arrive home I notice that Henry's car isn't parked in its usual spot. I'm relieved. I dread bumping into him after the way he talked to me in the street. As soon as I let myself through the front door Phoenix comes rushing out to greet me, his whole backside wagging, happy to see a friendly face. I bend down to make a fuss of him, then go upstairs to empty Rufus's laundry basket. As I'm tipping the contents onto the floor my phone buzzes. It's a text from Jo.

Hey, lovely. Is it okay for Paul to come over later to finally install that camera in your garden? He's been working away from home a lot this week or he'd have been over before. I'll come too and you can tell me how it went with Oliver today xx

Yes, please. That would be amazing, I reply.

Great. 7 p.m. okay?

Perfect.

My mood instantly lifts at the thought of seeing Jo and Paul and not spending the evening alone, as I'd envisaged. A camera in my back garden will give me peace of mind.

I place the phone next to me on the floor as I continue going through Rufus's clothes. I root inside the pockets of his jeans. Mostly the odd tissue and ticket stub from the gigs he's been to with Charlie. And then my fingers brush against something crisp, with a jagged edge. As I pull it out I feel a throb of pain to my finger. It's a newspaper cutting, folded up small, the edge slicing the fleshy part of my finger. I suck it, tasting blood, and then, with the other hand, I peel open the cutting and lay it out flat on Rufus's carpet. I read the headline and a wave of nausea washes over me.

BABY FOUND ON HOSPITAL STEPS

This was one of the articles pinned to the Morgans' wall, although I'd only been able to see part of the headline as it had been hidden by the other newspaper cuttings. My eyes dart over the next few paragraphs, words popping out at me. *St Calvert's. Newborn baby found on 22 February 1999. Abandoned. Cardboard box. Nurse. Simone Harvey.* That was my last week of training before I left my course. I scan the piece again. My name isn't mentioned. I was only talking to Oliver about this earlier. I remember him telling me about a journalist contacting him. I check the top of the newspaper and see that it's dated a few days after the baby was found.

For a moment, sitting there slumped against Rufus's bed, I experience a strange, disconnected out-of-body feeling. The room swims and I have to blink a few times to anchor myself to the here and now. Why has Rufus got this?

And then something so horrific occurs to me that I'm struck by a sudden wave of nausea. Was it Rufus I saw breaking into the Morgans' house the night I was there? The hooded figure had gone into the room with all the newspaper articles. Joan's spare key is missing from my drawer. Did Rufus take it? Confusion makes me feel dizzy. But I had the key that night. The person I saw broke in another way. It can't have been Rufus. He's a good boy. He'd never think of breaking into someone's home. And what would be his motive? It makes no sense.

But, then, nothing about any of this makes sense. Nothing at all.

50

'So, you use this app here to view the camera,' explains Paul, that evening. 'It's really straightforward.'

I'm trying to take in what he's saying but all I can think about is the article I found in Rufus's pocket. I haven't had the chance to tell Jo yet and, for the two hours before she arrived, I was stressing about what to do and what it could mean. I need to ask Rufus, but he's at his dad's and it's not a conversation I want us to have over the phone. Either way, having had time to think, despite the way it briefly looked, I don't believe Rufus broke into the Morgans' house and took the cutting. He must have found it somewhere. I know Rufus's every mannerism: little details like how he walks, round-shouldered with his arms dangling in front of him as though he doesn't want to be noticed, the way he inclines his head, or fluffs up his fringe with the palm of his hand. I don't know who that person, that *man*, I saw in the Morgans' house was, but it wasn't Rufus.

The patio doors are open, the vibrant orange sun descending behind the houses opposite even though it's nearly 10 p.m. A family of wood pigeons coo and flap around the higher branches of my silver birch and the air is still warm enough for me not to have to wear more than a T-shirt. I can smell a barbecue in the air and hear the faint clatter of cutlery, the clinking of glasses and laughter drifting from a few doors down. We are sitting at the patio table, Jo and I with glasses of prosecco, Paul with a Diet Coke. Jo is being loud and raucous in the heady, relieved Friday-night way that was once so familiar to me when I couldn't wait for the weekends to spend time with Charlie and Rufus. I wonder if the Morgans are in their back garden, and it makes me feel unnerved. Jo is discreet enough not to mention them, but I hope, if they're in the garden, Henry in particular will take heed if he hears us talking about the security camera.

Paul is sitting next to me, leaning over to show me my phone screen. A black-and-white image of us sitting in the garden looms out at me. 'And if you want to go back and see earlier footage you just press here,' he says, indicating an arrow on the screen. 'And likewise to go forward, frame by frame.'

I take the phone from him. 'Thanks so much, Paul. You're a lifesaver.'

Paul stays and chats with us for a bit, but I get the feeling he's not entirely comfortable being the only man. He and Charlie used to get on well and the four of us would often be at each other's houses for dinner. After twenty minutes or so Paul kisses his wife's cheek and announces he needs to pick up Charmaine. 'Ring me later when you want me to come and get you,' he says, stretching his legs and adjusting the waistband of his trousers.

I thank Paul again and he says, 'Any time,' his good-natured face beaming with pleasure that he's been able to help.

'You've got a good one there,' I say, when Paul has gone. 'He'd do anything for you.'

'Charlie was a good one too,' she says softly.

'Really?'

'Of course. God, Lena. He adored you.'

I chew my lip, which tastes of alcohol. It never seemed that way to me, at least not in the last few years. Now, in my prosecco-fuelled haze, I wonder if I was too hasty. 'I wished we'd just rowed. You know, like couples do. A proper blazing row, air all our grievances, put everything on the table.' I sigh.

'Paul and I bicker all the time. Or rather,' she laughs and stretches out her legs, kicking off her flip-flops, 'I rant at him, and he listens, bless him.'

I twirl my wine glass, heaviness pressing on my chest. 'Anyway, it's too late for all that now. It's been nearly eight months. He's moved on and so have I.'

She raises an eyebrow at me but doesn't say anything.

Phoenix is flopped at our feet and the night darkens. I lower my voice. 'Shall we go in?'

It's lovely and balmy outside – I'll miss the warm nights when the heatwave is over – but I want to tell Jo about Oliver and Simone. She gathers up the bottle of prosecco and her flip-flops and follows me inside. I close the patio doors, making sure to lock them, and we head into the living room, Phoenix at our heels.

Jo makes herself comfortable on the sofa, tucking her feet up. 'So, go on, then. I know you're dying to tell me all about your meeting with Oliver. What was it like seeing him again? Was the old attraction there?'

I shake my head. 'Not really. He said some interesting things, though – concerning, actually.' I tell her everything I talked about with Oliver: Simone going missing, the keyring I found in the Morgans' garden that he confirmed was hers, and the call from the journalist.

'Shit. So he thinks the Morgans might be connected somehow with the Hugh Warrington drugs scandal?'

'It's a possibility. And then last night I found something in Rufus's pocket.' I tell her about the newspaper cutting.

'There must be an explanation,' she says, echoing my thoughts. 'Have you asked him?'

'He's at Charlie's until Sunday and I don't want to talk to him about it over the phone.' I get up to fetch the article from where I'd slipped it into the book I'm currently reading and hand it to her. She takes it from me, bends down to retrieve a pair of reading glasses from her bag and slips them on. I watch her puzzled expression. When she's finished reading she looks up at me.

'This was the hospital where you did your training?'

'Yep. I was in my last week of the placement. The whole thing with Natalie and the drugs fraud put me off wanting to continue in midwifery.' I don't say that it was a rash decision I might not have made if I had my time all over again. But I was young, impulsive and idealistic. I was also insecure and unconfident in my abilities. 'I was there when Simone found the baby. Or, at least, just moments after.'

She rereads the article and pushes her glasses onto her hair. 'Do you think all those articles pinned to the Morgans' wall are connected to each other? I mean, there's the one about Simone and the electricians. And then this one with

Simone being the one to find the baby. Can you remember any of the others?'

'No. Annoyingly, I didn't get a chance to read them, and they were all overlapping so it was hard to make sense of them anyway.' I reach over to the coffee-table for my phone and scroll back to the photos I took on the night I let myself into their house.

BABY FOUND ON HOS . . .

. . . ORGANS FOR RESEARCH AT . . .

DRUGS LORD FOUND DEAD IN . . .

BRIGHT SPARKS WIN NATIONAL AWARD

'Here, look . . .'

I pass my phone to Jo. She lays the newspaper cutting on her lap and takes my mobile while simultaneously pushing her glasses from her head back onto her nose.

'It's hard to make them out exactly,' I say.

She looks up at me through her trendy oversized readers. 'The drugs-lord headline. That could be about Hugh Warrington? Or the gang Simone was running from?'

'Maybe. Oliver told me Hugh had died. I googled it when I got home and it's true. He was found dead in his house last summer from an overdose. He was sixty-four, divorced and, according to the reports I'd read online over the years, had been struck off the medical register so his career was over too. It was around the time Charlie and I were having all our problems so I must have missed it in the news.'

'And what about this organs one?'

'I haven't a clue.'

She hands me back my phone. 'Like I've said a million times, please be careful.' She hesitates.

'What?'

'On their wall? You didn't see anything about you?'

'What? No. Of course not. What makes you say that?'

'It's just . . . they have a few articles about St Calvert's and you worked there too.'

'For six weeks, twenty-five years ago.'

'That's true. But, please, stay away from them . . . Henry in particular. He sounds like a nasty piece of work.'

I stand in the shower, relishing the cold water that gushes over my head and down my back. I'd felt so hot after Jo left that I knew I wouldn't be able to sleep. Afterwards, I step out of the bathroom and the silence presses in on me: the house has that empty, hollow feeling. Phoenix is waiting patiently for me, stretched out on my bed, and the room is like a furnace, despite the two sash windows that overlook the street being open as far as they will go. I perch on the edge of the bed in just a towel, and the night air wafts in, brushing against my damp skin and leaving a faint metallic scent. For the first time today my body temperature is ambient, which I know won't last once the effect of the shower wears off.

It's gone midnight and I sit in the semi-darkness; the only light comes from the crescent moon and the street-lamps. I hear a car pull up and curiosity gets the best of me. I kneel at the window in time to see Henry pulling up in his Jaguar. He's alone. I crouch lower, hoping he can't see me, and watch as he gets out. He runs a hand lovingly over the bonnet, as though tracing a woman's curves, before making his way down his front path. Immediately a hallway light comes on. I wonder if Marielle is at home. I haven't seen her walking the 'baby' since I found out it was fake more than a week ago.

I close the curtains, leaving a gap so that air can still get through and throw on the vest and shorts that I sleep in, then lie on the bed on top of the sheet, Phoenix next to me. The silence, along with the coolness from the shower and the slight breeze, causes me to drift off.

I wake with a start. At first I don't know what's disturbed me and then I see that Phoenix is no longer on the bed. I get up, my heart quickening as I grab my mobile. I head to the top of the stairs. I can hear Phoenix growling and my heart gallops.

I forgot about the fucking dog.

With trembling hands I bring up the app that Paul installed for me just hours earlier and sink onto the top step. The garden looks ghostly through the lens of the security camera and my heart thuds painfully as I scan the screen. It's like looking through night-goggles and the effect is eerie. I see a cat dart across the grass but nothing for a while and then . . . My breath catches. The back gate is wide open and a figure is strolling brazenly across the lawn. There is something about the way he walks that I instantly recognize. I watch, in shock, as he peers through the glass of the patio doors, recoiling when Phoenix starts to bark. He retreats, pressing his back against the hedge. I

315

can't see his face, but I don't need to. I know exactly who it is.

It's Charlie.

51

HENRY

July 2024
Bristol

Henry lets himself into the house and switches on the hall light. He jumps when he sees Marielle sitting at the bottom of the stairs in her silk nightdress, looking ethereal. She's stroking the cat they've 'adopted' and nicknamed Caramac because of his colour. The cat leaps out of her arms when he sees Henry, who has never had any affinity with animals. It's always surprised him that Marielle does.

His hand goes to his heart. 'Bloody hell, Mari! I thought you were asleep.'

'It's time, Henry.'

He pauses by the radiator to take off his boat shoes, wondering why she always has to be so dramatic. He wants to shout at her that she's not living in her very own *film noir*. But he doesn't, of course. Not once in all the years they've been married has he ever raised his voice to her. He's never wanted to be like his father.

She stands up and walks down the remaining stairs to where he's standing. He's bone tired and just wants to go to bed. He'd hoped if he stayed out long enough she'd be asleep when he got home.

'Henry? Did you hear me? I said it's time.'

He turns to face her. 'I know.'

'Do you?'

He sighs. 'Yes. I do.'

She folds her arms, her expression closed. 'You don't think it will work, do you?'

He knows it won't. How can it? But he doesn't say so. He knows how much hope she has pinned to this. It's what's kept her going all these years.

She moves towards him, tucks her hand into his and presses her body against him. Straight away he feels desire surge. She's always known how to entice him. Wordlessly she leads him upstairs to their bedroom and starts to peel off his shirt.

'This will be the end of it?' he asks, as she reaches up to kiss his neck.

'I've said so, haven't I?' Her breath is hot against his sticky skin.

'You said that before.'

'I mean it this time.'

He just wants it to be over, even though he knows it never can be.

Hugh Warrington. That was his first mistake.

He should never have trusted that man. And he should have known he'd find a way to crawl out of the woodwork and back into his life. At least now Hugh can't do any more damage. He's been careful to go back over those clumsily dropped breadcrumbs, stamping them out. One by one.

Marielle pushes him back onto the bed. He knows the sudden passion she has for him is because of what she plans to do. Nothing excites her more. How can he tell her he's lost the taste for it? She was right when she accused him of being too old. It's true. He just wants a quiet life now. But that's never going to happen while he's with Marielle. She'll keep on and on and on and on until her last breath.

'Tomorrow, then,' she murmurs.

'Sure,' he mumbles, with a mixture of desire and dread. 'We'll do it tomorrow.'

52

LENA

I continue to watch in bewilderment as Charlie moves away from the hedge and makes his way back across the lawn and out through the gate, closing it behind him.

My first thought is Rufus. If Charlie is sneaking around in my garden at midnight then he's left our son alone. I know he's seventeen and perfectly capable of staying anywhere on his own, but what is the point of him being with Charlie this weekend if his dad is just going to sod off?

And why was Charlie prowling around my garden like a creeper? Did he knock over the plant pot the night I overheard the Morgans' conversation? But he would never have forgotten about Phoenix.

Rufus is bound to be awake this late on a Friday night, so I call him. He answers straight away. 'Mum?'

'Hi, love. Nothing to worry about. I was just wondering where your dad is.' I get up from where I'm still sitting on the top stair and head into my bedroom.

'What do you mean?'

I don't want to worry him with the truth. 'Is your dad there?'

'Um . . . he walked Rosie home. But he'll be back soon, and Freddie's here. We're watching a film.'

'Okay.' I go to the window and glance down the street, half expecting to see Charlie, but it's quiet and empty.

'Why are you looking for Dad?'

'It's all right, love, I'll talk to you properly when you get home on Sunday.' I hesitate. 'Also, just a quick question while you're on the phone. I was turning out your pockets before putting your jeans in the wash and you had this newspaper article . . .'

'You didn't throw it away, did you?' He sounds panicked.

'No. But what were you doing with it?'

'It's Kit's. He dropped it on the way out of our guitar lesson. I didn't see it until he'd already left, so I kept it to give back to him next time I saw him.'

Kit? Why would he be so interested in this story? And why would he have broken into the Morgans'? 'Okay. Don't worry, I've kept it safe. When are you seeing him next?'

'Sunday afternoon. He's coming over to give me another lesson when I get back from Dad's.'

'Okay. Great. You can give it to him then.'

'Cool. Mum, gotta go now. We're in the middle of *Nightcrawler.*'

He must have seen that film ten times. 'Have fun. Love you.'

I end the call and, sitting on the edge of the bed, I immediately scroll down for Charlie's number. When he doesn't pick up I send a text: *Why were you creeping around my garden? What the fuck, Charlie!*

When I wake up the next morning, Charlie still hasn't replied.

The heatwave has lasted nearly a full month now. I wake up irritable and hot after a fitful night's sleep where I dreamt of Charlie crawling through the gap in the hedge and into the Morgans' dark garden, where he's threatened by Henry, then Simone appearing in her scrubs, searching for her keys in long, wild grass, while Marielle is alone in the attic, the fake baby in her arms.

The sky is a hazy blue, the sun already up, a fireball of rage that matches my own emotions. I need caffeine even though it's too hot for a cup of tea. Thankfully the kitchen is still partly shaded and I make myself an iced coffee while thinking of what to say to Charlie when he eventually replies.

I'm just about to move away to get some breakfast when my mobile pings. I grab it eagerly, knowing it will be from Charlie. He's sent a text message.

No, not me. Everything okay?

I stare at his words in shock. I never took Charlie for a liar. He's many things, but never that. I don't know what to make of it. It was definitely 100 per cent him on my camera. When he drops Rufus home tomorrow I'll present him with the footage and see him try to wiggle his way out of it. I keep thinking about Kit too and why he has the newspaper cutting about the baby found at the hospital. If it was him who broke into the Morgans' house I don't want him anywhere near Rufus.

The doorbell rings and Phoenix instantly starts barking.

'Sssh,' I say to him, as I make my way down the hallway, the dog leaping alongside me as I go to open the door. I'm surprised to see Marielle on the step. She's smiling and, from behind her, I can see that Henry is loading suitcases into the boot of his Jaguar.

'Hi, Lena,' she says. 'I'm sorry to bother you so early, but we've got to go away for a few days. A family member has unfortunately become very ill . . .' She twists her hands in front of her.

'Oh, I'm sorry to hear that.'

Pain clouds her face, and I wonder if it's Savannah. I hope not. 'I was wondering if you'd mind feeding Caramac while we're away.'

I try to hide my surprise. 'Um, Caramac?'

'Our cat.'

'Sure. I love cats.'

'We've kind of adopted him. I don't know who he belongs to, but he seems to love our house and he calls in twice a day for food and cuddles.' She looks so innocent, standing there in an expensive lemon dress with a cream Peter Pan collar and matching pumps, talking about a beloved animal, yet this woman might know where Simone is or have done something to hurt her. She could be a criminal mastermind behind that smiley, butter-wouldn't-melt facade, but she could also be a victim of Henry. My stomach turns over when I remember my conversation with Oliver. The newspaper articles. The keyring. The fake baby. The lies. All the lies. Not to mention their conversation about 'getting caught'.

'Lena?'

I haven't said anything for a few seconds. 'Um, sorry.' I grip the edge of the door for support.

'The cat. Would you mind feeding him for us while we're away?'

I throw a worried glance towards Henry. Is he okay with this? He was so angry when he found out I'd let myself into their house. He'd threatened me. Told me to leave them alone. He obviously hasn't mentioned it to Marielle, and I'm grateful for that, at least. I turn my attention back to her. She is looking at me with concern.

'Sure. I'd be happy to.'

She smiles in relief. 'Thank you so much. That would be a big help. You're really the only neighbour we've got to know since moving in.' I'm tempted to ask how her grandson is, but she looks so jittery standing there. She presses the key into my hand. 'We should be back by Monday, all being well. I've left instructions in the house.'

'Great, thanks. Does the cat have specific mealtimes?'

'Just morning and evening. Any time.'

'Okay.' My gaze turns to Henry but he's looking straight ahead, his hands gripping the steering wheel.

'Thanks again, Lena.' She claps her hands together, rushes back to the car and gets in on the passenger side. I watch them drive away. Marielle waves, but Henry keeps his eyes firmly on the road, as though I don't exist.

'You'll never guess what,' I say to Jo, when I call her five minutes later. 'Marielle has given me a key. Wants me to feed her cat.'

'What? You're kidding!'

'Nope. Henry obviously hasn't told her about me letting myself in. I'll take more photos of the wall. See if there are other things that link Simone's disappearance to the Morgans. That newspaper cutting I found on Rufus actually belongs to his guitar teacher.' I recount my conversation last night, including finding Charlie in my back garden and his text denying it.

'It couldn't have been Charlie,' she says, too quickly.

'The camera doesn't lie, Jo.'

'Well, give him a chance to explain.'

Jo is my biggest champion, always supporting me. Granted, she never slagged Charlie off, but I knew, without her having to say it, that she was on my side. Yet now she's sticking up for him.

I bite back my irritation. I don't want to get into this. 'How much do I owe Paul for the camera?' I ask instead.

'Nothing. He's happy to do it. And, Lena . . .' she pauses '. . . leave it to Oliver to decide what he's going to do. You've told him everything, right? It's his responsibility now. Simone's his sister.'

53

I wait until six o'clock to let myself into the Morgans' house. I have to remind myself that I'm not doing anything illegal. They gave me their key and I have a legitimate reason to be there. Still, my mouth is dry as I step over the threshold. I pocket the key and stand in the hallway, watching as the light refracts through the glass droplets of their extravagant chandelier, casting a kaleidoscope of colours on the walls.

It's a strange feeling, being back here, and I'm suddenly struck with paranoia. As though they're watching me. I glance up at the ceiling to see if there are any hidden cameras. Is that how Henry knew I was here last time? I mentally shake myself. So what if there are cameras? I'm only doing what they asked.

I head into their immaculate kitchen. On the marble worktop sits a box of cat food and a cat's bowl. Marielle has written a note with instructions. I'm to use half a packet of Felix, then leave it outside their bifold doors for the cat to eat. I do as it says, then stand at their doors, looking out onto their manicured garden. I notice the gap in the hedge. I step onto the patio and cross the sun-dried lawn, peering down into the gap. I can see how easy it would be for Henry to ease himself through it and into my garden. And I think of how my back gate was left open before, and Charlie lurking in my garden last night.

I go back inside, closing the bi-folds behind me. I should just leave. Go home, but the temptation to snoop is too great.

'*It's too risky. We could get caught, Mari.*'

'*We didn't last time.*'

I can't resist going back into the small room at the bottom of the stairs.

The wall of articles is still there and I wonder why they haven't taken them down, knowing I'd be coming over to feed the cat. I walk further into the room to take more photos. I pat the pocket of my dress, looking for my phone. But only the two keys are there – my door key and the Morgans'. I check my other pocket but my phone isn't there either. Damn it, I must have left it behind as I rushed out. I'll go home in a minute and get it. I walk further into the room and examine the clippings, taking my time to read them properly. There's one here about a new birthing unit that opened in March 1999 at St Calvert's: I remember how it was surrounded in scaffolding while I was doing my placement, but I left before it was finished. Another about St Calvert's being involved in an organ-harvesting scandal, shortly before the place closed down in 2005. I lift it to read the one underneath, which is about Hugh Warrington's trial. The article above it is about his suicide last July. I scan another, and then another, lifting them carefully from where they overlap, the details jumping out at me, my unease growing as I read each one.

Every single one has some link to St Calvert's.

The click of a door makes me jump and I spin around. I freeze.

Marielle is standing there, leaning back against the closed door, blocking my way. The warm smile of earlier has vanished and her eyes are cold.

'Marielle?'

'I'm sorry, Lena.' Her voice is calm. 'I know you overheard us talking that day. Henry saw you.'

'I . . .' Confusion makes my brain woolly and it takes me a moment or two to register what she's saying. 'I . . . I didn't hear anything.'

'I know that's not true.'

'Look, whatever you're up to, it's none of my business.'

She folds her arms across her chest and clicks her tongue between her teeth. 'It is your business, Lena.'

My heart twists painfully, realizing, too late, that I've walked into a trap. They were never going away for the weekend. This was all a ruse to get me here.

'What's . . . what's going on?' I manage.

'You weren't supposed to overhear us, Lena. Especially as we were talking about you.'

My legs buckle beneath me. 'I don't understand . . .'

Her next words chill me to my core. She approaches me slowly. And then, in the hand that hangs by her side, I notice a syringe. '*You*, Lena. You were the plan. Why do you think we moved in next door?'

PART THREE

54

HENRY

August 1998
London

They were enjoying dinner at one of Henry's favourite restaurants on the King's Road when Marielle upended his world.

They were halfway through the starter. He still remembers what he was eating. Lobster. It turned to rubber in his mouth after she had spoken, making it impossible to swallow. He'd just stared at her, chewing, while she gabbled away.

She was pregnant, she said. Seven weeks. Baby was due mid-February.

He'd had to spit out the mouthful of lobster discreetly into a napkin before he could find his voice.

'It's a miracle, Henry. It's marvellous.'

'But you're forty. That's . . . that can be dangerous.'

'Don't be so silly, darling.' She laughed. 'Women are having children much later, these days. It's not like when our parents were young.'

He had to put his cutlery down. He'd lost his appetite. He had to pretend to be pleased, of course. He'd never considered, for one moment, that she might conceive naturally. Not when they were told there was such a tiny chance and she was getting older.

She reached across the table and clasped his hand. 'I'm so happy, Henry. I've never been so happy.'

He wondered if he might be sick. His mind raced with all the possibilities. Maybe it wouldn't be so bad. Perhaps they could get a live-in nanny. Marielle was bound to lose interest once the baby was born. She took her hand away and resumed eating.

'It's funny,' she continued. 'I've had no morning sickness. I feel great, actually.'

He appraised her. She looked great, radiant, in fact. Her skin was clear, her eyes shining, and her hair even more lustrous than usual. But as she came to life right there before him, he felt part of himself wither and die. He couldn't say what he really felt, not in the restaurant with other diners seated so close to them, and not to her, his beloved. His wife. He had no choice but to sit there and listen while she prattled away about how amazing it was going to be, how they would decorate the nursery, which cot they would choose – 'It has to be white, Henry. I love white for babies,' as though the baby was a mere accessory or a piece of furniture she'd been coveting for years. And he stared at her, utterly speechless the whole time, wondering how she could possibly be so deluded.

As he sat there, watching as she talked, he knew he had to do something. Anything. Because this couldn't happen.

This *really* couldn't happen. A baby couldn't be part of their lives. He needed to think. He was good under pressure – that was partly what made him an excellent surgeon – and he'd never felt as pressured as he did right then.

But his mind worked in brilliant, twisted ways. It always had done. It was his superpower.

And just like he knew it would, a plan was already beginning to take form.

55

LENA

My eyes open and I glance down to see that I'm laid out on a narrow bed. There isn't even a sheet on the stained mattress. I sit up groggily; my whole body feels as though I've just run a marathon and my head is spinning. The room is small but I recognize it instantly as the Morgans' attic. From the narrow windows I can make out the apricot-streaked sky. Soon it will be dark and then what?

How long have I been here? I must be in some nightmare. I can't believe this is happening. The last thing I remember is being in that room with Marielle and the syringe. She must have injected me with something.

I picture the fake baby and Marielle's pretence at having a grandson. Having children. Why? And all the lies. I don't understand what's going on.

All of this has something to do with St Calvert's. With Hugh and Simone. But why me? Why me, when I worked there for just six weeks nearly three decades ago?

Marielle's words come flooding back.

You, Lena. You were the plan.

Now that I'm here, what are they planning to do with me?

A rush of adrenaline and fear gives me the energy to move. I need to call someone. Charlie, Jo. I scan the room, frantically, but then I remember: I'd left my phone at home. I reach down and tap my pocket, relieved when my fingers make out the shape of my key. Thank goodness it's still there. Although that's not much help when I'm stuck here. I think of Rufus, returning home tomorrow to an empty house and wondering where I am. What if the Morgans decide to hurt him next? I can't allow those fucking psychos to harm him. I need to do something.

My mouth is so dry I'm finding it hard to swallow. I swing my legs out of bed and try to walk but they buckle and I end up crawling across the dusty floorboards, wincing when my knee scrapes a protruding nail. I stay on all fours until I get to the door and then I reach up and try the handle, but it's locked. I don't have the energy to scream and shout. I slump against the door in defeat.

I should have stayed away from them. My nosiness is going to cost me my life.

Why do you think we moved in next door?

And yet I can't see how this would have ended in any other way. It was obviously their plan from the very beginning.

56

HENRY

Henry watches as Marielle snaps on her blue latex gloves, wriggling her fingers, a smile of satisfaction on her face. No nurse's uniform this time. They don't need to pretend, like they did with Simone. Marielle has the glint of excitement in her eye, like a hunter about to shoot its prey. He hadn't wanted to do this. He'd tried to warn Lena to stay away – pushing while Marielle pulled. But he'd been naïve to think Marielle would forget about it. He knows she's not going to stop until she gets answers.

Except she'll never get answers. Because he is the only person who can give them to her. And he'd rather die than tell her the truth.

Marielle's standing at the kitchen counter with the syringe and she whips around to face him, holding it aloft. 'Well, come on, then, Henry. Don't just stand there. We need to get on with it. We don't have much time.'

'Marielle . . .'

'Don't bail on me now, Henry. Not when we've got this far. Lena knows what happened to our baby. She's our last chance.'

Of course she doesn't know! he wants to yell. But what would be the point?

He takes a deep breath. He'd tried all he could to dissuade her, to support her. He'd even let her have that ridiculous silicone baby and watched as she passed it off as their grandson. Anything, he reasoned, to make her happy. He had hoped her make-believe would keep her from the reality. But he'd soon realized it had been a temporary measure.

He pictures Lena, locked upstairs in the attic. She has a son who will miss her. A friend who is always checking up on her. Getting rid of her won't be as easy as it was with Simone. And it's not that Henry feels pity. He knows he doesn't have the same kind of feelings as other people. And that's okay. He's learned to accept his *limitations* over the years. Helped by Marielle. He understands he's devoid of most basic human emotions and that he's only ever loved one thing, one person, and that's his wife. His lack of empathy, of emotion, has made him a brilliant neurosurgeon. It was the driving force behind his ambition to deal with his abusive father. And when he met Marielle that Christmas all those years ago, it was the very thing he recognized in her.

He's often wondered over the years if not wanting a child was altruistic: to save the world from another sociopath. Or purely because he hadn't wanted to share Marielle with anyone else.

Marielle glares at him, flicking the syringe pointedly.

'What's that for? The last injection will be wearing off and she's not going to be able to answer any questions if she's drugged up, is she?'

'It's a deterrent, Henry. Follow me.'

This is useless, he wants to shout at her. But he follows her obediently up the stairs. He should never have allowed this charade to go on for as long as it has.

Lena won't give Marielle the answers she so desperately seeks, because the only people who know what he did are Hugh Warrington and Simone Harvey. And they're both dead.

He made sure of that.

57

LENA

I can hear footsteps on the stairs. I drag myself back across the floor, careful to avoid the protruding nail, and, with great effort, climb onto the bed, exhausted. It's useless. There's nowhere to hide and nothing in this room to use as a weapon. I'm totally at their mercy, trapped. I watch, frozen in horror, as I hear the sound of the key in the lock. The door swings open to reveal Marielle. She steps into the room and I can see she's brandishing a syringe. Henry is following close behind and it occurs to me that I wouldn't just have to overpower one of them but both. And even when I've not been drugged with something, that would be impossible.

'Why are you doing this?' I manage to say, annoyed that my voice sounds so weak and pathetic.

Marielle perches on the edge of my bed with the needle in her hand. Her face is devoid of compassion. It sends a sliver of fear through me.

'Do you really have no idea?' she asks. 'You don't remember what you did?'

I stare at her, confused. 'No.'

'I gave birth to a baby boy in your hospital. Hugh Warrington was the doctor who delivered my son. There was a midwife there too. Simone Harvey. Do you remember?'

'Yes, I remember them both, but I – I was only there for six weeks . . .' I try to picture her and Henry coming into the hospital, but I can't. I can only recall a handful of occasions when I was in the delivery room with Hugh and Simone – Natalie Grant's birth was the last.

She glances at Henry, who is guarding the door, then back at me.

'Hugh Warrington said my baby died. And I believed him. I was an older mother, there were a few complications. But a few years ago I read that in 1999 he went to prison for prescription fraud, among other things, and it confirmed what I already knew to be true in here.' She thumps her chest above her heart. 'He was a crook. A chancer. I don't know how he managed it, but he took my baby. He took my baby and sold him and I began collecting every article I could find about him and that horrible, seedy hospital where you worked. So many things came to light after it closed down. So many terrible, terrible things.'

She's totally delusional. Hugh and Simone might have been involved in many underhand, illegal activities but, as far as I knew, an adoption racket wasn't one of them. 'I'm sorry, Marielle, I really am, but I don't know anything about this.'

Her face contorts with rage. 'Don't lie to me. Simone told me that you knew all about what happened to my baby.'

My heart twists as the horror of what she's saying hits me. 'That's not true. Simone lied to you.'

'She couldn't help me, but you can. What did they do with my baby?'

Tears of panic and fear roll down my cheeks. She's obviously killed Simone and now she's going to kill me too. I have no clue what she's talking about. 'I promise you, Marielle, I know nothing about any of this.'

'Why would Simone tell me you were involved if it wasn't true?'

'Because she's a liar?' I cry. 'I don't know!'

'He was born on the twenty-first of February 1999,' she says, as though I haven't spoken. My heart sinks. That was a few days before I left St Calvert's and just a week after Natalie Grant died. I'd been so disillusioned by then and had had a blazing row with Simone outside my shared house in Walthamstow when I confronted her. She denied everything and told me that nobody would believe me anyway. The last image I have of her is her stalking off into the winter's night, in her burgundy fake-fur coat and her Dr Martens and I'd slumped against the wall, shaking from the confrontation. I'd made up my mind there and then to leave my course.

'That was my last week,' I say to Marielle. 'I know I definitely didn't help with your birth. Do you think you remember me or are you just taking Simone's word that I was there?'

The confusion in her face tells me everything. Simone made it up. Was throwing my name into the ring her revenge for my having confronted her? For being the first to suspect her? Or just a last-ditch attempt to save her own skin?

She sighs deeply. 'After I'd realized what sort of man Hugh was, it didn't take me long to find Simone. Her face is in here.' She taps the side of her head. 'I never forget a face. It took me a while to track her down but I found that article in the local paper when we were living in Salisbury last year. What are the chances that I'd end up living in the same place as her? Fate, that's what. And then, after her, it was easy to find you, thanks to Simone's information. She knew you'd married an ex-rock star. She must have been keeping tabs on you. Lena isn't a common name, even if you were no longer Bull but Fletcher. I had to bide my time, of course, work out how to play it. But Fate intervened again when the house next door to yours went up for sale. It was easy to keep an eye on you, being so close. I tried to get you talking, Lena, do you remember? I asked about your dreams, your hopes, but you never admitted to me that you used to be a mid-wife. Why was that?' She says all this calmly, which is even more chilling.

'Because I wasn't a midwife,' I mutter. 'I never completed my course. I left. Because of what Hugh and Simone were doing and the guilt I felt at not reporting it.'

'Their adoption racket?'

'What? No. The drugs. Please, Marielle. Let me go. I don't know anything about any illegal adoption. I promise. I have a son —'

'So did I!' screams Marielle, making me shrink back in terror.

Marielle closes her eyes and breathes in through her nose. She tucks her hair behind her ears. In the half-light, and from my position on the bed, she looks terrifying: gone is the poised, well-groomed woman I've known over the last few weeks and in her place is this banshee, with wild hair and raging eyes.

'Do you know what we did to get Simone to talk?' Her eyes snap open. She's calmer again now. 'I pretended to be a nurse. At first she thought she was in hospital. Until she learnt the truth, of course. I drugged her food, made her too weak to try to escape and started probing her for answers. I left little clues around the room, hoping she'd realize why she was there. A rabbit I'd bought for the baby and taken to the hospital in a maternity bag. But she didn't, of course, because she was as dense as you. I called my baby Peter. Did you know that? Peter.'

I remember her telling me she had a son called Peter.

'Marielle,' I sob, 'I'm so sorry you lost a son. I'm so sorry, but I promise I don't know anything about it.'

Henry comes up behind his wife and places a hand on her shoulder. 'Mari . . .'

And then I notice it. Uncertainty in his eyes. He doesn't want to do this. His resolve is weak. This has all been led by her. I've got it all so wrong. I thought he was bullying Marielle.

I remember his threats in the street. His insistence that I leave them alone. No wonder he was so angry when Drew confronted him about his sister. He must have met up with Drew in the park to try to placate him, and when Drew confronted him about his car Henry became angry and acted guilty because he *was* guilty. Not of doing anything to Sarah-Jane, but to someone else's sister.

She shrugs him off. 'Don't, Henry . . .'
And then they freeze.
Someone is banging loudly on their front door.

58

HENRY

February 1999
London

Henry had first met Hugh Warrington at medical school, and even though they were never great friends (Henry wasn't one for friends) they ending up sharing student digs together. Hugh was a narcissist: that was obvious to Henry early on. He wanted to play God. And Henry was good at dealing with narcissists, thanks to his father. He recognized parts of himself in Hugh. The morally grey parts. Like attracts like. After medical school they lost touch until, a year or so after Henry and Marielle married, she persuaded him to join some pretentious males-only members' club that her dad went to. Hugh was also a member and they reconnected.

Hugh liked a drink and he liked to brag, and it wasn't long before he admitted to Henry what he was up to at St Calvert's. Henry sometimes wondered if perhaps he gave off a kind of immoral aura, like a dark-hearted priest, because of the number of people who had confessed things to him over the years.

One night, while drinking at their club, Henry admitted to Hugh about Marielle wanting to try fertility treatment. Hugh had agreed to persuade her that it wouldn't work for them and she had believed him. And then she had fallen pregnant naturally.

It had been a shock and Henry had hoped it was a phantom pregnancy. But, no, their doctor had told them this could happen when a couple stopped trying. As the weeks went on and Marielle's belly continued to grow, Henry knew he was running out of options.

So, he went to Hugh with a plan and Hugh had agreed to help, for a large sum.

A few days before Marielle's due date Henry would give Marielle a solution of misoprostol to drink to induce her. Hopefully it should work within twenty-four hours and Hugh would book the day off so he could deliver the baby, but unofficially, so there would be no record of it. 'We can take her to the new natural birthing unit that is nearly finished,' he told Henry. 'The builders have always clocked off by three so we won't be seen. It's in a separate building to St Calvert's because,' he'd rolled his eyes, 'it's supposed to make the woman feel like she's giving birth at home. Anyway, some of the suites are already finished so we can use one of those. I'll have it ready. I've got a midwife who will be in on it with me. Someone I trust. She'll keep Marielle sedated until it's all done.'

Simone Harvey. He hadn't forgotten her name. A pretty little thing who had judged him, he was sure of it, when she ushered them into the unit that night. Marielle was a little bemused that they were going to St Calvert's instead of the fancy private maternity hospital she'd been booked in to but she was in so much pain, screaming at him that she'd made a huge mistake in getting pregnant, and didn't argue.

It had all worked so well. Hugh said he knew a couple who couldn't conceive and were desperate for a baby. As he whisked their little boy away from under an exhausted Marielle's nose, Henry left Hugh to organize the fake death certificate and pretend ashes he could give to Marielle.

Henry had continued to sedate Marielle at home, for weeks afterwards, in a bid to stop her asking too many questions. He pretended they'd had a small memorial for the baby, just the two of them, which she must have forgotten about, and they scattered the 'ashes' in Richmond Park, her favourite place. By this time her father had moved abroad with his new wife, and she was more or less estranged from her sister so there was nobody to involve.

The whole thing had cost him a lot of money. But it had been worth it. He was safe in the knowledge that his son was growing up somewhere with parents who would give him the emotional strength that he and Marielle never could.

He could never have predicted that twenty years later Hugh Warrington would rear his smarmy head again and derail his perfectly orchestrated life.

59

LENA

Someone knocks again, more insistent this time.

'Get rid of them, Henry,' Marielle barks, twisting around to face him.

If only I could knock the syringe out of her hand. I could scream, and then the person at the door might hear, even if I am three floors up.

'You go,' he says, in a low voice. He indicates me with a tilt of his head. 'She could overpower you.'

Marielle glances at me and grimaces. Then, wordlessly, she stands up, hands Henry the syringe and leaves the room, closing the door behind her.

My heart is beating so fast I feel dizzy. I take a few deep breaths, trying to calm myself. Henry stands awkwardly by the bed and I think how right I was about them all along.

He turns to me. 'I am sorry about all this,' he says, and the way he says it is almost comical, like he's apologizing for opening my post by mistake. 'I did try to make you stay away. I thought Marielle might change her mind, realize it was useless and that you knew nothing.'

'What . . .' I gulp '. . . what did you do to Simone? Did you kill her?'

He glares at me, his eyes hard. 'Marielle didn't mean to. She just wanted answers and to keep Simone sedated so she wouldn't run. She might have been pretending to be a nurse, but she isn't one. She gave her too much.'

'Too much?'

He holds up the syringe. Pins and needles begin at my feet and travel up my whole body. I dread to think what concoction he's got in that syringe. He's a doctor. He'll know just what to put in it to kill me.

'I'm afraid my wife is mentally ill. It's very sad, but we did lose a baby and she wants to find someone to blame. She needs to find a reason for it, do you see? She has never come to terms with the fact he was, sadly, stillborn. She believes that her baby was taken from her.' He shakes his head sorrowfully but, to me, his emotions aren't authentic. A wooden actor in a play. 'When she read about Hugh Warrington's death in the paper last year she remembered he had delivered our baby, and when she read about all the illegal activities he was involved in she began to suspect he'd taken our son.'

'But that's . . . Hugh wouldn't do that . . .' I trail off. I have no idea if that's even true. I hardly knew Hugh Warrington, but I do know he was morally corrupt.

'I know that,' he replies, crisply. 'As I've said, my wife is not of sound mind. I'm very sorry about all this, Lena.'

I need to divide and conquer. Henry knows this is madness. 'Please help me. I won't tell anyone about this.'

He arranges his features into a neutral expression, his

eyes on me again. 'You misunderstand me, Lena,' he replies coolly. 'I'm sorry you're in this situation, but I can't save you. I have to let Marielle take you. And then, hopefully, that will be the end of it.'

'What? You're just going to let her kill me like she did Simone? Why would she do that if she wants answers about her son?'

'Because it's obvious you have no answers,' he says. 'I just want this to be over. I tried to keep you away, Lena. I tried.' His words chill me. He's so cold. So pragmatic. How can he let this happen? Doesn't he have a conscience? He stands up, his hand with the syringe now at his side. 'I need to see what's taking her so long.'

'Was it you in my garden that night?' I ask, as he goes to the door.

He turns to look at me over his shoulder. 'I saw you'd recorded us. I couldn't be certain how much you'd over-heard. I wanted to get my hands on that equipment.' He leaves the room and I hear the key in the lock.

This is my only chance. They're both as psychotic as each other and I don't doubt for one moment that they will kill me. My eye goes to the nail in the floorboards. It's the only thing I can think of. I scrabble from the bed, go to it and try frantically to prise it from the wood, but it's old, rusty and won't budge. 'Come on, come on,' I mutter. I need to act fast, before they come back. It takes all my force to pull it out and when I do I fall back on my heels, the nail in my hand. It's big and sharp. I rack my brains, trying to remember the class about human anatomy when I was a student nurse. The jugular. Piercing that with the end of this nail will do the most damage. I fold it in my hand and get back onto the bed. I feel as if I might vomit but I have no choice. It's either me or them.

I wait, poised on the bed with the nail in my hand. Where are they? They're taking a while to get rid of whoever is at their front door. Could the person be in the house? Maybe it's worth me banging and screaming. I get up and go to the door, pressing my ear to it. I can hear the low mumble of voices coming from somewhere in the bowels of the house.

I muster all my energy to bang my fists against the door. 'HELP ME!' I yell. 'HELP! I'M UP HERE! HELP!' I keep banging and yelling. Finally I hear footsteps on the stairs and the key in the lock. I step back. Marielle's furious face appears in the doorway.

'I should fucking kill you now,' she hisses. She shoves me further into the room and closes the door behind her. 'It was just old Mr Cannick from number seventy-two wanting to borrow something from Henry, so don't get excited you're about to be saved, because he's gone.'

My heart falls. I can feel the nail digging into the palm of my hand, but I hide it in the folds of my dress.

'Get back on the bed.'

I do as she asks.

Henry bursts into the room looking hot and bothered. He wipes a hand across his brow. I notice he doesn't have the syringe.

Marielle notices too. 'Henry!'

He looks down at his empty hands. 'Right. Yes, sorry. I'll be back.' He disappears out through the door again.

Marielle starts pacing the room, agitated.

'Marielle . . . please. I really don't know anything about your son. I –'

'Shut up!' In one swift movement Marielle lunges at me and grabs me around the throat. 'Don't lie to me, you little witch. Now, for the last time, tell me where my son is.'

She's never going to accept it. Henry's right. She squeezes my windpipe harder and I struggle to breathe. I need to strike now. I bring the hand up that is still clutching the nail and drive it into the side of her neck. She screams and clamps her hand around the nail as blood spurts out. I've missed her jugular but at least I've managed to stop her. She stumbles backwards, the nail poking out of her skin, and I take the opportunity to leap from the bed. The room spins: the drugs aren't yet out of my system, but I make a run for it, slamming the door behind me. The key is still in the door and I quickly turn it, locking Marielle in.

A burst of adrenaline overrides the woozy effects of the injection. Carefully, I lean over the banister. I'm surprised by how dark it is now. I must have been in the attic for hours. I can't see Henry. I tiptoe down the first flight of stairs. I don't have long. Henry might have heard the commotion. I flatten myself against the wall, listening for him. I'm scared he'll hear my hammering heart as I make my way across the landing.

And then I hear his foot on the stairs.

I dart into the nursery, trying to decide on the best way of getting out of the house. Henry is now coming up the stairs. I can just about make out his bare calves and his shoes that squeak when he walks. He's whistling to himself as he passes the nursery door. He has the syringe in his hand, holding it aloft. He's come to kill me and he's whistling. The knowledge makes my insides turn to ice.

I wait, holding my breath. My heart is thumping so much I can feel it reverberating through my whole body, like tiny electric pulses. He's going up the next staircase now. I take a deep breath and count silently. One, two . . .

My hands are tingling with panic. I've got one chance to get this right.

Three . . .

And then I run.

60

HENRY

July 2023

Henry killed Hugh Warrington on 16 July 2023. It was a Sunday.

He'd had no choice. Marielle was getting suspicious, and he had to act quickly to stop her finding out everything.

Five years earlier he'd received a phone call from Hugh out of the blue. He hadn't heard from him since he was sent to prison back in 1999 for prescription fraud and stealing drugs from St Calvert's to sell.

'I've tried to make ends meet,' Hugh had said, sounding decades older since they'd last spoken. 'But it's difficult now I'm no longer able to work as a doctor. I need cash, Henry. And I know you have plenty of that. I've been following your career from afar. I know your lovely wife would never understand what you've done, but I can be paid to keep quiet. For the right amount.'

Henry had agreed to pay him a monthly sum. Thankfully, he dealt with all the outgoings, so Marielle never saw monies going out to H. E. Warrington every four weeks.

And then Hugh started getting greedy, demanding more and more. Once, he had travelled over a hundred miles from his place in Nottingham to where Henry was living in Reading, after Henry stopped answering his calls. Henry had been furious. Marielle knew Hugh was the doctor who had delivered their baby, and if she'd recognized him she would have bombarded him with questions about the birth. Henry had managed to keep her away from the court case all those years ago by moving them to a remote village in Scotland and shielding her from the news. Marielle had been so grief-stricken that she hadn't put up much of a fight or taken an interest in the world around her.

But it hadn't ended there. Of course it hadn't. Blackmailers never stopped. They kept on and on and on until their victim snapped. And Henry believed he was a victim in all of this, he really did. Hugh didn't have as much to lose as Henry if the police became involved. After all, Hugh had already lost his career, thanks to his drugs conviction, and his marriage had ended. Henry couldn't risk Marielle ever finding out what he'd done.

It all came to a head when Marielle saw Hugh lurking in their street.

Marielle never forgot a face, even if that face was jowly and twenty years older.

She began questioning Henry, asking to speak to Hugh, telling him how much of a fog it had been after losing Peter. 'He might be able to give us answers, Henry. I didn't know you were still in touch with him.' When he put her off, she started her own investigations, trying to find his address.

Henry knew he had to act fast. He couldn't risk Marielle finding Hugh.

He planned it carefully. He drove to Nottingham late one night on the pretence that he wanted to talk to Hugh about the money situation. He got his old adversary drunk and injected him with a lethal dose of fentanyl. Hugh died slumped in his armchair. Not a bad death, Henry reasoned, as he arranged the scene to make it look self-inflicted.

They moved again. This time to Salisbury. Marielle had decided to retire by then and was happy to move somewhere more rural.

He really hoped that would be the end of it.

Until Marielle found that photograph in the local newspaper of Simone Harvey.

61

LENA

I run as fast as I can along the landing, almost tripping over my feet in my hurry to get away. I hear Henry shout something. I take the stairs two at a time. I can hear Henry's footsteps behind me, sense him making a grab for me. If he gets close enough to inject me, that's it. Game over. I jump down the remainder of the stairs and hit the tiles hard. I wince with pain, but I get up and grapple with the front door, just as Henry is behind me. I'm all fingers and thumbs. Why won't it open?

He reaches out, his fingernails sharp against my bare shoulder and I scream.

I pull at the door with all my strength, relieved when it opens and I collide with someone. A man who is blocking my escape. Oh, God.

'What's going on?'

I look up into the man's face. It's Kit, Rufus's guitar teacher. What is he doing here? I remember the newspaper article he stole from their house.

He glances past me to Henry and then back to me again, his features contorted in confusion.

'Kit. Thank God. You have to help me, please,' I gasp.

'It's okay, it's okay, Lena,' he says, putting an arm protectively around my shoulders. 'What are you doing to her?' he demands, glaring at Henry, who is hiding the syringe behind his back. 'What the hell is going on here?'

I sag against Kit in relief. He backs out of the door, his arm still around me, guiding me to safety.

'I can explain,' begins Henry.

'I'm taking her home,' says Kit, and I'm impressed by his authoritarian tone.

I throw the key to Henry, where it clatters onto the tiles at his feet. 'Your wife is locked in the attic. She might need medical attention, but then, you are a doctor.'

Henry just stands there, gawping at us. Kit closes the door on him and leads me down the path towards my house. 'Are you okay? What just happened? Shall I call the police?'

'I just want to go home.' My whole body is trembling and I have to hand Kit my front-door key so he can let us in. 'Thank God you showed up. Kit, they're fucking psychos, both of them.'

'What did they do?' he asks, as he helps me into the kitchen and onto a chair before fetching me a glass of water.

I put my hand to my head. I feel shivery, like I've caught the flu. 'They . . . oh God, where to start?'

'I'm going to call Charlie.'

'No! It's okay, I . . .'

But he's firm and before I can stop him he's got out his mobile and is dialling my ex-husband's number, asking him to come over urgently. When he ends the call he flashes me a concerned look. 'You can't be on your own, Lena. I don't know what's going on with the people next door, but you look as white as a ghost and you're shaking. You're obviously in shock.'

I sip my water, my mind swimming.

He takes a seat next to me. 'What happened?' he probes gently.

I want to ask him about the article and why he went to the Morgans', but I dismiss it for now. I can ask him about that later.

'Oh, God, Kit. It's so much worse than I even thought.' I recount everything that happened and his eyes get bigger and rounder as my story progresses. 'And then I managed to escape by sticking the nail into the side of Marielle's neck and locking her in the attic. Henry would have jabbed me with God knows what if you hadn't shown up. You saved my life, Kit. I can't thank you enough.'

Ten minutes later Charlie arrives with Rufus. We're all in my living room and someone, I'm assuming Kit, has draped a throw over my shoulders. I can't stop trembling even though I'm trying to play it down in front of Rufus, who is wide-eyed with terror.

'It's the shock,' says Charlie, handing me a can of Coke from the fridge. 'Drink this. The sugar will be good.' Rufus is sitting so close to me he's almost on my lap, reminding me of when he was little and nervous if we were somewhere unfamiliar.

Kit is hovering by the window. He keeps glancing down the street. 'I'm going around there,' he says, turning to us with a look of determination. 'I'll call the police and make sure they don't abscond or anything. Henry's Jag is still outside.'

'It's my word against theirs,' I say, my teeth chattering. 'Marielle is the one with the wound. They'll blame me.'

'I'll make sure to tell the police what I witnessed, don't worry,' Kit assures me, but I notice something like doubt pass across his face. Does he believe me? He saw how scared I was.

'Thanks, Kit,' says Charlie. And then he turns to me. 'Do you mind if I stay here tonight? I don't want to leave you on your own.'

'I can look after her,' says Rufus, putting his arm protectively around me.

'I know, son,' says Charlie, 'but I'd like to be here too, if that's okay.'

I'm not sure how I feel about that after finding footage of Charlie sneaking around my garden late at night. But I don't want to say anything in front of Rufus.

'Of course.'

Kit walks towards the living-room door. 'Right, I'm going to call the police. It will be fine, Lena. But before I go there's something you should know.' He looks down at his hands. 'The reason I was at their door in the first place.' His expression is hard to read in the glow of the corner lamp. He reaches into his pocket and pulls out a newspaper cutting, which he passes to me. Rufus must have given it back to him. 'The baby . . . it's me.'

I stare at him as I try to reconcile this strapping lad with the tiny newborn Simone had found on those hospital steps all those years ago. Of course. Why hadn't I realized? Why else would he have been so interested in that newspaper story?

Rufus doesn't look surprised – Kit must already have told him. Charlie just appears confused, and I hand him the cutting so he can read it for himself.

'So you were the one in the Morgans' house that night?' I ask.

He looks shocked. 'Which night?'

'Last Friday. I was there too, and I saw someone rooting around.'

He flushes with guilt but doesn't ask why I was there. I suspect it was Kit who stole Joan's key from my kitchen drawer a few days later, then discovered they'd changed the locks. 'Yep. I didn't mean any harm. I was just trying to find out what I could about them. I already knew I was adopted and found on the steps of St Calvert's Hospital. When my adoptive mother died I decided to look into it and that was when I discovered through my records that I was abandoned and found by a midwife, Simone Harvey.'

I remember what Oliver had told me about a call from a 'journalist'. 'Did you contact her brother, Oliver?'

'I did. I've been searching for my real parents for over a year, and I've discovered . . . well, I've discovered a lot.' He glances from Charlie to Rufus. 'I'm sorry I used you guys to find out more from Lena.'

'What? Why?' Charlie looks up in surprise.

Rufus doesn't say anything but moves even closer to me.

'It's almost impossible to find out about your real parents when you've been abandoned,' Kit says, in a small voice. I glance at him with his floppy hair, and I can see the lost little boy who lurks beneath this handsome young man. 'After a lot of digging I found someone who showed me old hospital records from the time I was found. Simone's name was there, of course, because she'd been the one to find me, but also your name came up, Lena.'

'Because I was with Simone when she reported the abandoned baby.'

He nods. 'They'd recorded your name too. When I couldn't find Simone I found you, hoping you'd know something about my parents. I befriended Charlie and Rufus, hoping to get close enough to confide in you and ask you questions. It was a long shot. I certainly didn't expect you to lead me right to them.'

I remember the Barnardo's sticker on his guitar case.

It all clicks into place. The date: 22 February 1999. That was the day after Marielle said she'd given birth to her baby. She had been right. Her baby never died. But who faked the baby's death? Simone? Hugh? Simone must have pretended to find him on the steps of the hospital after she and Hugh had taken him from Marielle. He hadn't been abandoned, but stolen.

'And . . . your birth parents?'

He throws me a knowing look. 'You've already guessed, haven't you?'

62

'Why don't you go up to bed, love?' I say to Rufus. 'I'll be okay here with Dad.'

Kit has gone next door to keep an eye on the Morgans, calling the police on the way over. I suspect he also wants to tell Marielle and Henry the truth about who he is. I wonder how much he knows about the circumstances of his birth and hope he isn't in for a nasty shock.

Rufus kisses my cheek and leaves the room. I sip my Coke, feeling on the edge of tears. Charlie gets up from the chair and takes the seat next to me, made warm by Rufus.

'I'm so relieved you're okay,' he says, his face pinched with worry. 'The police should be here soon. You should be checked over by a hospital. They did drug you.' I just want to be at home. I lean forwards to place my can on the table. When I sit back Charlie takes my hand. 'God, Lena, you could have died. Those people. I can't believe it.'

'Marielle killed Simone.' I gulp. 'Henry was so adamant that the baby was stillborn, but how do you make a mistake like that? He must have been in on it. I just don't understand why Henry would do something so horrific.'

'Let the police deal with it now. I'm just thankful you're safe.'

I snatch my hand away from Charlie, suddenly angry. 'What were you doing in my garden last night? Why were you sneaking around?'

He turns away from me and looks down into his lap. He had just finished a gig when he received the call from Kit, and he smells of dry ice and fresh sweat, but it's not unpleasant. I miss the smell of him. He looks up at me, his face earnest. 'I'm sorry . . . it was stupid. But I – I wanted to see if you were with anyone.'

'With anyone? I don't understand.'

'With another man?'

I laugh in disbelief. 'What? You're the one in a new relationship, not me.'

'What about that guy?'

'What guy? Do you mean Drew? Oh, my God, Charlie. Drew is . . . was a client. He's a nice guy, but he's just a friend, if that.'

He shrugs. 'Well, I don't know.' In the half-light his eyes look dark and sad. 'You were the one who ended our marriage.'

I stare at him in shock. 'Not because I'd met someone else but because I felt I was dealing with everything on my own. That you'd checked out emotionally. The whole thing with Rufus being bullied –'

'He was never being bullied.'

'See?' I cry. 'You've always got your head in the sand and –'

He takes my hand again. 'Rufus was never being bullied,' he repeats, softer this time, his eyes not leaving mine. 'I'm going to be blunt. Rufus was struggling with his sexuality and his feelings for Jackson.'

'What? But . . . No. That's not what was going on. How do you know this?'

He exhales deeply. 'Because Rufus told me.'

It's like a blade to the heart. 'What? Why didn't he tell me?'

'He was going to tell you, but then you got it into your head he was being bullied and he went along with it rather than admit the truth. Then you went marching over to this boy's mother, accusing her son of all sorts, and, well, he was mortified.'

Shame inches its way up my body and I throw off the blanket, suddenly hot. 'I didn't listen . . .'

'You went all mama bear, which is what you do, and I don't mean that as a criticism.' He squeezes my hand. 'But then Rufus was too embarrassed to tell you the truth.'

I groan. 'He did try to tell me a few times. But I was so obsessed with the Morgans that I didn't listen.'

'Well, you were right to be obsessed with them, as it happens.'

'But my instincts weren't right about Rufus.'

'You can't be right about everything.' His eyes twinkle. 'And I'm no longer with Rosie. That was a stupid rebound thing. It was never serious. I . . . well, I . . .' His cheeks colour. 'I ended things with her because I still love you.'

I stare at him in surprise. Then I take my hand from his and touch his cheek. 'I still love you too, Charlie. I always will. But . . . I'm not sure we're right together any more. I don't think we bring out the best in one another.'

He sighs. 'I know. I'm just having trouble letting go, that's all.'

'Charlie . . .' I hesitate, removing my hand from his face. 'This was never about another man. You do believe that, don't you?'

'I do. And for what it's worth, I'm sorry.'

'For what?'

'For not being what you wanted me to be, in the end.'

'You're a good man,' I say, my voice catching. 'This is just one of those things.'

He throws me a self-conscious grin. 'I know that, deep down. I'll probably write a song about it.' He winks at me and I can't help but laugh.

He pulls me into his arms, and we stay like that, clinging to each other as though we never want to let go, even though we know we have to.

63

The living room is dimly lit and my head rests on Charlie's shoulder as we sit on the sofa waiting for the police to arrive. It's finally started to rain and the blissful scent of petrichor drifts in through the open window. We listen in silence to the drumming on the bonnets of cars and splashing over roof tiles.

Eventually I lift my head from Charlie's shoulder. 'Do you think Kit's okay? It's been over an hour.'

'That's what I was wondering too,' says Charlie, standing up and going to the window. 'I can't see any police, but a car is parked outside the Morgans' that wasn't there earlier.' He moves closer to the glass. 'A black saloon. Maybe it's an unmarked police car.'

'I hope they haven't done anything to Kit . . .'

'They won't hurt him if he tells them he's their son,' Charlie says. 'The police could be in there now, questioning them.' He returns to his seat next to me on the sofa. 'They'll be here soon.'

'I'm so tired,' I say, my eyes drooping.

'Maybe we should go to the hospital . . .' I can hear the concern in his voice, but I assure him I'm fine. I pull the throw back over me and snuggle down in the crevices of the sofa, my feet on Charlie's lap. I must drop off because the next thing I know I wake with a jolt when I hear the bang of a car door. Have more police arrived? I reach over and shake Charlie, who has also fallen asleep and is snoring gently, his chin to his chest.

'Wha . . . what's going on?' His eyes ping open. 'Is everything okay?'

'I don't know.' I rush over to the window. The black saloon is gone. I glance at the clock. It's nearly 1 a.m. Kit left to go to the Morgans at eleven. Why haven't the police called to talk to me? Have they just left?

Charlie reaches for his mobile. 'I'm calling Kit,' he says, phone pressed to his ear.

I perch on the arm of the chair with a sense of dread.

'He's not picking up. It's just ringing out.' Charlie frowns as he ends the call. 'I'm going to call the police myself, find out what's going on. No, don't get up. I'll do it.' He wanders out of the room and I follow him into the kitchen. I don't want to be on my own, even for a minute. I just hope the Morgans have been arrested and are in a prison cell right now.

'Fuck it,' Charlie says, placing his mobile on the worktop and turning to me. 'The police know nothing about it. Why didn't Kit report them?'

'What if something's happened to him? He might not have had the chance to call the police.'

'But we saw him on the phone as he walked over to their house.' He scratches his stubble. 'He must have been pretending. Why the fuck didn't he report them? Out of some sense of duty because they're his parents?'

My heart plunges. 'Maybe. I don't know.'

'I should go over there and see –'

'No way!' I cut him off. 'Leave it to the police, Charlie.'

'They'll be here soon,' he reassures me. 'And then they can throw the book at both of them.'

'What book?' And we both snigger because it was something we always said to each other when we heard cops using it on TV police dramas. And then we sober up as the reality of the situation hits us again.

We have no choice but to wait. I make a cup of tea. Rufus comes down the stairs, claiming he can't sleep, and sits with us at the kitchen table. Charlie goes through to the living room to close the windows: the rain is heavier.

'Dad's told you about Jackson, hasn't he?' Rufus pipes up, and I wonder if that's another reason why he can't get to sleep.

I nod and reach for his hand. 'I wish you'd told me.'

'I wanted to.'

'I know, and I'm sorry I didn't listen. So . . . you and Jackson? Are you an item?'

'An item?' He laughs, and it's such a lovely sight.

'Sorry, it's what Nanny Pat always says.' I grin, referring to Charlie's mum.

Rufus swallows, then blushes. 'I don't know. It's complicated.'

'Well, if you ever want to talk about it . . .'

'Thanks. But, Mum, I do think you should apologize to Jackson's mum. Some of his friends found out and made my life a bit hellish for a while, and Jackson and I did have a fight about it because everyone was poking their noses in so I went along with the bullying story. I was glad to leave school and not go on to sixth form there, but Jackson was never mean. You saw the bruises and jumped to conclusions.'

I squirm when I think of how rude I was to Collette about her son. 'Of course,' I say. 'And I really am sorry. So, Freddie? He's just a friend?'

He pulls a face. 'God, yeah. Of course. He has a girl-friend.'

'Right. Okay.'

Charlie rushes back into the kitchen. 'Two police cars have pulled up outside,' he says, and anxiety makes my heart race. I glance at Rufus and we all troop back into the living room. Charlie pulls aside the curtains to look out. 'I think they've kicked the door down,' he whispers. He turns away from the window to look at us, then says to Rufus, 'Do you think you should go to bed?'

'No way!' he exclaims. 'I hope Kit's okay.'

'We should have insisted we called the police,' I say, 'and not left it to Kit.'

The doorbell rings and we all jump. 'I'll get it,' insists Charlie. 'Stay here.'

I hear him go into the hallway and open the door, then the murmur of voices and footsteps before he returns with two detectives. A man and a woman. They are both wearing matching grave expressions.

'Elena Fletcher?' asks the woman officer. When I nod, she continues, 'We need to take a statement from you about what happened tonight. This is now a murder inquiry.'

I jolt in shock, my chest tightening. 'Murder? Who – who's been murdered?' Surely they wouldn't have hurt Kit, their own son.

Her eyes narrow. 'Henry Morgan. Your neighbour.'

64

LENA

Four months later

Henry Morgan died from a stab wound to the chest. A massive police hunt is still under way but, as yet, Marielle hasn't been found. And neither has Kit. It was like he disappeared into thin air. Nobody knows what happened to him after he left our house. I had to give a statement explaining everything, and for a while I was worried the police would think I had killed Henry. After all, the only witness to me running away from Henry that day was Kit. But, thankfully, Kit and Marielle's fingerprints were found on the knife and the fact she's gone on the run makes her the number-one suspect. Kit remains a person of interest.

Simone Harvey's body was found two weeks later after police searched their house and found a key to a lock-up in Wiltshire. Her body had been kept in a freezer. Oliver rang to tell me and I'd surprised myself by crying. I'll never forgive her for trying to pass the buck to me, putting my life in danger. Yet after my kidnapping experience I can well imagine the terror she must have felt, being a prisoner in their home, knowing she was about to die.

I often think about Kit and wonder if he's okay. Did he help Marielle escape or did she hurt him too? I have to accept there are things I'll never get to the bottom of. I remember how Henry had tried to convince me that Marielle was mad for believing her child was still alive when all the time he knew the truth. I still don't understand how he could have done that to his own wife. His own baby. Although I'm less surprised that Hugh and Simone were involved: it's become obvious they would have done anything for money. Now I understand why Kit was so instantly familiar when I met him. He reminded me of Henry.

Charlie and I have agreed to sell the house when Rufus goes to university next year. With my share I'll have enough money for a flat nearby with a spare bedroom for Rufus when he's back from uni. I have decided I would like to go back to training as a midwife. I should never have left because of Hugh and Simone. Before I became disillusioned I'd thrived on it and, I believe, I was good at it.

Charlie and I are still trying to figure out the rules of our new-found friendship. It will take a while to adjust from being romantically involved to platonic, but we still care about each other and want to be there for Rufus. I no longer feel so afraid of the future and have accepted that things will change when he leaves for university next year, but it will be a new and, hopefully, exciting chapter in my life too. There is so much to look forward to, now that I have escaped the shackles of my past.

I sometimes see Drew. We've been out for dinner a couple of times and have grown closer, as friends for the moment, although he's made it obvious he'd like more. I don't know if anything will happen between us but it's nice to have someone to spend time with. Jo has met him and likes him, which is important to me. I'm not ready for a new relationship but I'm happy my social network has grown. I feel less alone and ready to face the future.

I was shocked to discover that the Morgans never owned their home, only rented it from the developers for six months. Today, a Friday, the new neighbours will be moving in. It's my day off, Rufus is at college and I've got some work to catch up with. I left Citizens Advice three months ago and I'm now working four days a week at Jo's chambers, which means we get to meet for lunch more regularly. As much as I enjoy it, I know it's not my vocation and I plan to apply for the midwifery course in January.

It's raining and the mid-morning light is dim. Out of the corner of my eye I see a car pull up and can't help but look up from my laptop. A couple, not much younger than me, stands at the gate of the Morgans' old home. The woman is very attractive with slick dark hair pulled back in a high ponytail. Her partner is tall and blond and they are both holding cardboard boxes. They have a boy with them, around ten or eleven. Maybe tomorrow, when they've had the chance to settle in a bit, I'll go over and introduce myself.

I watch as they carry the boxes down the front path. The woman brings up the rear and she stops, halfway to the door, her eyes going to my window. She sees me and smiles, nodding. I smile and wave back, watching as she goes into the house.

I wonder what their story is.

I turn back to my laptop, smiling to myself. I've got too much going on in my own life to have time to be nosy about the new neighbours.

65

PETER

Peter watches his mother pegging out the washing from inside the lodge. Her auburn hair is hidden beneath a scarf and hat, her cheeks ruddy from the harsh Scottish elements. There is nobody around to see them: they're safe here for the winter at least. She turns to smile at him. Marielle Morgan. His mother. He can't believe he's found her at last. He no longer calls himself Kit. He should never have been given that name in the first place.

He's Peter – Peter Morgan – now.

It wasn't like he had a bad life as Kit Cooper. His adoptive parents were kind, if a little bland. But he'd never felt he fitted in, and he had spent his life wondering what his real parents were like and if, perhaps, he'd taken after them.

He thinks back to that balmy night four months ago.

When he'd turned up at the Morgans' house, Henry was in the kitchen attending to Marielle's neck wound. Their front door had been left slightly ajar, and he wondered if they were getting ready to run away.

'What's going on? Why aren't you leaving?' he'd asked.

'Who are you?' snapped Henry. 'A cop?'

And Kit had laughed. 'No, Dad. I'm the son you abandoned on the steps of the hospital back in 1999.'

Henry just stared at him, his jaw slack with shock. Marielle, who had been watching him intently, stood up, brushing Henry's hand away from her neck. 'Peter?' she'd gasped. 'Oh, my God, it's Peter. Henry, he's come back. I knew it. I knew he wasn't dead. He's got your eyes, Henry.' She stood before Kit, reaching up to touch his face. She looked wild with her unruly hair and the large padded plaster on the side of her neck.

'How . . . how did you know?' Henry asked as he joined Marielle. Kit could hear the doubt in his voice.

'Look at him, Henry,' she marvelled. 'He's the spitting image of you when you were younger.'

Kit cleared his throat, trying to remember his prepared speech. He'd imagined this moment for a long time but had never thought it would happen, that he would find them. He had Lena to thank for that. 'My adoptive parents had always been honest with me about how I was found on the steps of a hospital,' he began. 'Old records from St Calvert's mentioned Simone and Lena. I searched for them both, but Lena was easier to find, thanks to Charlie. I hoped she could give me some answers, but when her son told me she was suspicious of the two of you and she thought you might have kidnapped a woman, well . . .' he shrugged '. . . I was intrigued. I broke in here one night and found the newspaper cutting.' He reached into his jeans pocket and handed it to them. 'Your wall of newspaper articles tells quite the story. I didn't know for certain, of course, but things started to click, especially when I saw you, Henry. I was leaving Lena's house and you were washing your car and I noticed our resemblance. Why would you abandon me?'

Marielle grabbed his hands. 'We never abandoned you, Peter. They said you'd died.'

'Who said?'

'Hugh Warrington and Simone Harvey. That's why . . .' She swallowed, not finishing her sentence. She turned to her husband. 'Didn't they, Henry? Tell him.'

Kit saw a look of defeat in Henry's face and watched as his father slumped onto a chair.

'Henry?' Marielle rounded on him. 'Henry, tell him.'

Henry groaned, head in hands. 'I can't do this any more,' he mumbled through his fingers. 'I'm so tired of it.' He removed his hands from his face, revealing anguished eyes. 'I'm sorry, Mari, I really am. If I had my time again I might not have done it.'

'Done what? You're not making any sense, Henry.'

'It was you, wasn't it?' said Kit. 'You arranged this. Why?'

'I thought . . . Hugh told me they'd found a family for you. I never thought they'd pretend you were abandoned. That wasn't part of the deal.'

The air in the kitchen stilled as his words sank in. Then Kit heard a noise that sent chills down his back. It was coming from Marielle. They both turned to where she stood by the worktop.

'You took the one thing from me I'd always wanted, Henry!' she wailed. 'What kind of man are you?'

'We're the same, my love,' Henry replied, standing up and going to her. 'We're both the same.'

The way he spoke made Kit feel sick.

'No, we're not!' Marielle screamed. 'You're the murderer, Henry. Not me. I know what you did to Hugh. To Simone. I understand it all, now. You let me believe I'd killed her, but it was you, wasn't it? You killed her to stop her telling me the truth about what you did. How much did you pay Hugh Warrington to take our baby and pretend he had died? That's why he was hanging around our house last year, wasn't it? He was blackmailing you. How could you have done such a wicked, wicked thing?'

In one swift movement Marielle grabbed a knife from a wooden block and waved it in front of Henry's face.

'Put down the knife, Mari . . .'

Kit stood, waiting, a tiny thrill at what was unfolding in front of him growing in the pit of his stomach. These, he realized, were his people. For so long he'd felt adrift, directionless, different from everyone in the world because of the kind of thoughts, *desires* he had.

Marielle lowered the knife, but she still gripped it tightly.

'I did it because I loved you,' Henry said eventually. 'And you love me, for all my faults. Because we're the same . . .'

'Will you stop saying that!' she cried. 'We are *not* the same, Henry.'

'We are. I know you killed Violet all those years ago. You're no different from me.'

Kit stared at his mother in shock. She'd killed someone too?

'What are you talking about? Of course I didn't kill Violet. I'm not saying I wasn't glad she died. I hated her, as you know. She was a horrible stepmother to me. But I didn't kill her. She drowned after taking too many pills.'

Kit watched as the colour drained from Henry's face. He could tell that Henry believed her. In that moment he looked as if he had lost everything he ever thought to be true. He stepped closer. 'No, that's . . . but I always thought . . .'

'I'm not a killer, Henry. You are.'

'You helped me kidnap Simone. What did you expect we were going to do with her? Let her go again after you got answers?'

'Well, yes. She'd hardly have gone to the police, would she? She was on the run.'

Henry looked visibly shaken. Marielle was still clutching the knife. 'Mari, darling, I love you so much. Nothing else matters to me but you,' he said softly.

'You took my baby and let me believe he'd died,' she yelled. 'And why? Because you were threatened by how much I would love him?' She reached for Kit's hand and squeezed it. 'I knew you weren't dead,' she whispered to Kit. 'I knew it. I always knew.' Then she turned back to Henry. 'I hate you. I hate you for what you did.'

'Marielle, please . . .'

'You don't know what love is. This, how a mother feels about her child, that's love. And you tried to take it away from me.'

'No, Marielle.'

Henry suddenly lunged at her, knocking the knife out of her hand. The three of them watched as it clattered to the floor. 'You don't mean what you're saying,' Henry cried. 'The love we have trumps everything.'

'No, Henry.'

It happened so quickly. Henry and Kit pounced on the knife at the same time, but Kit was stronger and managed to wrestle it out of his father's hand. The three stood frozen for a few seconds. Kit gripped the knife, not sure what to do next. He glanced at Marielle, his mother, and their eyes locked, understanding passing between them.

Henry must have noticed because the next thing Kit knew, Henry leapt at him, his piercing blue eyes full of hatred, as though he blamed Kit for all of this.

Kit didn't think twice. He plunged the knife into Henry's chest.

Henry's eyes widened, and he stumbled backwards, blood blooming from his wound and seeping through his linen shirt. He crumpled to the floor.

Marielle turned to Kit, her face ashen. 'What have you done, Peter?'

'He would have hurt you, Mum. Didn't you see? He went for the knife. He would have killed you and maybe me as well.'

She softened at the word 'Mum'. She touched his cheek gently. 'You're right. You're right, Peter.'

'We need to go,' he urged. 'I've got a car outside.'

Marielle glanced down at Henry lying comatose on the kitchen floor, blood darkening his shirt, his face unnaturally pale, his eyes closed. Kit doubted his father was dead. If they called an ambulance now they could save him.

Or they could leave him bleeding out on the kitchen floor.

He knew which option he preferred.

He wondered if Marielle would waver. He watched, his breath in his throat, as she knelt beside her husband and stroked the side of his cheek. 'Goodbye, Henry,' she whispered. And then she got to her feet. 'Okay,' she said to Kit, matter-of-factly. 'Let's go.'

It didn't take Kit long to shake off his old, fake identity – the face he had presented to the world to fit in – and become Peter, the son of psychopath Henry Morgan, who had only ever loved one thing, even if that love was warped and twisted and sick. He doesn't know what the future holds, but it doesn't matter because he's with his real family now. Not the too nice but soft adoptive parents to whom he had always felt such a disappointment, a freak because of the darkness that ran through his veins. But he's with his mother, his *real* mother, who understands him, just like she once understood Henry.

And he doesn't have to pretend any more.

ACKNOWLEDGEMENTS

It was so much fun writing this book and getting into the minds of Henry and Marielle Morgan, but Lena in particular is special to me because, even though we are very different (my neighbours will be pleased to know I won't be spying on them!), she and I both faced the prospect of our adult children about to fly the nest. The character of Lena's best friend and voice of reason, Jo, was named after the lovely Jo Robertson, who entered a Facebook competition last year to have a character named after them. Jo is a wonderful blogger who has been so supportive of my books from the very beginning. I hope you like your namesake, Jo.

Getting a book to publication really is a collaborative process and I'm indebted to the amazing team at Penguin Michael Joseph. Thank you so much to my wonderful editor Maxine Hitchcock, who is always so enthusiastic and kind, even when faced with my messy first drafts, who is always there to reassure and brainstorm tricky plot points with me over a cake before lunch, and who has taken my career from strength to strength. Thank you also to Clare Bowron and Stella Newing who also provided invaluable notes and advice. This book is so much better than it would have been thanks to you all. Also to the rest of the amazing team: Ellie Morley, Ellie Hughes, Frankie Banks, Vicky Photiou, Beatrix McIntyre, Deirdre O'Connell, Hannah Padgham, and Katie Corcoran. To Lee Motley for the beautiful and striking book jackets. To the audio team who do such a fantastic job on the audiobooks, and to Hazel Orme for her meticulous copy-edits. I'm so grateful to you all.

A huge thank you also to Juliet Mushens, dream agent and first reader. Thank you so much for helping me with one of the twists in this book and providing such insightful and encouraging feedback. What a journey we've had together since 2013, and I can't thank her enough for taking a chance on me all those years ago. Thank you also to Liza DeBlock, Kiya Evans, Rachel Neely, Catriona Fida, Alba Arnau Prado, Emma Dawson, and the rest of the brilliant team at Mushens Entertainment and to Jenny Bent and Mary Pender in the US.

To my German editor Duygu Maus and publicist Stefanie Leimsner at Penguin Verlag for taking such great care of me and my daughter when we visited for my first book tour in November 2024 and taking us shopping when the airline lost our bags. I had such an amazing week in Germany meeting readers and booksellers at events and spending time with Duygu, Stefanie, Gabi, and the Penguin Verlag team. Thank you all so much.

Also, a huge thanks to my US editor Sarah Stein and the team at Harper, and all at HarperCollins Canada.

To all my lovely friends who have been so supportive over the years and to all the authors who have given their time so generously to read and quote for my books.

To the West Country author crew Gilly Macmillan, Tim Weaver, C L Taylor and Chris Ewan. Thank you for the lunches, laughs, and support.

To the booksellers and librarians for getting my books into readers' hands, and to book bloggers for the reviews and cover reveals.

To my readers who have been on this journey with me and continue to read and recommend my books, for your lovely messages on social media, for your reviews and posts. I still have to pinch myself I get to write full-time and I couldn't do it without you.

To my husband, Ty, for all the brainstorming and listening patiently while I run by another plot twist with you; to my children, Claudia and Isaac, and to my mum, dad, sister, nieces, in-laws and step family.

And last but not least, to my lovely step-mum, Laura, for your support, generosity and love. This book is for you.